# PHOTO-FINISH

DAME NGAIO MARSH, one of the world's most popular detective novelists, has written twenty-five of her classical whodunnits since she published *A Man Lay Dead* in 1934.

Now in her seventies, she is New Zealand born and bred. Her first name (pronounced 'Nye-oh') is a Maori word which can mean a tree, a bug that lives on it, a light on the water – or simply 'clever'.

Many of her stories have theatrical settings, for Ngaio Marsh's real passion is Shakespeare. Almost single-handedly she revived the New Zealand public's interest in live theatre, and it was for this work that she received what she calls her 'damery' in 1966.

Her most recent detective story is *Photo-Finish*.

*Available in Fontana by the same author*

Black as He's Painted
Final Curtain
Grave Mistake
Last Ditch
Tied up in Tinsel
Vintage Murder
Died in the Wool
Swing Brother Swing
The Nursing Home Murder

NGAIO MARSH

# Photo-Finish

FONTANA/Collins

First published in 1980 by William Collins Sons & Co. Ltd
First issued in Fontana Paperbacks 1982

© Ngaio Marsh Limited 1980

Made and printed in Great Britain by
William Collins Sons & Co. Ltd, Glasgow

For Fredaneve
with love

# CONTENTS

# CAST OF CHARACTERS
## (in order of appearance)

ISABELLA SOMMITA
  (née Pepitone)
BEN RUBY                                    *Her manager*
MONTAGUE V. REECE                           *Her friend*
RUPERT BARTHOLOMEW                          *Her protégé*
MARIA                                       *Her maid*

CHIEF SUPERINTENDENT
  RODERICK ALLEYN CID
TROY ALLEYN RA                              *His wife*
HIS ASSISTANT-
  COMMISSIONER,
  SCOTLAND YARD

BERT                                        *A chauffeur*
LES                                         *A launchman*
MARCO                                       *A manservant*
NED HANLEY                                  *Mr Reece's secretary*

SIGNOR BEPPO LATTIENZO                      *The Sommita's Master of*
                                               *Singing*
HILDA DANCY                                 *A contralto*
ERU JOHNSTONE                               *A bass*
SYLVIA PARRY                                *A mezzo-soprano*
ROMANO RODOLFO                              *A tenor*
SIR DAVID BAUMGARTNER                       *A critic*
MRS BACON                                   *Housekeeper*
DR JOHN CARMICHAEL, MD                      *A guest*

INSPECTOR HAZELMERE                         *Rivermouth Constabulary*
DETECTIVE-SERGEANT                          *Rivermouth Constabulary*
  FRANKS
DETECTIVE-SERGEANT                          *Rivermouth Constabulary*
  BARKER

*Chapter One*

## THE SOMMITA

I

One of the many marvels of Isabella Sommita's technique was her breathing: it was totally unobservable. Even in the most exacting passages, even in the most staggering flights of coloratura, there was never the slightest disturbance of the corsage.

'You could drop an ice cube down her cleavage,' boasted her Manager, Ben Ruby, 'and not a heave would you get for your trouble.'

He had made this observation when sitting in a box immediately above the diva at the Royal Festival Hall and had spoken no more than the truth. Off-stage, when moved by one of her not infrequent rages, La Sommita's bosom would heave with the best of them.

It did so now, in her private suite at the Château Australasia in Sydney. She was *en negligé* and it was sumptuously evident that she was displeased and that the cause of her displeasure lay on the table at her elbow: a newspaper folded to expose a half-page photograph with a banner headline, CROSS-PATCH? and underneath, LA SOMMITA IS NOT AMUSED!

It had been taken yesterday in Double Bay, Sydney. The photographer, wearing a floppy white hat, a white scarf over his mouth and dark spectacles had stepped out from an alleyway and gone snap. She had not been quick enough to turn her back but her jaw had dropped and her left eye had slewed; its habit when rage overtook her. The general effect was that of a gargoyle at the dentist's: an elderly and infuriated gargoyle. The photograph was signed Strix.

She beat on the paper with her largish white fist and her rings cut into it. She panted lavishly.

'Wants horsewhipping,' Montague Reece mumbled. He was generally accepted as the Sommita's established lover and he filled this role in the manner commonly held to be appropriate, being large, rich, muted, pale, dyspeptic and negative. He was said to wield a great deal of power in his own world.

'Of course he needs horsewhipping,' shouted his dear one. 'But where's the friend who will go out and do it?' She laughed and executed a wide contemptuous gesture that included all present. The newspaper fluttered to the carpet.

'Personally,' Ben Ruby offered, 'I wouldn't know one end of a horsewhip from the other.' She dealt him a glacial stare. 'I didn't mean to be funny,' he said.

'Nor were you.'

'No.'

A young man of romantic appearance in a distant chair behind the diva clasped a portfolio of music to his midriff and said in a slightly Australian voice: 'Can't something be done? Can't they be sued?'

'What for?' asked Mr Ruby.

'Well—libel. Look at it, for God's sake!' the young man brought out. 'Well, I mean to say, *look!*'

The other two men glanced at him, but the Sommita without turning her head said: 'Thank you, darling,' and extended her arm. The intention was unmistakable: an invitation, nay, a command. The young man's beautiful face crimsoned, he rose and, maintaining a precarious hold on his portfolio, advanced crouchingly to imprint a kiss upon the fingers. He lost control of his portfolio. Its contents shot out of their confine and littered the carpet: sheet upon sheet of music in manuscript.

He fell on his knees and scrabbled about the floor, 'I'm so sorry,' he gabbled. 'Oh hell, I'm so bloody sorry.'

The Sommita had launched a full-scale attack upon the

Australian press. Rupert, she said, indicating the young man, was absolutely right. The press should be sued. The police should be called in. The photographer should be kicked out of the country. Was he to be suffered to wreck her life, her career, her sanity, to make her the laughing-stock of both hemispheres? (She was in the habit of instancing geographical data.) Had she not, she demanded, consented to the Australian appearances soley as a means of escape from his infamy?

'You are sure, I suppose,' said Mr Reece in his pallid manner, 'that it's the same man? Strix?'

This produced a tirade. 'Sure! Sure!' Had not the detested Strix bounced out of cover in all the capitals of Europe as well as in New York and San Francisco? Had he not shot her at close quarters and in atrocious disarray? *Sure!* She drew a tempestuous breath. Well, she shouted, what were they going to do about it? Was she to be protected or was she to have a breakdown, lose her voice and spend the rest of her days in a strait-jacket? She only asked to be informed.

The two men exchanged dead-pan glances.

'We can arrange for another bodyguard,' Montague Reece offered without enthusiasm.

'She didn't much fancy the one in New York,' Mr Ruby pointed out.

'Assuredly I did not,' she agreed, noisily distending her nostrils. 'It is not amusing to be closely followed by an imbecile in unspeakable attire who did nothing, but nothing, to prevent the outrage on Fifth Avenue. He merely goggled. As, by the way did you all.'

'Sweetheart, what else could we do? The fellow was a passenger in an open car. It was off like a bullet as soon as he'd taken his picture.'

'Thank you, Benny. I remember the circumstances.'

'But *why?*' asked the young man called Rupert, still on his knees assembling his music. 'What's got into him? I mean to say, it doesn't make sense and it must cost a lot of money to follow you all over the globe. He must be bonkers.'

9

He recognized his mistake as soon as it escaped his lips and began to gabble. Perhaps because he was on his knees and literally at her feet the Sommita who had looked explosive leant forward and tousled his blond hair. 'My poorest!' she said. 'You are quite, *quite* ridiculous and I adore you. I haven't introduced you,' she added as an afterthought. 'I've forgotten your surname.'

'Bartholomew.'

'Really? Very well, Rupert Bartholomew,' she proclaimed, with an introductory wave of her hand.

'. . . d'you do,' he muttered. The others nodded.

'Why does he do it? He does it,' Montague Reece said impatiently, reverting to the photographer, 'for money. No doubt the idea arose from the Jacqueline Kennedy affair. He's carried it much further and he's been successful. Enormously so.'

'That's right,' Ruby agreed. 'And the more he does it the more—' he hesitated— 'outrageous the results become.'

'He re-touches,' the Sommita intervened. 'He distorts. I know it.'

They all hurriedly agreed with her.

'I'm going,' she said unexpectedly, 'to dress. Now. And when I return I wish to be given an intelligent solution. I throw out, for what they are worth, my suggestions. The police. Prosecution. The Press. Who owns this—' she kicked the offending newspaper and had some difficulty in disengaging her foot— 'this garbage? Who is the proprietor? Attack him.' She strode to the bedroom door. 'And I warn you, Monty. I warn you, Benny. This is my final word. Unless I am satisfied that there is an end to my persecution I shall not sing in Sydney. They can,' said the Sommita, reverting to her supposed origins, 'stuff their Sydney Opera House.'

She made her exit and did not neglect to slam the door.

'Oh dear,' said Benjamin Ruby quietly.

'Quite,' said Montague Reece.

The young man called Rupert Bartholomew, having reinstated his portfolio, got to his feet.

'I reckon I'd better — ?'

'Yes?' said Mr Reece.

'Take myself off. I mean to say, it's a bit awkward.'

'What's awkward?'

'Well, you see, Madame — Madame Sommita asked me — I mean to say, she said I was to bring this — ' he indicated, precariously, his portfolio.

'Look out,' said Ben Ruby. 'You'll scatter it again.' He did not try to suppress a note of resignation. 'Is it something you've written?' he said. It was more a statement than an inquiry.

'This is right. She said I could bring it.'

'When,' Reece asked, 'did she say it?'

'Last night. Well — this morning. About one o'clock. You were leaving that party at the Italian Embassy. You had gone back to fetch something: her gloves, I think, and she was in the car. She saw me.'

'It was raining.'

'Heavily,' said the young man proudly. 'I was the only one.'

'You spoke to her?'

'She beckoned me. She put the window down. She asked me how long I'd been there. I said three hours. She asked my name and what I did. I told her. I play the piano in a small orchestra and give lessons. And I type. And then I told her I had all her recordings and — well, she was so wonderful. I mean to me, there in the rain. I just found myself telling her I've written an opera — short — a one-acter — sort of dedicated to her, *for* her. Not, you know, not because I dreamt she would ever hear of it. Good God no!'

'And so,' Benjamin Ruby suggested, 'she said you could show it to her.'

'This is right. This morning. I think she was sorry I was so wet.'

'And have you shown it to her?' asked Mr Reece. 'Apart from throwing it all over the carpet?'

'No. I was just going to when the waiter came up with this morning's papers and—she saw that thing. And then you came. I suppose I'd better go.'

'It's hardly the moment perhaps—' Mr Reece began when the bedroom door opened and an elderly woman with ferociously black hair came into the room. She held up a finger at Rupert, rather in the manner of summoning a waiter.

'She wanta you,' said the woman. 'Also the music.'

'All right, Maria,' said Mr Ruby, and to the young man, 'Maria is Madame's dresser. You'd better go.'

So Rupert, whose surname was Bartholomew, clutching his opera, walked into La Sommita's bedroom as a fly, if he'd only known it, into a one-way web.

'She'll eat that kid,' Mr Ruby said dispassionately, 'in one meal.'

'Half way down her throat already,' her protector agreed.


## II

'I've wanted to paint that woman,' said Troy Alleyn, 'for five years. And now look!'

She pushed the letter across the breakfast table. Her husband read it and raised an eyebrow. 'Remarkable,' he said.

'I know. Especially the bit about you. What does it say, exactly? I was too excited to take it all in. Who's the letter *from*, actually? Not from *her*, you'll notice?'

'It's from Montague Reece, no less.'

'Why, "no less". Who's Montague Reece?'

'I wish,' said Alleyn, 'he could hear you ask.'

'Why?' Troy repeated. 'Oh, I know! Isn't he very well off?'

'You may say so. In the stinking-of-it department. Mr Onassis Colossus, in fact.'

'I remember now. Isn't he her lover?'

'That's it.'

'All is made clear to me. I think. Do read it, darling. Aloud.'

'All of it?'

'Please.'

'Here goes,' said Alleyn and read:-

'Dear Mrs Alleyn,

I hope that is the correct way to address you. Should I perhaps have used your most celebrated soubriquet?

'I write to ask if from November 1st you and your husband will be my guests at Waihoe Lodge, an island retreat I have built on a lake in New Zealand. It is recently completed and I dare to hope it will appeal to you. The situation is striking and I think I may say that my guests will be comfortable. You would have, as your studio, a commodious room, well-lit, overlooking the lake, with a view of distant mountains and, of course, complete freedom as to time and privacy.'

'He sounds like a land-and-estate agent — all mod. cons. and the usual offices. Pray continue,' said Troy.

'I must confess that this invitation is the prelude to another and that is for you to paint a portrait of Madame Isabella Sommita who will be staying with us at the time proposed. I have long hoped for this. In my opinion, and I am permitted to say in hers also, none of her portraits hitherto has given us the true "Sommita".

'We are sure that a "Troy" would do so quite marvellously!

'Please say you approve the proposal. We will arrange transport, as my guest, of course, by air, and will settle details as soon as we hear, as I so greatly hope, that you will come. I shall be glad if you will be kind enough to inform me of your terms.

'I shall write, under separate cover, to your husband whom we shall be delighted to welcome with you to the Lodge.

'I am, believe me, dear Mrs Alleyn,
'Yours most sincerely,
(in spiky writing) 'Montague Reece.'

After a longish pause Troy said: 'Would it be going too far to paint her singing? You know, mouth wide open for a top note.'

'Mightn't she look as if she were yawning?'

'I don't *think* so,' Troy brooded, and then with a sidelong grin at her husband, 'I could always put a balloon coming out of her mouth with "A in alt" written in it.'

'That would settle any doubts, of course. Except that I fancy it refers to male singers.'

'You haven't looked at your letter. Do look.'

Alleyn looked. 'Here it is,' he said. 'Over-posh and posted in Sydney.' He opened it.

'What's he say?'

'The preamble's much the same as yours and so's the follow-up: the bit about him having to confess to an ulterior motive.'

'Does he want *you* to paint *his* portrait, my poor Rory?'

'He wants me to give them "my valued opinion" as to the possibility of obtaining police protection "in the matter of the persecution of Madame Sommita by a photographer of which I am no doubt aware." Well, of all the damn cheek!' said Alleyn. 'Travel thirteen thousand miles to sit on an island in the middle of a lake and tell him whether or not to include a copper in his house-party.'

'Oh! Yes. The penny's dropped. All that stuff in the papers. I didn't really read it.'

'You must be the only English-speaking human being who didn't.'

'Well, I did, really. Sort of. But the photographs were so hideous they put me off. Fill me, as I expect they say in Mr Reece's circles, in.'

'You remember how Mrs Jacqueline Kennedy, as she was then, was pestered by a photographer?'

'Yes.'

'It's the same situation but much exaggerated. The Kennedy rumpus may have put the idea into this chap's head. He signs himself "Strix". He's actually followed the Sommita

14

all over the world. Wherever she has appeared in opera or on the concert stage: Milan, Paris, Covent Garden, New York, Sydney. At first the photographs were the usual kind of thing with the diva flashing gracious smiles at the camera, but gradually differences crept in. They became more and more unflattering and he became more and more intrusive. He hid behind bushes. He trespassed on private ground and cropped up when and where he was least expected. On one occasion he joined the crowd round the stage door with the rest of the press, and contrived to get right up to the front.

'As she came into the doorway and did her usual thing of being delighted and astonished at the size of the crowd he aimed his camera and at the same time blew a piercingly loud whistle. Her jaw dropped and her eyes popped and in the resulting photograph she looked as if someone had thumped her between the shoulder-blades.

'From then on the thing ripened into a sort of war of attrition. It caught the fancy of her enormous public, the photos became syndicated and the man is said to be making enormous sums of money. Floods of angry letters from her fans to the papers concerned. Threats. Unkind jokes in the worst possible taste. Bets laid. Preposterous stories suggesting he's a cast-off lover taking his revenge or a tenor who fell out with her. Rumours of a nervous breakdown. Bodyguards. The lot.'

'Isn't it rather feeble of them not to spot him and manhandle him off?'

'You'd have thought so, but he's too smart for them. He disguises himself—sometimes bearded and sometimes not. Sometimes in the nylon stocking mask. At one time turned out like a City gent, at another like a Skid Row drop-out. He's said to have a very, *very* sophisticated camera.'

'Yes, but when he's done it, why hasn't somebody grabbed him and jumped on the camera? And what about her celebrated temperament? You'd think she'd set about him herself.'

'You would, but so far she hasn't done any better than

yelling pen-and-ink.

'Well,' Troy said, 'I don't see what you could be expected to do about it.'

'Accept with pleasure and tell my AC that I'm off to the antipodes with my witch-wife? Because,' Alleyn said, putting his hand on her head, 'you are going, aren't you?'

'I do madly want to have a go at her: a great big flamboyant rather vulgar splotch of a thing. Her arms,' Troy said reminiscently, 'are indecent. White and flowing. You can see the brush strokes. She's so shockingly sumptuous. Oh yes, Rory love, I'm afraid I must go.'

'We could try suggesting that she waits till she's having a bash at Covent Garden. No,' said Alleyn, watching her, 'I can see that's no go, you don't want to wait. You must fly to your commodious studio and in between sittings you must paint pretty peeps of snowy mountains reflected in the lucid waters of the lake. You might knock up a one-man show while you're about it.'

'You shut up,' said Troy, taking his arm.

'I think you'd better write a rather formal answer giving your terms, as he so delicately suggests. I suppose I decline under separate cover.'

'It might have been fun if we'd dived together into the flesh-pots.'

'The occasions when your art and my job have coincided haven't been all that plain-sailing, have they, my love?'

'Not,' she agreed, 'so's you'd notice. Rory, do you mind? My going?'

'I always mind but I try not to let on. I must say I don't go much for the company you'll be keeping.'

'Don't you? High operatic with tantrums between sittings? Will that be the form, do you suppose?'

'Something like that, I dare say.'

'I shan't let her look at the thing until it's finished and if she cuts up rough, her dear one needn't buy it. One thing I will *not* do,' said Troy calmly. 'I will not oblige with asinine alterations. If she's that sort.'

'I should think she well might be. So might he.'

'Taking the view that if he's paying he's entitled to a return for his cash? What is he? English? New Zealand? American? Australian?'

'I've no idea. But I don't much fancy you being his guest, darling, and that's a fact.'

'I can hardly offer to pay my own way. Perhaps,' Troy suggested, 'I should lower my price in consideration of board and lodging.'

'All right, smarty-pants.'

'If it turns out to be a pot-smoking party or worse, I can always beat a retreat to my pretty peepery and lock the door on all comers.'

'What put pot into your fairly pretty little head?'

'I don't know. Here!' said Troy. 'You're not by any chance suggesting the diva is into the drug scene?'

'There have been vague rumours. Probably false.'

'He'd hardly invite *you* to stay if she was.'

'Oh,' Alleyn said lightly, 'their effrontery knows no bounds. I'll write my polite regrets before I go down to the Factory.'

The telephone rang and he answered it with the noncommittal voice Troy knew meant the Yard.

'I'll be down in a quarter of an hour, sir,' he said and hung up. 'The AC,' he explained. 'Up to something. I always know when he goes all casual on me.'

'Up to what, do you suppose?'

'Lord knows. Undelicious by the sound of it. He said it was of no particular moment but would I drop in: an ominous opening. I'd better be off.' He made for the door, looked at her, returned and rounded her face between his hands. 'Fairly pretty little head,' he repeated and kissed it.

Fifteen minutes later his Assistant Commissioner received him in the manner to which he had become accustomed: rather as if he was some sort of specimen produced in a bad light to be peered at, doubtfully. The AC was as well furnished with mannerisms as he was with brains and that would be underestimating them.

'Hullo, Rory,' he said. 'Morning to you. Morning. Troy well? Good.' (Alleyn had not had time to answer.) 'Sit down. Sit down. Yes.'

Alleyn sat down. 'You wanted to see me, sir?' he suggested.

'It's nothing much, really. Read the morning papers?'

'*The Times*.'

'Seen last Friday's *Mercury*?'

'No.'

'I just wondered. That silly stuff with the press photographer and the Italian singing woman. What's-her-name?'

After a moment's pause Alleyn said woodenly: 'Isabella Sommita.'

'That's the one,' agreed the AC, one of whose foibles it was to pretend not to remember names. 'Silly of me. Chap's been at it again.'

'Very persistent.'

'Australia. Sydney or somewhere. Opera House, isn't it?'

'There is one: yes.'

'On the steps at some sort of function. Here you are.'

He pushed over the newspaper folded to expose the photograph. It had indeed been taken a week ago on the steps of the magnificent Sydney Opera House on a summer's evening. La Sommita, gloved in what seemed to be cloth of gold topped by a tiara, stood among VIPs of the highest calibre. Clearly she was not yet poised for the shot. The cameraman had jumped the gun. Again, her mouth was wide open but on this occasion she appeared to be screaming at the Governor-General of Australia. Or perhaps shrieking with derisive laughter. There is a belief held by people of the theatre that nobody over the age of twenty-five should allow themselves to be photographed from below. Here, the camera had evidently been half a flight beneath the diva who therefore appeared to be richly endowed with chins and more than slight *embonpoint*. The Governor-General, by some momentary accident, seemed to regard her with

18

incredulity and loathing.

A banner headline read: WHO DO YOU THINK YOU ARE!

The photograph, as usual, was signed 'Strix' and was reproduced, by arrangement, from a Sydney newspaper.

'That, I imagine,' said Alleyn, 'will have torn it!'

'So it seems. Look at this.'

It was a letter addressed to 'The Head of Scotland Yard, London' and written a week before the invitations to the Alleyns on heavy paper endorsed with an elaborate monogram: I.S. lavishly entwined with herbage. The envelope was bigger than the ones received by the Alleyns but of the same make and paper. The letter itself occupied two and a half pages, with a gigantic signature. It had been typed, Alleyn noticed, on a different machine. The address was Château Australasia, Sydney.

'The Commissioner sent it down,' said the AC. 'You'd better read it.'

Alleyn did so. The typed section merely informed the recipient that the writer hoped to meet one of his staff, Mr Alleyn, at Waihoe Lodge, New Zealand, where Mr Alleyn's wife was commissioned to paint the writer's portrait. The writer gave the dates proposed. The recipient was of course aware of the outrageous persecution— 'and so on along the already familiar lines. Her object in writing to him, she concluded, was because she hoped Mr Alleyn would be accorded full authority by the Yard to investigate this outrageous affair and she remained—'

'Good God,' said Alleyn quietly.

'You've still got a postcript,' the AC observed.

It was handwritten and all that might be expected. Points of exclamation proliferated. Underscorings doubled and trebled to an extent that would have made Queen Victoria's correspondence appear by contrast a model of stony reticence. The subject-matter lurched into incoherence but the general idea was to the effect that if the 'Head of Scotland Yard' didn't do something pretty smartly he would have only

19

himself to blame when the writer's career came to a catastrophic halt. On her knees she remained distractedly and again in enormous calligraphy, sincerely, Isabella Sommita.

'Expound,' the AC invited with his head on one side. He was being whimsical. 'Comment. Explain in your own words.'

'I can only guess that the letter was typed by a secretary who advised moderation. The postscript seems to be all her own and written in a frenzy.'

'*Is* Troy going to paint the lady? And do you propose to be absent without leave in the antipodes?'

Alleyn said: 'We got our invitations this morning. I was about to decline, sir, when you rang up. Troy's accepting.'

'*Is* she?' said the AC thoughtfully. '*Is* she, now? A good subject, um? To paint? What?'

'Very,' Alleyn said warily. What *is* he on about? he wondered.

'Yes. Ah well,' said the AC, freshening his voice with a suggestion of dismissal. Alleyn started to get up. 'Hold on,' said the AC. 'Know anything about this man she lives with? Reece, isn't it?'

'No more than everyone knows.'

'Strange coincidence, really,' mused the AC.

'Coincidence?'

'Yes. The invitations. Troy going out there and all this.' He flipped his finger at the papers on his desk. 'All coming together as it were.'

'Hardly a coincidence, sir, would you say? I mean, these dotty letters were all written with the same motive.'

'Oh, I don't mean *them*,' said the AC contemptuously. 'Or only in so far as they turn up at the same time as the other business.'

'What other business?' said Alleyn, and managed to keep the weary note out of his voice.

'Didn't I tell you? Stupid of me. Yes. There's a bit of a flap going on in the international Drug Scene: the USA in particular. Interpol picked up a lead somewhere and passed it on to the French who talked to the FBI who've been talking to our lot. It seems there's been some suggestion that the diva might be a big, big girl in the remotest background. Very nebulous it sounded to me but our Great White Chief is slightly excited.' This was the AC's habitual manner of alluding to the Commissioner. 'He's been talking to the Special Squad. And, by the way, to MI6.'

'How do they come into it?'

'Somewhere along the line. Cagey, as usual, I gather,' said the AC. 'But they did divulge that there was a leak from an anonymous source to the effect that the Sommita is thought to have operated in the past.'

'What about Reece?'

'Clean as a whistle, as far as is known.'

'Montague Reece,' Alleyn mused. 'Almost too good to be true. Like something out of *Trilby*. Astrakhan coat-collar and glistening beard. Anything about his origin, sir?'

'Thought to be American-Sicilian.'

During the pause that followed the AC hummed, uncertainly, the habañera from *Carmen*. 'Ever heard her in that?' he said. 'Startling. Got the range — soprano, mezzo, you name it, got the looks, got the sex. Stick you like a pig for tuppence and make you like it.' He shot one of his disconcerting glances at Alleyn. 'Troy'll have her hands full,' he said. 'What?'

'Yes,' Alleyn agreed, and with a strong foreboding of what was in store, added: 'I don't much fancy her going.'

'Quite. Going to put your foot down, are you, Rory?'

Alleyn said: 'As far as Troy's concerned I haven't got feet.'

'Tell that to the Fraud Squad,' said the AC and gave a slight whinny.

'Not where her work's concerned. It's a must. For both of us.'

'Ah,' said the AC. 'Mustn't keep you,' he said, and shifted without further notice into the tone that meant business. 'It just occurs to me that in the circumstances you might, after all, take this trip. And by the way you know New Zealand, don't you? Yes?' And when Alleyn didn't answer: 'What I meant when I said "coincidence". The invitation and all that. Drops like a plum into our lap. We're asked to keep a spot of very inconspicuous observation on this article and here's the article's boy-friend asking you to be his guest and Bob, so to speak, is your uncle. Incidentally, you'll be keeping an eye on Troy and her termagant subject, won't you? Well?'

Alleyn said: 'Am I to take it, sir, that this is an order?'

'I must say,' dodged the AC, 'I thought you would be delighted.'

'I expect I ought to be.'

'Very well, then,' said the AC testily. 'Why the hell aren't you?'

'Well, sir, you talked about coincidences. It so happens that by a preposterous series of them Troy has been mixed up to a greater and lesser degree in four of my cases. And—'

'And by all accounts behaved quite splendidly. Hul-*lo*!' said the AC. 'That's it, is it? You don't like her getting involved?'

'On general principles, no, I don't.'

'But, my dear man, you're not going out to the antipodes to involve yourself in an investigation. You're on observation. There won't,' said the AC, 'as likely as not, be anything to observe. Except, of course, your most attractive wife. You're not going to catch a murderer. You're not going to catch anyone. What?'

'I didn't say anything.'

'All right. It's an order. You'd better ring your wife and tell her. Morning to you.'


III


In Melbourne all was well. The Sydney season had been a fantastic success artistically, financially and, as far as Isabella Sommita was concerned, personally. 'Nothing to

22

equal it had been experienced,' as the press raved, 'within living memory.' One reporter labouriously joked that if cars were motivated by real instead of statistical horse-power the quadrupeds would undoubtedly have been unhitched and the diva drawn in triumph and by human propulsion through the seething multitudes.

There had been no further offensive photography.

Young Rupert Bartholomew had found himself pitch-forked into a milieu that he neither understood nor criticized but in which he floundered in a state of complicated bliss and bewilderment. Isabella Sommita had caused him to play his one-act opera. She had listened with an approval that ripened quickly with the realization that the soprano role was, to put it coarsely, so large that the rest of the cast existed only as trimmings. The opera was about Ruth and the title was *The Alien Corn*. ('Corn,' muttered Ben Ruby to Monty Reece, but not in the Sommita's hearing, 'is dead right.') There were moments when the pink clouds amid which Rupert floated thinned and a small, ice-cold pellet ran down his spine and he wondered if his opera was any good. He told himself that to doubt it was to doubt the greatest soprano of the age and the pink clouds quickly re-formed. But the shadow of unease did not absolutely leave him.

Mr Reece was not musical. Mr Ruby, in his own untutored way, was. Both accepted the advisability of consulting an expert and such was the pitch of the Sommita's mounting determination to stage this piece that they treated the matter as one of top urgency. Mr Ruby, under pretence of wanting to study the work, borrowed it from the Sommita. He approached the doyen of Australian music critics, and begged him, for old times' sake, to give his strictly private opinion on the opera. He did so and said that it stank.

'Menotti-and-water,' he said. 'Don't let her touch it.'

'Will you tell her so?' Mr Ruby pleaded.

'Not on your Nelly,' said the great man, and as an afterthought, 'What's the matter with her? Has she fallen in love with the composer?'

'Boy,' said Mr Ruby deeply, 'you said it.'

It was true. After her somewhat tigerish fashion the Sommita was in love. Rupert's Byronic appearance, his melting glance, and his undiluted adoration had combined to do the trick. At this point she had a flaring row with her Australian secretary who stood up to her and when she sacked him said she had taken the words out of his mouth. She then asked Rupert if he could type and when he said yes promptly offered him the job. He accepted, cancelled all pending appointments, and found himself booked in at the same astronomically expensive hotel as his employer. He not only dealt with her correspondence. He was one of her escorts to the theatre and was permitted to accompany her at her practices. He supped with her after the show and stayed longer than any of the other guests. He was in Heaven.

On a night when this routine had been observed and Mr Reece had retired early, in digestive discomfort, the Sommita asked Rupert to stay while she changed into something comfortable. This turned out to be a ruby silken negligée which may indeed have been comfortable for the wearer but which caused the beholder to shudder in an agony of excitement.

He hadn't a hope. She had scarcely embarked upon the preliminary phases of her formidable techniques when she was in his arms, or more strictly, he in hers.

An hour later he floated down the long passage to his room, insanely inclined to sing at the top of his voice.

'My first!' he exulted. 'My very first. And, incredibly — Isabella Sommita.'

He was, poor boy, as pleased as Punch with himself.


IV


As far as his nearest associates could discover Mr Reece was not profoundly disturbed by his mistress's goings-on. Indeed he appeared to ignore them but, really, it was impossible to tell, he was so remarkably uncommunicative. Much of his time, most of it, in fact, was spent with a secretary, manipulating, it was widely conjectured, the Stock Markets and receiving long-distance telephone calls. His manner towards Rupert Bartholomew was precisely the same as his manner towards the rest of the Sommita's following: so neutral that it could scarcely be called a manner at all. Occasionally when Rupert thought of Mr Reece he was troubled by stabs of uncomfortable speculation, but he was too far gone in incredulous rapture to be greatly concerned.

It was at this juncture that Mr Reece flew to New Zealand to inspect his island lodge, now completed.

On his return, three days later, to Melbourne, he found the Alleyns' letters of acceptance and the Sommita in a high state of excitement.

'Dar-leeng,' she said, 'you will show me everything. You have photographs, of course? Am I going to be pleased? Because I must tell you I have great plans. But such plans!' cried the Sommita and made mysterious gestures. 'You will never guess.'

'What are they?' he asked in his flat-voiced way.

'Ah-ah!' she teased. 'You must be patient. First the pictures which Rupert, too, must see. Quick, quick, the pictures.'

She opened the bedroom door into the sitting-room and in two glorious notes sang, 'Rupert!'

Rupert had been coping with her fan mail. When he came in he found that Mr Reece had laid out a number of glossy coloured photographs on the bed. They were all of the island lodge.

The Sommita was enchanted. She exclaimed, purred, exulted. Several times she burst into laughter. Ben Ruby arrived and the photographs were re-exhibited. She embraced all three men severally and more or less together.

And then with a sudden drop into the practical she said, 'The music room. Let me see it again. Yes. How big is it?'

'From memory,' said Mr Reece, 'sixty feet long and forty

25

wide.' Mr Ruby whistled. 'That's quite a size,' he remarked. 'That's more like a bijou theatre than a room. You settling to give concerts, honey?'

'Better than that!' she cried. 'Didn't I tell you, Monty my dar-leeng, that we have made plans. Ah, we have cooked up *such* plans, Rupert and I. Haven't we, *caro*? Yes?'

'Yes,' Rupert said with an uncertain glance at Mr Reece. 'I mean— Marvellous.'

Mr Reece had an extremely passive face but Rupert thought he detected a shade of resignation pass over it. Mr Ruby, however, wore an expression of the deepest apprehension.

The Sommita flung her right arm magnificently across Rupert's shoulders. 'This dear child,' she said and if she had made it: 'this adorable lover' she could have scarcely been more explicit, 'has genius. I tell you— I who know. *Genius.*' They said nothing and she continued. 'I have lived with his opera. I have studied his opera. I have studied the leading role. The "Ruth". The arias, the solos, the duets—there are two—and the *ensembles*. All, but all, have the unmistakable stigmata of genius. I do not,' she amended, 'use the word "stigmata" in the sense of martyrdom. Better, perhaps, to say "they bear the banner of genius". *Genius!*' she shouted.

To look at Rupert at this moment one might have thought that 'marytrdom' was, after all, the more appropriate word. His face was dark red and he shifted in her embrace. She shook him, none too gently. 'Clever, *clever* one,' she said and kissed him noisily.

'Are we to hear your plan?' Mr Reece asked.

The hour being seven o'clock she hustled them into the sitting-room and told Rupert to produce cocktails. He was glad to secrete himself in the chilly cabinet provided for drinks, ice and glasses. A few desultory and inaudible remarks came from the other three. Mr Ruby cleared his throat once or twice. Then, so unexpectedly that Rupert spilt Mr Reece's whisky and soda over his hands, the piano in the sitting-room sketched the opening statement of what he had hoped would be the big aria from his opera: and the superb voice, in heart-rending pianissimo, sang: 'Alone, alone amidst the alien corn.'

It was at that moment with no warning at all that Rupert was visited by a catastrophic certainty. He had been mistaken in his opera. Not even the most glorious voice in all the world could ever make it anything but what it was—third rate.

It's no good, he thought. It is ridiculously commonplace. And then: She has no judgement. She is not a musical woman.

He was shattered.

*Chapter Two*

## THE LODGE

### I

Early on a fine morning in the antipodean spring the Alleyns were met at their New Zealand airport by a predictably rich car and were driven along roads that might have been ruled across the plains to vanishing points on the horizon. The Pacific was out of sight somewhere to their left and before them rose foothills. These were the outer ramparts of the Southern Alps.

'We're in luck,' Alleyn said. 'On a grey day when there are no hills to be seen, the plains can be deadly. Would you want to paint?'

'I don't think so,' Troy said after considering it. 'It's all a bit inhuman, isn't it? One would have to find an idiom. I get the feeling that the people only move across the surface. They haven't evolved with it. They're not included,' said Troy, 'in the anatomy. What cheek!' she exclaimed, 'to generalize when I've scarcely arrived in the country.'

The driver, who was called Bert, was friendly and anxious for his passengers to be impressed. He pointed out mountains that has been sheep-farmed by the first land-holders.

'Where we're going,' Troy asked, 'to Waihoe Lodge — is that sheep country?'

'No way. We're going into Westland, Mrs Alleyn. The West Coast. It's all timber and mining over there. Waihoe's quite a lake. And the Lodge! You know what they reckon it's cost him? Half a million. And more. That's what they reckon. Nothing like it anywhere else in N'yerzillun. You'll be surprised.'

'We've heard about it,' Alleyn said.

'Yeah? You'll still be surprised.' He slewed his head towards Troy. 'You'll be the painting lady,' he said. 'Mr Reece reckoned you might get the fancy to take a picture up at the head of the Pass. Where we have lunch.'

'I don't think that's likely,' Troy said.

'You're going to paint the famous lady: is that right?' His manner was sardonic. Troy said yes, she was.

'Rather you than me,' said the driver.

'Do you paint, then?'

'Me? Not likely. I wouldn't have the patience.'

'It takes a bit more than patience,' Alleyn said mildly.

'Yeah? That might be right, too,' the driver conceded. There was a longish pause. 'Would she have to keep still, then?' he asked.

'More or less.'

'I reckon it'll be more "less" than "more",' said the driver. 'They tell me she's quite a celebrity,' he added.

'Worldwide,' said Alleyn.

'What they reckon. Yeah,' said the driver with a reflective chuckle, 'they can keep it for mine. Temperamental! You can call it that if you like.' He whistled. 'If it's not one thing it's another. Take the dog. She had one of these fancy hound things, white with droopy hair. The boss give it to her. Well, it goes crook and they get a vet and he reckons it's hopeless and it ought to be put out of its misery. So *she* goes crook. Screechin' and moanin', something remarkable. In the finish the boss says get it over with, so me and the vet take it into the hangar and he chloroforms it and then gives it an injection and we bury it out of sight. Cripes!' said the driver. 'When they told her you'd of thought they'd committed a murder.' He sucked his teeth reminiscently.

'Maria,' he said presently, 'that's her personal help or maid or whatever it's called—she was saying there's been some sort of a schemozzle over in Aussie with the papers. But you'll know about that, Mr Alleyn. Maria reckons you've taken on this situation. Is that right?'

'I'm afraid not,' said Alleyn. Troy gave him a good nudge.

'What she reckons. You being a detective. 'Course Maria's a foreigner. Italian,' said the driver. 'You can't depend on it with that mob. They get excited.'

'You're quartered there, are you? At the Lodge?'

'This is right. For the duration. When they pack it in there'll only be a caretaker and his family on the island. Monty Reece has built a garage and boathouse on the lake shore and his launch takes you over to the Lodge. He's got his own chopper, mind. No trouble. Ring through when required.'

The conversation died. Troy wondered if the driver called his employer 'Monty Reece' to his face and decided that quite possibly he did.

The road across the plains mounted imperceptibly for forty miles and a look backward established their height. Presently they stared down into a wide riverbed laced with milky-turquoise streaks.

At noon they reached the top where they lunched from a hamper with wine in a chiller-kit. Their escort had strong tea from a Thermos flask. 'Seeing I'm the driver,' he said, 'and seeing there's the Zig-Zag yet to come.' He was moved to entertain them with stories about fatal accidents in the gorge.

The air up here was wonderfully fresh and smelt aromatically of manuka scrub patching warm tussocky earth. They were closer now to perpetual snow.

'We better be moving,' said the driver. 'You'll notice a big difference when we go over the head of the Pass. Kind of sudden.'

There was a weathered notice at the top: CORNISHMAN'S PASS. 1000 METRES.

The road ran flat for a short distance and then dived into a new world. As the driver had said: it was sudden. So sudden, so new and so dramatic that for long afterwards Troy would feel there had been a consonance between this moment and the events that were to follow, as if, on crossing over the Pass, they entered a region that was prepared and waiting.

It was a world of very dark rain forest that followed, like velvet, the convolutions of the body it enfolded. Here and there waterfalls glinted. Presiding over the forests, snow-tops caught the sun, but down below the sun never reached and there, thread-like in its gorge, a river thundered. 'You can just hear 'er,' said the driver who had stopped the car.

But all they heard at first was birdsong — cool statements, incomparably wild. After a moment Troy said she thought she could hear the river. The driver suggested they go to the edge and look down. Troy suffered horridly from height-vertigo but went, clinging to Alleyn's arm. She looked down once as if from a gallery in a theatre on an audience of tree-tops, and saw the river.

The driver, ever-informative, said that you could make out the roof of a car that six years ago went over from where they stood. Alleyn said, 'So you can,' put his arm round his wife and returned her to the car.

They embarked upon the Zig-Zag.

The turns in this monstrous descent were so acute that vehicles travelling in the same direction would seem to approach each other and indeed did pass on different levels. They had caught up with such a one and crawled behind it. They met a car coming up from the gorge. Their own driver pulled up on the lip of the road and the other sidled past on the inner running with half an inch to spare. The drivers wagged their heads at each other.

Alleyn's arm was across Troy's shoulders. He pulled her ear. 'First prize for intrepidity, Mrs A.,' he said. 'You're being splendid.'

'What did you expect me to do? Howl like a banshee?'

Presently the route flattened out and the driver changed into top gear. They reached the floor of the gorge and drove beside the river, roaring in its courses, so that they could scarcely hear each other speak. It was cold down there.

31

'Now you're in Westland,' shouted the driver.

Evening was well advanced when, after a two-hour passage through the wet loam-scented forest that New Zealanders call 'bush' they came out into more open country and stopped at a tiny railway station called Kai-kai. Here they collected the private mailbag for the Lodge and then drove parallel with the railway for twenty miles, rounded the nose of a hill and there lay a great floor of water: Lake Waihoe.

'There you are,' said the driver, 'That's the Lake for you. *And* the Island.'

'Stay me with flagons!' said Alleyn and rubbed his head.

The prospect was astonishing. At this hour the lake was perfectly unruffled and held the blazing image of an outrageous sunset. Fingers of land reached out bearing elegant trees that reversed themselves in the water. Framed by these and far beyond them was the Island and on the island Mr Reece's Lodge.

It was a house designed by a celebrated architect in the modern idiom but so ordered that one might have said it grew organically out of its primordial setting. Giants that carried their swarthy foliage in clusters stood magnificently about a grassy frontage. There was a jetty in the foreground with a launch alongside. Grossly incongruous against the uproarious sunset, like some intrusive bug, a helicopter hovered. As they looked it disappeared behind the house.

'I don't believe in all this,' said Troy. 'It's out of somebody's dream. It can't be true.'

'You reckon?' asked the driver.

'I reckon,' said Troy.

They turned into a lane that ran between tree-ferns and underbrush down to the lake edge where there was a garage, a landing-stage, a boathouse and a bell in a miniature belfry. They left the car and walked out into evening smells of wet earth, fern and moss and the cold waters of the lake.

The driver rang the bell, sending a single echoing note across the lake. He then remarked that they'd been seen from the Island. Sure enough the launch put out. So still was the evening they could hear the putt-putt of the engine. 'Sound travels a long way over the water,' said the driver.

The sunset came to its preposterous climax. Everything that could be seen, near and far, was sharpened and gilded. Their faces reddened. The far-off windows of the Lodge turned to fire. In ten minutes it had all faded and the landscape was cold. Troy and Alleyn walked a little way along the water's edge and Troy looked at the house and wondered about the people inside it. Would Isabella Sommita feel that it was a proper showplace for her brilliance and what would she look like posing in the 'commodious studio' against those high windows, herself flamboyant against another such sunset as the one that had gone by?

Troy said. 'This really *is* an adventure.'

Alleyn said: 'Do you know, in a cockeyed sort of way it reminds me of one of those Victorian romances by George Macdonald where the characters find a looking-glass and walk out of this world into another one inhabited by strange beings and unaccountable on-goings.'

'Perhaps,' said Troy, 'the entrance to that great house will turn out to be our own front door and we'll be back in London.'

They talked about the house and the way in which it rose out of its setting in balanced towers. Presently the launch, leaving an arrowhead of rippled silk in its wake, drew in to the landing-stage. It was a large, opulent craft. The helmsman came out of his wheelhouse and threw a mooring rope to the car driver.

'Meet Les Smith,' said the driver.

'Gidday,' said Les Smith. 'How's tricks, then, Bert? Good trip?'

'No trouble, Les.'

'Good as gold,' said the helmsman.

Alleyn helped them stow the luggage. Troy was handed on board and they puttered out on the lake.

The driver went into the wheelhouse with Les Smith. Troy

and Alleyn sat in the stern.

'Here we go,' he said. 'Liking it?'

'It's a lovely beginning,' said Troy. 'It's so lovely it hurts.'

'Keep your fingers crossed,' he said lightly.

## II

Perhaps because their day had been so long and had followed so hard on their flight from England, the first night at the Lodge went by rather like a dream for Troy.

They had been met by Mr Reece's secretary and a dark man dressed like a tarted-up ship's steward who carried their baggage. They were taken to their room to 'freshen up'. The secretary, a straw-coloured youngish man with a gushing manner, explained that Mr Reece was on the telephone but would be there to meet them when they came down and that everyone was 'changing' but they were not to bother as everybody would 'quite understand'. Dinner was in a quarter of an hour. There was a drinks tray in the room and he suggested that they should make use of it and said he knew they would be angelic and excuse him as Mr Reece had need of his services. He then, as an apparent afterthought, was lavish in welcome, flashed smiles and withdrew. Troy thought vaguely that he was insufferable.

'I don't know about you,' she said 'but I refuse to be quite understood and I'm going to shift my clothes. I require a nice wash and a change. And a drink, by the way.'

She opened her suitcase, scuffled in it and lugged out a jump suit which was luckily made of uncrushable material. She then went into the bathroom which was equipped like a plumber-king's palace. Alleyn effected a lightning change at which exercise he was a past master and mixed two drinks. They sat side by side on an enormous bed and contemplated their room.

'It's all been done by some super American interior decorator, wouldn't you say?' said Troy, gulping down her brandy-and-dry.

34

'You reckon?' said Alleyn, imitating the driver.

'I reckon,' said Troy. 'You have to wade through the carpet, don't you? Not walk on it.'

'It's not a carpet: it's about two hundred sheepskins sewn together. The local touch.

'All jolly fine for us to snigger. It's pretty smashing, really, let's face it. Not human, though. If only there was something shabby and out of character somewhere.'

'Us,' Alleyn said. 'We're all of that. Drink up. We'd better not be late.'

On their way downstairs they took in the full effect of the hall with its colossal blazing fireplace, display on the walls of various lethal weapons and hangings woven in the Maori fashion, and a large semi-abstract wood sculpture of a pregnant nude with a complacent smirk. From behind one of the doors there came sounds of conversation. An insistent male voice rose above the rest. There followed a burst of multiple laughter.

'Good Lord,' said Alleyn, 'it's a house-party.'

The dark man who had taken their baggage up was in the hall.

'In the drawing-room, sir,' he said unnecessarily and opened the door.

About a dozen or so people, predominantly male, were grouped at the far end of a long room. The focal point seemed to be a personage with a grey imperial beard and hair *en brosse*, wearing a velvet jacket and flowing tie, an eyeglass and a flower in his lapel. His manner was that of a practised *raconteur* who, after delivering a *mot*, is careful to preserve an expressionless face. His audience was barely recovered from its fits of merriment. The straw-coloured secretary, indeed, with glass in hand, gently tapped his fingers against his left wrist by way of applause. In doing this he turned, saw the Alleyns and bent over someone in a sofa with its back to the door.

A voice said: 'Ah yes,' and Mr Reece rose and came to greet them.

He was shortish and dark and had run a little to what is sometimes called expense-account fat. His eyes were large, and his face closed: a face that it would be easy to forget since it seemed to say nothing.

He shook hands and said how glad he was to receive them: to Troy he added that it was an honour and a privilege to welcome her. There were, perhaps, American overtones in his speech but on the whole his voice, like the rest of him seemed neutral. He introduced the Alleyns formally to everybody. To the *raconteur* who was Signor Beppo Lattienzo and who kissed Troy's hand. To a rotund gentleman who looked like an operatic tenor and turned out to be one: the celebrated Rodolfo Romano. To Mr Ben Ruby who was jocular and said they all knew Troy would do better than *that*: indicating a vast academic portrait of La Sommita's gown topped up by her mask. Then came a young man of startling physical beauty who looked apprehensive — Rupert Bartholomew; a pretty girl whose name Troy, easily baffled by mass introductions, didn't catch, and a largish lady on a sofa who was called Miss Hilda Dancy and had a deep voice, and finally there loomed up a gentleman with an even deeper voice and a jolly brown face who proclaimed himself a New Zealander and was called Mr Eru Johnstone.

Having discharged his introductory duties Mr Reece retained his hold on Alleyn, supervised his drink, led him a little apart and, as Troy could see by the sort of attentive shutter that came over her husband's face, engaged him in serious conversation.

'You have had a very long day, Mrs Alleyn,' said Signor Lattienzo who spoke with a marked Italian accent, 'Do you feel as if all your time signals had become —' he rotated plump hands rapidly round each other — 'jumbled together?'

'Exactly like that,' said Troy. 'Jet hangover, I think.'

'It will be nice to retire?'

'Gosh, yes!' she breathed, surprised into ardent agreement.

'Come and sit down,' he said, and led her to a sofa removed

from that occupied by Miss Dancy

'You must not begin to paint before you are ready,' he said. 'Do not permit them to bully you.'

'Oh, I'll be ready, I hope, tomorrow.'

'I doubt it and I doubt even more if your subject will be available.'

'Why?' asked Troy quickly. 'Is anything the matter? I mean—'

'The *matter*? That depends on one's attitude.' He looked fixedly at her. He had very bright eyes. 'You have not heard evidently of the great event,' he said. 'No? Ah. Then I must tell you that the night after next we are to be audience at the first performance on any stage of a brand-new one-act opera. A world première, in fact,' said Signor Lattienzo and his tone was exceedingly dry. 'What do you think about that?'

'I'm flabbergasted,' said Troy.

'You will be even more so when you have heard it. You do not know who I am, of course.'

'I'm afraid I only know that your name is Lattienzo.'

'Ah-ha.'

'I expect I ought to have exclaimed, "No! Not *the* Lattienzo?" '

'Not at all. I am that obscure creature a vocal pedagogue. I take the voice and teach it to know itself.'

'And did you—?'

'Yes. I took to pieces the most remarkable vocal instrument of these times and put it together again and gave it back to its owner. I worked her like a horse for three years and I am probably the only living person to whom she pays the slightest professional attention. I am commanded here because she wishes me to fall into a rapture over this opera.'

'Have you seen it? Or should one say "read it"?'

He cast up his eyes and made a gesture of despair.

'Oh dear,' said Troy.

'Alas, alas,' agreed Signor Lattienzo. Troy wondered if he was habitually so unguarded with complete strangers.

'You have, of course,' he said, 'noticed the fair young man with the appearance of a quattrocento angel and the expression of a soul in torment?'

'I have indeed. It's a remarkable head.'

'What devil, one asks oneself, inserted into it the notion that it could concoct an opera. And yet,' said Signor Lattienzo, looking thoughtfully at Rupert Bartholomew, 'I fancy the first-night horrors the poor child undoubtedly suffers are not of the usual kind.'

'No?'

'No. I fancy he has discovered his mistake and feels deadly sick.'

'But this is dreadful,' Troy said. 'It's the worst that can happen.'

'Can it happen to painters, then?'

'I think painters know while they are still at it, if the thing they are doing is no good. I know I do,' said Troy. 'There isn't perhaps the time-lag that authors and, from what you tell me, musicians can go through before they come to the awful moment of truth. Is the opera really so bad?'

'Yes. It is bad. Nevertheless, here and there, perhaps three times, one hears little signs that make one regret he is being spoilt. Nothing is to be spared him. He is to conduct.'

'Have you spoken to him? About it being wrong?'

'Not yet. First I shall let him hear it.'

'Oh,' Troy protested, 'but why! Why let him go through with it. Why not tell him and advise him to cancel the performance.'

'First of all, because she would pay no attention.'

'But if he refused?'

'She has devoured him, poor dear. He would not refuse. She has made him her secretary-accompanist-composer, but beyond all that and most destructively, she has taken him for her lover and gobbled him up. It is very sad,' said Signor Lattienzo and his eyes were bright as coal nuggets. 'But you see,' he added, 'what I mean when I say that La Sommita will be too much *engagée* to pose for you until all is over.

And then she may be too furious to sit still for thirty seconds. The first dress-rehearsal was yesterday. Tomorrow will be occupied in alternately resting and making scenes and attending a second dress-rehearsal. And the next night — the performance! Shall I tell you of their first meeting and how it has all come about?'

'Please.'

'But first I must fortify you with a drink.'

He did tell her, making a good story of it. 'Imagine! Their first encounter. All the ingredients of the soap opera. A strange young man, pale as death, beautiful as Adonis, with burning eyes and water pouring off the end of his nose, gazes hungrily at his goddess at one a.m. during a deluge. She summons him to the window of her car. She is kind and before long she is even kinder. And again, kinder. He shows her his opera — it is called *The Alien Corn*, it is dedicated to her and since the role of Ruth is virtually the entire score and has scarcely finished ravishing the audience with one coloratura embellishment before another sets in, she is favourably impressed. You know, of course, of her celebrated A above high C.'

'I'm afraid not!'

'No? It's second only to the achievement recorded in the *Guinness Book of Records*. This besotted young man has been careful to provide for it in her aria. I must tell you by the way that while she sings like the Queen of Heaven, musically speaking this splendid creature is as stupid as an owl.'

'Oh, come!'

'Believe me. It is the truth. You see before you the assembled company engaged at vast cost for this charade. The basso: a New Zealander and a worthy successor to Inia te Wiata. He is the Boaz and, believe me, finds himself knee deep in corn for which "alien" is all too inadequate a description. The dear Hilda Dancy on the sofa is the Naomi who escapes with a duet, a handful of recitatives and the contralto part in an enfeebled pastiche of "*Bella figlia del amore*". There she is joined by a mezzo-soprano—(the little Sylvia Parry now talking to the composer). She is, so to speak, Signora Boaz. Next comes the romantic element in the person of Rodolfo Romano who is the head gleaner and adores the Ruth at first sight. She, I need not tell you, dominates the quartet. You find me unsympathetic, perhaps?' said Signor Lattienzo.

'I find you very funny,' said Troy.

'But spiteful? Yes?'

'Well—ruthless, perhaps.'

'Would we were all.'

'What?'

' "Ruth"—less, my dear.'

'Oh, *really*!' said Troy and burst out laughing.

'I am very hungry. She is twenty minutes late as usual and our good Monty consults his watch. Ah! we are to be given the full performance—the Delayed Entrance. Listen.'

A musical whooping could at that moment be heard rapidly increasing in volume.

'The celestial fire-engine,' said Signor Lattienzo, 'approaches.' He said this loudly to Alleyn who had joined them.

The door into the hall was flung wide, Isabella Sommita stood on the threshold and Troy thought: This is it. O, praise the Lord all ye lands, this is it.

The first thing to be noticed about the Sommita was her eyes. There were enormous, black and baleful, and set slant-wise in her magnolia face. They were topped by two jetty arcs, thin as a camel hair brush but one knew that if left to themselves they would bristle and meet angrily above her nose. Her under lip was full, her teeth slightly protuberant with the little gap at the front which is said to denote an amorous disposition.

She wore green velvet and diamonds and her celebrated bosom, sumptuously displayed, shone like marble.

Everyone who had been sitting rose. Alleyn thought: A bit more of this and the ladies would fall to the ground in curtseys.

He looked at Troy and recognized the quickened attention, the impersonal scrutiny that meant his wife was hooked.

'Dar-leengs!' sang La Sommita. 'So late! Forgive, forgive.' She directed her remarkably searching gaze upon them all, and let it travel slowly, rather, Alleyn thought, in the manner of a lighthouse, until it rested upon him, and then upon Troy. An expression of astonishment and rapture dawned. She advanced upon them both with outstretched arms and cries of excitement, seized their hands, giving them firm little shakes as if she was congratulating them on their union and found her joy in doing so too great for words.

'But you have COME!' she cried at last and appealed to everyone else. 'Isn't it wonderful!' she demanded. 'They have COME!' She displayed them, like trophies, to her politely responsive audience.

Alleyn said 'Hell' inaudibly and as a way of releasing himself kissed the receptive hand.

There followed cascades of welcome. Troy was gripped by the shoulders and gazed at searchingly and asked if she (the Sommita) would 'do' and told that already she knew they were *en rapport* and that she (the Sommita) always '*knew*'. Didn't Troy always *know*? Alleyn was appealed to: 'Didn't she?'

'Oh,' Alleyn said, 'she's as cunning as a bagload of monkeys, Madame. You've no idea.'

Further melodious hoots, this time of laughter, greeted the far from brilliant sally. Alleyn was playfully chided.

They were checked by the entry at the far end of the room of another steward-like personage who announced dinner He carried a salver with what was no doubt the mail that had come with the Alleyns and took it to the straw-coloured secretary who said: 'On my desk.' The man made some inaudible reply and seemed to indicate a newspaper on his salver. The secretary looked extremely perturbed and repeated, loudly enough for Alleyn to hear. 'No, no. I'll attend to it. In the drawer of my desk. Take it away.'

The man bowed slightly and returned to the doors.

The guests were already in motion and the scene now resembled the close of the first act of an Edwardian comedy, voices pitched rather high, movements studied, the sense, even, of some approach to a climax which would develop in the next act.

It developed, however, there and then. The bass, Mr Eru Johnstone, said in his enormous voice: 'Do I see the evening paper? It will have the results of the Spring Cup, won't it?'

'I should imagine so,' said Mr Reece. 'Why?'

'We had a sweep on Top Note. It seemed a clear indication,' and he boomed up the room. 'Everybody! The Cup!'

The procession halted. They all chattered in great excitement but were, as actors say, 'topped' by the Sommita demanding to see the paper there and then. Alleyn saw the secretary, who looked agitated, trying to reach the servant but the Sommita had already seized the newspaper and flapped it open.

The scene that followed bore for three or four seconds a far-fetched resemblance to an abortive ruck in Rugby football. The guests, still talking eagerly surged round the prima donna. And then, suddenly, fell silent, backed away and left her isolated, speechless and crosseyed, holding out the open newspaper as if she intended to drop kick it to eternity. Alleyn said afterwards that he could have sworn she foamed at the mouth.

Across the front page of the paper a banner-head-line was splashed.

## SOMMITA SAYS NO FALSIES

And underneath:-

SIGNED STATEMENT: BY FAMOUS PRIMA-DONNA.
HER CURVES ARE ALL HER OWN. BUT ARE THEY????

Boxed in a heavy outline, at the centre of the page, were about nine lines of typescript and beneath them the enormous signature—

Isabella Sommita

Dinner had been catastrophic, a one-man show by the
Sommita. To say she had run through the gamut of the passions
would be a rank understatement: she began where the
gamut left off and bursts of hysteria were as passages-of-rest
in the performance. Occasionally she would come to an
abrupt halt and wolf up great mouthfuls of the food that
had been set before her, for she was a greedy lady. Her
discomforted guests would seize the opportunity to join her,
in a more conservative manner, in taking refreshment. The
dinner was superb.

Her professional associates were less discomforted, the
Alleyns afterwards agreed, than a lay audience would have
been and indeed seemed more or less to take her passion in
their stride, occasionally contributing inflamatory remarks
while Signor Romano who was on her left made wide ineffable
gestures and when he managed to get hold of it, kissed her
hand. Alleyn was on her right. He was frequently appealed
to and came in for one or two excruciating prods in the ribs
as she drove home her points. He was conscious that Troy
had her eyes on him and when he got the chance, made a
lightning grimace of terror at her. He saw she was on the
threshold of giggles.

Troy was on Mr Reece's right. He seemed to think that in
the midst of this din he was under an obligation to make
conversation and remarked upon the lack of journalistic
probity in Australia. The offending newspaper, it seemed,
was an Australian weekly with a wide circulation in New
Zealand.

When the port had been put before him and his dear one
had passed for the time being into a baleful silence, he
suggested tonelessly that the ladies perhaps wished to withdraw.

The Sommita made no immediate response and a tricky
hiatus occurred during which she glowered at the table.
Troy thought: Oh, to hell with all this, and stood up. Hilda

43

Dancy followed with alacrity and so after a moment's hesitation did wide-eyed Sylvia Parry. The men got to their feet.

The Sommita rose, assumed the posture of a Cassandra about to give tongue, appeared to change her mind and said she was going to bed.

About twenty minutes later Alleyn found himself closeted in a room that looked like the setting for a science-fiction film but was Mr Reece's study. With him were Mr Reece himself, Mr Ben Ruby, Rupert Bartholomew and the straw-coloured secretary whose name turned out to be Hanley.

The infamous sheet of newsprint was laid out on a table round which the men had gathered. They read the type-written letter reproduced in the central box.

> To The Editor
> *The Watchman*
> Sir: I wish, through your column, to repudiate utterly an outrageous calumny which is circulating in this country. I wish to state, categorically, that I have no need of, and therefore have never resorted to, cosmetic surgery or to artificial embellishment of any kind whatsoever. I am, and I present myself to my public, as God made me. Thank you.
> > Isabella Sommita.
> > (*Picture on page 30*)

'And you tell me,' Alleyn said, 'that the whole thing is a forgery?'

'You bet it's a forgery,' said Ben Ruby. 'Would she ever help herself to a plateful of poisonous publicity! My God, this is going to make her the big laugh of a lifetime over in Aussie. *And* it'll spread overseas, you better believe it.'

'*Have* there in fact been any rumours, any gossip of this sort?'

'Not that we have knowledge of,' said Mr Reece, 'And if it

44

had been at all widespread, we certainly would have heard Wouldn't we, Ben?'

'Well, face it, old boy, anyone that's seen her would know it was silly. I meantersay, look at her cleavage? Speaks for itself.' Mr Ruby turned to Alleyn. 'You've seen. You couldn't miss it. She's got the best twin set you're likely to meet in a lifetime. Beautiful! Here! Take a look at this picture.'

· He turned to page 30 and flattened it out. The 'picture' was a photograph of the Sommita in profile with her head thrown back, her hands behind her resting on a table and taking the weight. She was in character as Carmen and an artificial rose was clenched between her teeth. She was powerfully décolletée and although at first glance there seemed to be no doubt of the authenticity of the poitrine, on closer examination there were certain curious little marks in that region suggestive of surgical scars. The legend beneath read 'Seeing's believing!'

'She never liked that picture,' Mr Ruby said moodily. 'Never. But the press did, so we kept it in the handouts. Here!' he exclaimed jamming a forefinger at it. 'Here, take a look at this, will you? This has been interfered with. This has been touched up. This has been tinkered with. Those scars are phoney.'

Alleyn examined it. 'I think you're right,' he said and turned back to the front page.

'Mr Hanley,' he said, 'do you think that typewriter could have been one belonging to anybody in Madame Sommita's immediate circle? Can you tell that?'

'Oh? Oh!' said the secretary and stooped over the paper. 'Well,' he said after a moment, 'it wasn't typed on my machine.' He laughed uncomfortably. 'I can promise you that much,' he said. 'I wouldn't know about hers. How about it, Rupert?'

'Bartholomew,' explained Mr Reece in his flattened way, 'is Madame's secretary.' He stood back and motioned Rupert to examine the page.

Rupert who had a tendency to change colour whenever

Mr Reece paid him any attention, did so now. He stooped over the paper.

'No,' he said, 'it's not our—I mean my—machine. The letter p is out of alignment in ours. And anyway it's not the same type.'

'And the signature? That looks convincing enough, doesn't it?' Alleyn asked his host.

'Oh yes,' he said. 'It's Bella's signature.'

'Can any of you think of any cause Madame Sommita may have had to put her signature at the foot of a blank sheet of letter paper?'

Nobody spoke.

'Can she type?'

'No,' they all said and Ben Ruby added irritably, 'Ah, for Chrissake, what's the point of labouring at it? There've been no rumours about her bosom, pardon my candour, and, hell, she never wrote that bloody letter. It's got to be a forgery and, by God, in my book it's got to be that sodding photographer at the bottom of it.'

The two young men made sounds of profound agreement.

Mr Reece raised his hand and they were silenced. 'We are fortunate enough,' he announced, 'to have Mr Alleyn, or rather Chief Superintendent Alleyn, with us. I suggest that we accord him our full attention, gentlemen.'

He might have been addressing a board meeting. He turned to Alleyn and made a slight inclination. 'Will you—?' he invited.

Alleyn said: 'Of course, if you think I can be of use. But I expect I ought just to mention that if there's any idea of calling in the police it will have to be the New Zealand police. I'm sure you will understand that.'

'Oh, quite so, quite so,' said Mr Reece. 'Let us say we will value, immensely, your unofficial expertise.'

'Very well. But it won't be at all startling.'

The men took chairs round the table, as if, Alleyn thought, they were resigning themselves to some damned lecture. The whole scene, he thought, was out of joint.

They might have arranged between themselves how it should be played but were not quite sure of their lines.

He remembered his instructions from the AC. He was to observe, act with extreme discretion, fall in with the terms of his invitation and treat the riddle of the naughty photographer as he would any case to which he had been consigned in the ordinary course of his duties.

He said: 'Here goes then. First of all: if this was a police job one of the first things to be done would be to make an exhaustive examination of the letter which seems to be a reproduction in print of an original document. We would get it blown up on a screen, search the result for any signs of fingerprints or indications, of what sort of paper the original might be. Same treatment for the photograph with particular attention to the rather clumsy faking of surgical scars.

'At the same time someone would be sent to the offices of *The Watchman* to find out everything available about when the original letter was received and whether by post or pushed into the correspondence box at the entrance or wherever of *The Watchman*'s office. And also who dealt with it. *The Watchman*, almost certainly, would be extremely cagey about this and would, when asked to produce the original, say it had not been kept which might or might not be true. Obviously,' Alleyn said, 'they didn't ask for any authorization of the letter or take any steps to assure themselves that it was genuine.'

'It's not that sort of paper,' said Ben Ruby. 'Well, look at it. If we sued for libel it'd be nothing new to *The Watchman*. The scoop would be worth it.'

'Didn't I hear,' Alleyn asked, 'that on one occasion the photographer—"Strix" isn't it?—dressed as a woman, asked for her autograph and then fired his camera at point-blank range and ducked out?'

Mr Ruby slammed the table. 'By God, you're right,' he shouted, 'and he got it. She signed. He got her signature.'

'It's too much, I suppose, to ask if she remembers any particular book or whether she ever signed at the bottom of a blank page or how big the page was.'

'She remembers! Too right she remembers!' Mr Ruby shouted. 'That one *was* an outsize book. Looked like something special for famous names. She remembers it on account it was not the usual job. As for the signature she's most likely to have made it extra big to fill out the whole space. She does that.'

'Were any of you with her? she was leaving the theatre, wasn't she? At the time?'

'I was with her,' Mr Reece offered. 'So were you, Ben. We always escort her from the stage door to her car. I didn't actually see the book. I was looking to make sure the car was in the usual place. There was a big crowd.'

'I was behind her,' said Mr Ruby. '*I* couldn't see anything. The first thing *I* knew was the flash and the rumpus. She was yelling out for somebody to stop the photographer. Somebody else was screaming "Stop that woman!" and fighting to get through. And it turned out afterwards, the screamer was the woman herself who was the photographer Strix if you can follow me.'

'Just,' said Alleyn.

'He's made monkeys out of the lot of us; all along the line he's made us look like monkeys,' Mr Ruby complained.

'What does *he* look like? Surely someone must have noticed something about him?'

But, no, it appeared. Nobody had come forward with a reliable description. He operated always in a crowd where everyone's attention was focused on his victim and cameramen abounded. Or unexpectedly he would pop round a corner with his camera held in both hands before his face, or from a car that shot off before any action could be taken. There had been one or two uncertain impressions — he was bearded, he had a scarf pulled over his mouth, he was dark. Mr Ruby had a theory that he never wore the same clothes twice and always went in for elaborate make-ups but there was nothing to support this idea.

'What action ' Mr Reece asked Alleyn, 'would you advise?'

'To begin with: *not* an action for libel. Can she be persuaded against it, do you think?'

'She may be all against it in the morning. You never know,' said Hanley, and then with an uneasy appeal to his employer: 'I *beg* your pardon, sir, but I mean to say you *don't*, do you? Actually?'

Mr Reece, with no change of expression in his face, merely looked at his secretary who subsided nervously.

Alleyn had returned to *The Watchman*. He tilted the paper this way and that under the table lamp. 'I think,' he said, 'I'm not *sure* but I *think* the original paper was probably glossy.'

'I'll arrange for someone to deal with *The Watchman* end,' said Mr Reece, and to Hanley: 'Get through to Sir Simon Marks in Sydney,' he ordered. 'Or wherever he is. Get him.'

Hanley retreated to a distant telephone and huddled over it in soundless communication.

Alleyn said: 'If I were doing this as a conscientious copper I would now ask you all if you have any further ideas about the perpetrator of these ugly tricks — assuming for the moment that the photographer and the concoctor of the letter are one and the same person. Is there anybody you can think of who bears a grudge deep enough to inspire such persistent and malicious attacks? Has she an enemy, in fact?'

'Has she a hundred bloody enemies?' Mr Ruby heatedly returned. 'Of course she has. Like the homegrown baritone she insulted in Perth or the top hostess in Los Angeles who threw a high-quality party for her and asked visiting royalty to meet her.'

'What went wrong?'

'She didn't go.'

'Oh dear!'

'Took against it at the last moment because she'd heard the host's money came from South Africa. We talked about a sudden attack of migraine, which might have answered if she hadn't gone to supper at Angelo's and the press hadn't

49

reported it with pictures the next morning.'

'Wasn't "Strix" already in action by then, though?'

'That's true,' agreed Mr Ruby gloomily. 'You've got something there. But enemies! My oath!'

'In my view,' said Mr Reece, 'the matter of enmity doesn't arise. This has been from first to last a profitable enterprise. I've ascertained that "Strix" can ask what he likes for his photographs. It's only a matter of time, one imagines, before they reappear in bookform. He's hit on a money-spinner and unless we can catch him in the act he'll go on spinning as long as the public interest lasts. Simple as that.'

'If he concocted the letter,' Alleyn said, 'it's hard to see how he'd make money out of that. He could hardly admit to forgery.'

Rupert Bartholomew said: 'I think the letter was written out of pure spite. She thinks so, too: you heard her. A sort of black practical joke.'

He made this announcement with an air of defiance, almost of proprietorship. Alleyn saw Mr Reece look at him for several seconds with concentration as if his attention had been unexpectedly aroused. He thought: That boy's getting himself into deep water.

Hanley had been speaking into the telephone. He stood up and said, 'Sir Simon Marks, sir.'

Mr Reece took the call inaudibly. The others fell into an unrestful silence, not wishing to seem as if they listened but unable to find anything to say to each other. Alleyn was conscious of Rupert Bartholomew's regard which as often as he caught it was hurriedly turned away. He's making some sort of appeal, Alleyn thought and went over to him. They were now removed from the others.

'Do tell me about your opera,' he said. 'I've only gathered the scantiest picture from our host of what is going to happen but it all sounds most exciting.'

Rupert muttered something about not being too sure of that.

'But,' said Alleyn, 'it must be an enormous thing for you.

isn't it? For the greatest soprano of our time to bring it all about? A wonderful piece of good fortune, I'd have thought.'

'Don't,' Rupert muttered. 'Don't say that.'

'Hullo! What's all this? First night nerves?'

Rupert shook his head. Good Lord, Alleyn thought, a bit more of this and he'll be in tears. Rupert stared at him and seemed to be on the edge of speech when Mr Reece put back the receiver and rejoined the others. 'Marks will attend to *The Watchman*,' he said. 'If the original is there he'll see that we get it.'

'Can you be sure of that?' Ruby asked.

'Certainly. He owns the group and controls the policy.'

They began to talk in a desultory way and for Alleyn their voices sounded a long way off and disembodied. The spectacular room became unsteady and its contents swelled, diminished and faded. I'm going to sleep on my feet, he thought and pulled himself together.

He said to his host, 'As I can't be of use, I wonder if I may be excused? It's been a long day and one didn't get much sleep on the plane.'

Mr Reece was all consideration. 'How very thoughtless of us,' he said. 'Of course. Of course.' He made appropriate hospitable remarks about hoping the Alleyns had everything they required, suggested that they breakfasted late in their room and ring when they were ready for it. He sounded as if he was playing some sort of internal cassette of his own recording. He glanced at Hanley who advanced, all eager to please.

'We're in unbelievable bliss,' Alleyn assured them, scarcely knowing what he said. And to Hanley: 'No, please don't bother. I promise not to doze off on my way up. Good night, everyone.'

He crossed the hall which was now dimly lit. The pregnant woman loomed up and stared at him through slitted eyes. Behind her the fire, dwindled to a glow, pulsated quietly.

As he passed the drawing-room door he heard a scatter of

desultory conversation: three voices at the most, he thought, and none of them belonging to Troy.

And, sure enough, when he reached their room he found her in bed and fast asleep. Before joining her he went to the heavy window curtains, parted them and saw the lake in moonlight close beneath him, stretching away like a silver plain into the mountains. Incongruous, he thought, and impertinent, for this little knot of noisy, self-important people with their self-imposed luxury and serio-comic concerns to be set down at the heart of such an immense serenity.

He let the curtain fall and went to bed.

He and Troy were coming back to earth in Mr Reece's aeroplane. An endless road rushed towards them. Appallingly far below, the river thundered and water lapped at the side of their boat. He fell quietly into it and was immediately fathoms deep.

*Chapter Three*

REHEARSAL

I

Troy slept heavily and woke at ten o'clock to find Alleyn up and dressed and the room full of sunshine.

'I've never known you so unwakeable,' he said. 'Deep as the lake itself. I've asked for our breakfast.'

'Have you been up long?'

'About two hours. The bathroom's tarted up to its eyebrows. Jets of water smack you up where you least expect it. I went downstairs. Not a soul about apart from the odd slave who looked at me as if I was dotty. So I went outside and had a bit of an explore. Troy, it really is quite extraordinarily beautiful, this place; so still; the lake clear, the trees motionless, everything new and fresh and yet, or so one feels, empty and belonging to primordial time. Dear me,' said Alleyn, rubbing his nose, 'I'd better not try. Let's tell each other about what went on after that atrocious dinner-party.'

'I've nothing to tell. When we left you the diva merely said in a volcanic voice: 'Excuse me, ladies,' and swept upstairs. I gave her time to disappear and then followed suit. I can scarcely remember getting myself to bed. What about you?'

Alleyn told her.

'If you ask me,' Troy said, 'it needs only another outrage like this and she'll break down completely. She was literally shaking all over as if she had a rigor. She can't go on like that. Don't you agree?'

'Not really. Not necessarily. Have you ever watched two Italians having a discussion in the street? Furious gestures, shrieks, glaring eyes, faces close together. Any moment, you

53

think, it'll be a free-for-all and then without warning they burst out laughing and hit each other's shoulders in comradely accord. I'd say she was of the purest Italian — perhaps Sicilian — peasant stock and utterly uninhibited. Add to that the propensity of all public performers to cut up rough and throw temperaments right and left when they think they've been slighted and you've got La Sommita. You'll see.' .

But beyond staring bemusedly out of the windows, Troy was not given much chance of seeing for herself. Instead, she and Alleyn were to be taken on a tour of the house by Mr Reece, beginning with the 'studio' which turned out to be on the same level as their bedroom. Grand pianos being as chicken-feed to Mr Reece, there was one in here and Troy was given to understand that the Sommita practiced at it and that the multiple-gifted Rupert Bartholomew acted as her accompanist, having replaced an Australian lady in that capacity. She found, with astonishment, that an enormous easel of sophisticated design and a painter's table and stool had been introduced into the room for her use. Mr Reece was anxious, he said, to know if they suited. Troy, tempted to ask if they were on sale or return, said they did and was daunted by their newness. There was also a studio throne with a fine lacquer screen on it. Mr Reece expressed a kind of drab displeasure that it was not large enough to accommodate the grand piano as well. Troy, who had already made up her mind what she wanted to do with her subject, said it was of no consequence. When, she asked, would she be able to start? Mr Reece, she thought, was slightly evasive. He had not spoken this morning to Madame, he said, but he understood there would be rehearsals for the greater part of the day. The orchestra was to arrive. They had been rehearsing, with frequent visits from Bartholomew, and would arrive by bus. The remaining guests were expected tomorrow.

The studio window was of the enormous plate-glass kind. Through it they had a new view of lake and mountains. Immediately beneath them, adjoining the house, was a patio and close by an artificially enclosed swimming pool, round which and in which members of the house-party were displayed. On the extreme right, separated from the pool and surrounded by native bush, was an open space and a hangar which, Mr Reece said, accommodated the helicopter.

Mr Reece was moved to talk about the view which he did in a grey, factual manner, stating that the lake was so deep in many parts that it had never been sounded and that the region was famous for a storm, known locally as The Rosser, which rose unheralded in the mountains and whipped the lake into fury and had been responsible for many fatal accidents.

He also made one or two remarks on the potential for 'development' and Alleyn saw the look of horrified incredulity on his wife's face. Fortunately, it appeared, pettifogging legislation about land-tenure and restrictions on imported labour would prohibit what Mr Reece called 'worthwhile touristic planning' so that the prospect of marinas, highrise hotels, speedboats, loud music and floodlit bathing pools did not threaten those primordial shores. Sandflies by day and mosquitoes by night, Mr Reece thought, could be dealt with and Troy envisaged low-flying aircraft delivering millions of gallons of kerosene upon the immaculate face of the lake.

Without warning she was overcome by a return of fatigue and felt quite unable to face an extended pilgrimage of this unending mansion. Seeing her dilemma, Alleyn asked Mr Reece if he might fetch her gear and unpack it. There was immediate talk of summoning a 'man' but they managed to avoid this. And then a 'man' in fact did appear, the dark, Italiate-looking person who had brought their breakfast. He had a message for Mr Reece. Madame Sommita wished to see him urgently.

'I think I had better attend to this,' he said. 'We all meet on the patio at eleven for drinks. I hope you will both join us there.'

So they were left in peace. Alleyn fetched Troy's painting gear and unpacked it. He opened up her old warrior of a paint-box, unstrapped her canvases and set out her sketch-book, and the collection of materials that were like signatures written across any place where Troy worked. She sat in a chair by the window and watched him and felt better.

Alleyn said: 'This room will be de-sterilized when it smells of turpentine and there are splotches of flake white on the ledge of that easel and paint rags on the table.'

'At the moment it can *not* be said to beckon one to work. They might as well have hung Please Don't Touch notices on everything.'

'You won't mind once you get going.'

'You think? P'raps you're right,' she said, cheering up. She looked down at the house-party round the pool. 'That's quite something,' she said. 'Very frisky colour and do notice Signor Lattienzo's stomach. Isn't it superb!'

Signor Lattienzo was extended on an orange-coloured chaise-longue. He wore a green bathrobe which had slid away from his generous torso upon which a book with a scarlet cover was perched. He glistened.

Prompted, perhaps, by that curious telepathy which informs people that they are being stared at, he threw back his head, saw Troy and Alleyn and waved energetically. They responded. He made eloquent Italianate gestures which he wound up by kissing both his hands at once to Troy.

'You've got off, darling,' said Alleyn.

'I like him, I think. But I'm afraid he's rather malicious. I didn't tell you. He thinks that poor beautiful young man's opera is awful. Isn't that sad?'

'Is *that* what's the matter with the boy!' Alleyn exclaimed. 'Does *he* know it's no good?'

'Signor Lattienzo thinks he might.'

'And yet they're going on with all this wildly extravagant business.'

'She insists, I imagine.'

'Ah.'

'Signor Lattienzo says she's as stupid as an owl.'

'Musically?'

'Yes. But I rather gathered generally, as well

'The finer points of attitudes towards a hostess don't seem to worry Signor Lattienzo.'

'Well, if we're going to be accurate, I suppose she's not his hostess. She's his ex-pupil.'

'True.'

Troy said: 'That boy's out of his depth altogether. She's made a nonsense of him. She's a monster and I can't wait to get it on canvas. A monster,' Troy repeated with relish.

'He's not down there with the rest of them,' Alleyn pointed out. 'I suppose he's concerned with the arrival of his orchestra.'

'I can't bear to think of it. Imagine! All these musical VIPs converging on him and he knowing, if he *does* know, that it's going to be a fiasco. He's going to conduct. Imagine!'

'Awful. Rubbing his nose in it.'

'We'll have to be there.'

'I'm afraid so, darling.'

Troy had turned away from the window and now faced the door of the room. She was just in time to see it gently closing.

'What's wrong?' Alleyn asked quickly.

Troy whispered: 'The door. Someone's just shut it.'

'Really?'

'Yes. Truly.'

He went to the door and opened it. Troy saw him look to his right.

'Hullo, Bartholomew,' he said. 'Good morning to you. Looking for Troy, by any chance?'

There was a pause and then Rupert's Australian voice, unevenly pitched, not fully audible: 'Oh, good morning. I — yes -- matter of fact — message — '

'She's here. Come in.'

He came in, white-faced and hesitant. Troy welcomed him

with what she felt might be overdone cordiality and asked if his message was for her.

'Yes,' he said, 'yes, it is. She — I mean Madame Sommita — asked me to say she's very sorry but in case you might be expecting her she can't — she's afraid she won't be able — to sit for you today because — because —'

'Because of rehearsals and everything? Of course. I wasn't expecting it and in fact I'd rather *not* start today.'

'Oh,' he said, 'yes. I see. Good-oh, then. I'll tell her.'

He made as if to go but seemed inclined to stay.

'Do sit down,' said Alleyn, 'unless you're in a hurry, of course. We're hoping someone — you, if you've time — will tell us a little more about tomorrow night.'

He made a movement with both hands almost as if he wanted to cover his ears but checked it and asked if they minded if he smoked. He produced a cigarette case; gold with a jewelled motif.

'Will you?' he said to Troy and when she declined, turned to Alleyn. The open case slipped out of his uncertain grasp. He said: 'Oh. Sorry,' and looked as if he'd been caught shoplifting. Alleyn picked it up. The inside of the lid was inscribed. There in all its flamboyance was the now familiar signature: Isabella Sommita.

Rupert was making a dreadfully clumsy business of shutting the case and lighting his cigarette. Alleyn, as if continuing a conversation, asked Troy where she would like him to put the easel. They improvised an argument about light and the possibility of the bathing pool as a subject. This enabled them both to look out of the window.

'Very tricky subject,' Troy said. 'I don't think I'm up to it!'

'Better maintain a masterly inactivity, you think?' Alleyn cheerfully rejoined. 'You may be right.'

They turned back into the room and there was Rupert Bartholomew, sitting on the edge of the model's throne and crying.

He possessed male physical beauty to such a remarkable degree that there was something unreal about his tears.

They trickled over the perfect contours of his face and might have been drops of water on a Greek mask. They were distressing but they were also incongruous.

Alleyn said: 'My dear chap, what's the matter?' and Troy: 'Would you like to talk about it? We're very discreet.'

He talked. Disjointedly at first and with deprecating interruptions — they didn't want to hear all this — he didn't want them to think he was imposing — it could be of no interest to them. He wiped his eyes, blew his nose, drew hard on his cigarette and became articulate.

At first it was simply a statement that The Alien Corn was no good, that the realization had come upon him out of the blue and with absolute conviction. 'It was ghastly,' he said. 'I was pouring out drinks and suddenly, without warning, I knew. Nothing could alter it: the thing's punk.'

'Was this performance already under consideration?' Alleyn asked him.

'She had it all planned. It was meant to be a — well — a huge surprise. And the ghastly thing is,' said Rupert, his startlingly blue eyes opened in horror, 'I'd thought it all fantastic. Like one of those schmaltzy young-genius-makes-it films. I'd been in — well — in ecstasy.'

'Did you tell her, there and then?' asked Troy.

'Not then. Mr Reece and Ben Ruby were there. I — well, I was so — you know — shattered. Sort of. I waited,' said Rupert, and blushed, 'until that evening.'

'How did she take it?'

'She didn't take it. I mean she simply wouldn't listen. I mean she simply swept it aside. She said — my God, she said genius always had moments like these, moments of what she called divine despair. She said *she* did. Over her singing. And then, when I sort of tried to stick it out, she — was — well, very angry. And you see — I mean she had cause. All her plans and arrangements. She'd written to Beppo Lattienzo and Sir David Baumgartner and she'd fixed up with Rodolfo and Hilda and Sylvia and the others. And the press. The big names. All that. I did hang out for a bit but —'

He broke off, looked quickly at Alleyn and then at the floor. 'There were other things. It's more complicated than I've made it sound,' he muttered.

'Human relationships can be hellishly awkward, can't they?' Alleyn said.

'You're telling me,' Rupert fervently agreed. Then he burst out: 'I think I must have been mad! Or ill, even. Like running a temperature and now it's gone and— and—I'm cleaned out and left with tomorrow.'

'And you *are* sure?' Troy asked. 'What about the company and the orchestra? Do you know what they think? And Signor Lattienzo?'

'She made me promise not to show it to him. I don't know if *she's* shown it. I think she has. He'll have seen at once that it's awful, of course. And the company: they know all right. Rodolfo Romano very tactfully suggests alterations. I've seen them looking at each other. They stop talking when I turn up. Do you know what they call it? They think I haven't heard but I've heard all right. The call it *Corn*. Very funny. Oh,' Rupert cried out, 'she shouldn't have done it! It hasn't been a fair go: I hadn't got a hope. Not a hope in hell. My God, she's making me *conduct*. There I'll stand, before those VIPs, waving my arms like a bloody puppet and they won't know which way to look for embarrassment.'

There was a long silence, broken at last by Troy.

'Well,' she said vigorously, 'refuse. Never mind about the celebrities and the fuss and the phoney publicity. It'll be very unpleasant and it'll take a lot of guts but at least it'll be honest. To the devil with the lot of them. Refuse.'

He got to his feet. He had been bathing and his short yellow robe had fallen open. He's apricot-coloured, Troy noted, not blackish tan and coarsened by exposure like most sun addicts. He's really too much of a treat. No wonder she grabbed him. He's a collector's piece, poor chap.

'I don't think,' Rupert said, 'I'm any more chicken than the next guy. It's not that. It's her—Isabella. You saw last night what she can be like. And coming on top of this letter

60

business—look, she'd either break down and make herself ill or—or go berserk and murder somebody. Me, for preference.'

'Oh, come *on*!' said Troy.

'No,' he said, 'it's not nonsense. Really. She's a Sicilian.'

'Not *all* Sicilians are tigers,' Alleyn remarked.

'Her kind are.'

Troy said, 'I'm going to leave you to Rory. I think this calls for male-chauvinist gossip.'

When she had gone, Rupert began apologizing again. What, he asked, would Mrs Alleyn think of him?

'Don't start worrying about that,' Alleyn said. 'She's sorry, she's not shocked and she's certainly not bored. And I think she may be right. However unpleasant it may be, I think perhaps you should refuse. But I'm afraid it's got to be your decision and nobody else's.'

'Yes, but you see you don't know the worst of it. I couldn't bring it out with Mrs Alleyn here. I—Isabella— we—'

'Good Lord, my dear chap—' Alleyn began and then pulled himself up. 'You're lovers, aren't you?' he said.

'If you can call it that,' he muttered.

'And you think if you take this stand against her you'll lose her? That it?'

'Not exactly—I mean, yes, of course, I suppose she'd kick me out.'

'Would that be such a very bad thing?'

'It'd be a bloody good thing,' he burst out.

'Well, then—'

'I can't expect you to understand. I don't understand myself. At first it was marvellous: magical. I felt equal to anything. Way up. Out of this world. To hear her sing, to stand at the back of the theatre and see two thousand people go mad about her and to know that for *me* it didn't end with the curtain calls and flowers and ovations but that for *me* the best was still to come. Talk about the crest of the wave—gosh, it was super.'

'I can imagine.'

'And then, after that—you know—that moment of truth

about the opera, the whole picture changed. You could say that the same thing happened about her. I saw all at once what she really is like and that she only approved of that bloody fiasco because she saw herself making a success in it and that she ought never, *never* to have given me the encouragement she did. And I knew she had no real musical judgement and that I was lost.'

'All the more reason—' Alleyn began and was shouted down.

'You can't tell me anything I don't know. But I was *in* it. Up to my eyes. Presents—like this thing, this cigarette case. Clothes, even. A fantastic salary. At first I was so far gone in—I suppose you could call it—rapture, that it didn't seem degrading. And now, in spite of seeing it all as it really is, I can't get out. I can't.'

Alleyn waited. Rupert got to his feet. He squared his shoulders, pocketed his awful cigarette case and actually produced a laugh of sorts.

'Silly, isn't it?' he said, with an unhappy attempt at lightness. 'Sorry to have bored you.'

Alleyn said: 'Are you familiar with Shakespeare's sonnets?'

'No. Why?'

'There's a celebrated one that starts off by saying the expense of spirit in a waste of shame is lust in action. I suppose it's the most devastating statement you can find of the sense of degradation that accompanies passion without love. *La Belle Dame Sans Merci* is schmaltz alongside it. That's your trouble, isn't it? The gilt's gone off the gingerbread but the gingerbread is still compulsive eating. And that's why you can't make the break.'

Rupert twisted his hands together and bit his knuckles.

'You could put it like that,' he said.

The silence that followed was interrupted by an outbreak of voices on the patio down below: exclamations, sounds of arrival and unmistakably the musical hoots that were the Sommita's form of greeting.

'Those are the players,' said Rupert. 'I must go down We have to rehearse.'

## II

By midday Troy's jet-lag had begun to fade and with it the feeling of unreality in her surroundings. A familiar restlessness replaced it and this, as always, condensed into an itch to work. She and Alleyn walked round the island and found that, apart from the landing-ground for the helicopter and the lawnlike frontage with its sentinal trees, it was practically covered by house. The clever architect had allowed small areas of original bush to occur where they most could please. On the frontal approach from the lake to the Lodge, this as well as the house itself served to conceal a pole from which power lines ran across the lake to a spit of land with a dado of trees that reached out from the far side of the island.

'For the moment,' said Troy, 'don't let's think about what it all cost.'

They arrived at the bathing-pool as eleven o'clock; drinks were being served. Two or three guests had arrived at the same time as the quartet of players who turned out to be members of a South Island Regional Orchestra. The musicians, three men and a lady, sticking tight to each other and clearly overawed, were painstakingly introduced by Rupert. The Sommita, in white sharkskin with a tactful tunic, conversed with them very much *de haut en bas* and then engulfed the Alleyns, particularly Troy whose arm and hand she secured, propelling her to a canopied double seat and retaining her hold after they had occupied it. Troy found all this intensly embarrassing but at least it gave her a good opportunity to notice the markedly asymmetric structure of the face, the distance between the corner of the heavy mouth and that of the burning eye being greater on the left side. And there was a faint darkness, the slightest change of colour on the upper lip. You couldn't have a better face for Carmen, Troy thought.

The Sommita talked of the horrible letter and the touched-up photograph and what they had done to her and how shattering it was that the activities of the infamous photographer — for of course he was at the bottom of it — should have extended to New Zealand and even to the Island when she had felt safe at last from persecution.

'It *is* only the paper, though,' Troy pointed out. 'It's not as though the man himself was here. Don't you think it's quite likely that now the tour of Australia is over he may very well have gone back to his country of origin, wherever that may be? Mightn't the letter have just been his final effort? You had gone and he couldn't take any more photographs so he cooked up the letter?'

The Sommita stared at her for a long time and in a most uncomfortable manner, gave her hand a meaningful squeeze and released it. Troy did not know what to make of this.

'But,' the Sommita was saying, 'we must speak of your art, must we not? And of the portrait. We begin the day after tomorrow, yes? And I wear my crimson décolleté which you have not yet seen. It is by Saint-Laurent and is dramatic. And for the pose — this.'

She sprang to her feet, curved her sumptuous right arm above her head, rested her left palm upon her thigh, threw back her head and ogled Troy frowningly in the baleful, sexy manner of Spanish dancers. The posture provided generous exposure to her frontage and gave the lie to any suggestions of plastic surgery.

'I think,' Troy said, 'the pose might be a bit exacting to maintain. And if it's possible I'd like to make some drawings as a sort of limbering-up. Not posed drawings. Only slight notes. If I could just be inconspicuously on the premises and make scribbles with a stick of charcoal.'

'Yes? Ah! Good. This afternoon there will be rehearsal. It will be only a preparation for the dress-rehearsal tonight. You may attend it. You must be very inconspicuous, you understand.'

'That will be ideal,' said Troy. 'Nothing could suit me better.'

'My poor Rupert,' the Sommita suddenly proclaimed, again fixing Troy with that disquieting regard, 'is nervous. He has the sensitivity of the true artist, the creative temperament. He is strung like a violin.'

She suspects something, Troy thought. She's pumping. Damn.

She said: 'I can well imagine.'

'I'm sure you can,' said the Sommita with what seemed to be all too meaningful an emphasis.

'Darling Rupert,' she called to him: 'if your friends are ready perhaps you should show them — ?'

The players gulped down the rest of their drinks and professed themselves ready.

'Come!' invited the Sommita, suddenly all sparkle and gaiety. 'I show you now our music-room. Who knows? There may be inspiration for you, as for us. We bring also our great diviner who is going to rescue me from my persecutors.'

She towed Troy up to Alleyn and unfolded this proposition. Her manner suggested the pleasurable likelihood of his offering to seduce her at the first opportunity. 'So you come to the salon too,' she said, 'to hear music?' And in her velvet tones the word 'music' was fraught with much the same meaning as 'china' in *The Country Wife*.

Troy hurried away to get her sketching-block, charcoal and conté pencil. Alleyn waited for her and together they went to the 'music-room'.

It was entered by double doors from the rear of the main hall. It was, as Mr Ruby had once indicated, more like a concert chamber than a room. It were tedious to insist upon the grandiloquences of Waihoe Lodge: enough to say that the stage occupied one end of this enormous room, was approached from the auditorium by three wide steps up to a projecting apron and thence to the main acting area. Beautifully proportioned pillars were ranged across the back flanking curtained doorways. The musicians were in a little huddle by a grand piano on the floor of the auditorium and in the angle of the apron. They were tuning their instruments and Rupert, looking ill, was with them. The singers came in and sat together in the auditorium.

There was a change now in the Sommita; an air of being in her own professional climate and with no nonsense about it. She was deep in conversation with Romano when the Alleyns came in. She saw them and pointed to chairs half way down the auditorium. Then she folded her arms and stood facing the stage. Every now and then she shouted angry instructions. As if on some stage director's instruction, a shaft of sunlight from an open window found her. The effect was startling. Troy settled herself to make a drawing.

Now the little orchestra began to play: tentatively at first with stoppages when they consulted with Rupert. Then with one and another of the soloists, repeating passages, making adjustments. Finally the Sommita said, 'We take the aria, darling,' and swept up to stage centre.

Rupert's back was turned to the audience and facing the musicians. He gave them the beat conservatively. They played and were stopped by the Sommita. 'More authority,' she said. 'We should come in like a lion. Again.'

Rupert waited for a moment. Troy saw that his left hand was clenched so hard that the knuckles shone white. He flung back his head, raised his right hand and gave a strong beat. The short introduction was repeated with much more conviction, it reached a climax of sorts and then the whole world was filled with one long sound: '*Ah!*' sang the Sommita. '*A-a-a-h!*' and then: '*What joy is here, what peace, what plentitude!*'

At first it was impossible to question the glory, so astonishing was the sound, so absolute the command. Alleyn thought: Perhaps it hardly matters what she sings. Perhaps she could sing 'A bee-eye-ee-eye-ee sat on a wall-eye-all-eye-all' and distil magic from it. But before the aria had come to its end he thought that even if he hadn't been warned he would have known that musically it was no great shakes. He thought he could detect clichés and banalities. And the words! He supposed in opera they didn't matter all that much but the thought occurred that she might more appropriately have sung: 'What joy is here, what peace, what platitude.'

Troy was sitting two seats in front of Alleyn, holding her breath and drawing in charcoal. He could see the lines that ran out like whiplashes under her hand, the thrown-back head and the wide mouth. Not a bit, he thought, remembering their joke, as if the Sommita was yawning: the drawing itself sang. Troy ripped the sketch off her pad and began again. Now her subject talked to the orchestra who listened with a kind of avid respect, and Troy drew them in the graphic shorthand that was all her own.

Alleyn thought that if Rupert was correct in believing the players had rumbled the inadequacies of the music, the Sommita had ravished them into acceptance, and he wondered if, after all, she could work this magic throughout the performance and save poor Rupert's face for him.

A hand was laid on Alleyn's shoulder. He turned his head and found Mr Reece's impassive countenance close to his own. 'Can you come out?' he said very quietly. 'Something has happened.'

As they went out the Sommita and Rudolfo Romano had begun to sing their duet.

The servant who had brought the Alleyns their breakfast was in the study looking uneasy and deprecating.

'This is Marco,' said Mr Reece. 'He has reported an incident that I think you should know about. Tell Chief Superintendent Alleyn exactly what you told me.'

Marco shied a little on hearing Alleyn's rank, but he told his story quite coherently and seemed to gather assurance as he did so. He had the Italian habit of gesture but only a slight accent.

He said that he had been sent out to the helicopter hanger to fetch a case of wine that had been brought in the previous day. He went in by a side door and as he opened it heard a scuffle inside the hangar. The door dragged a little on the floor. There was, unmistakably, the sound of someone running. 'I think I said something, sir, "Hullo" or something, as I pushed the door open. I was just in time to catch sight of a man in bathing costume, running out at the open end of the hangar. There's not much room when the chopper's there. I had to run back and round the tail and by the time I got out he was gone.'

Alleyn said: 'The hangar, of course, opens on to the cleared space for take-off.'

'Yes, sir. And it's surrounded by a kind of shrubbery. The proper approach follows round the house to the front. I ran along it about sixty feet but there wasn't a sign of him so I returned and had a look at the bush as they call it. It was very overgrown and I saw at once he couldn't have got through it without making a noise. But there wasn't a sound. I peered about in case he was lying low and then I remembered that on the far side of the clearing there's another path through the bush going down to the lakeside. So I took this path. With the same result: nothing: Well, sir,' Marco amended, and an air of complacency if not of smugness crept over his face, 'I say "nothing". But that's not quite right. There was something. Lying by the path. There was this.'

With an admirable sense of timing he thrust forward his open palm. On it lay a small round metal or plastic cap.

'It's what they use to protect the lens, sir. It's off a camera.'


III


'I don't think,' Alleyn said, 'we should jump to alarming conclusions about this but certainly it should be followed up. I imagine,' he said drily, 'that anything to do with photography is a tricky subject at the Lodge.'

'With some cause,' said Mr Reece.

'Indeed. Now then, Marco. You've given us a very clear account of what happened and you'll think I'm being unduly fussy if we go over it all again.'

Marco spread his hands as if offering him the earth.

'First of all, then: this man. Are you sure it wasn't one of the guests or one of the staff?'

'No, no, no, no, no,' said Marco rapidly, shaking his finger sideways as if a wasp had stung it. 'Not possible. No!'

'Not, for instance, the launchman?'

'No, sir. No! Not anyone of the household. I am certain. I would swear it.'

'Dark or fair?'

'Fair. Bareheaded. Fair. Certainly a blond.'

'And bare to the waist?'

'Of course. Certainly.'

'Not even a camera slung over his shoulder?'

Marco closed his eyes, bunched his fingers and laid the tips to his forehead. He remained like that for some seconds.

'Well? What about it?' Mr Reece asked a trifle impatiently.

Marco opened his eyes and unbunched his fingers. 'It could have been in his hands,' he said.

'This path,' Alleyn said. 'The regular approach from the front of the house round to the hangar. As I recollect, it passes by the windows of the concert chamber?'

'Certainly,' Mr Reece said and nodded very slightly at Alleyn. 'And this afternoon they were not curtained.'

'And open?'

'And open.'

'Marco,' Alleyn said, 'did you at any point hear anything going on in the concert chamber?'

'But yes!' Marco cried, staring at him. 'Madame, sir. It was Madame. She sang. With the voice of an angel.'

'Ah.'

'She was singing still, sir, when I returned to the clearing.'

'After you found this cap, did you go on to the lakeside?'

69

'Not quite to the lakeside, sir, but far enough out of the bush to see that he was not there. And then I thought I should not continue but that I should report at once to Signor Reece. And that is what I did.'

'Very properly.'

'Thank you, sir.'

'And I,' said Mr Reece, 'have sent the house staff to search the grounds, and most of the guests.'

'If I remember correctly,' Alleyn said, 'at the point where Marco emerged from the bush it is only a comparatively short distance across from the Island to that narrow tree-clad spit that reaches out from the mainland towards the Island and is linked to it by your power lines?'

'You suggest he might have swum it?' Mr Reece asked.

'No, sir,' Marco intervened. 'Not possible. I would have seen him.' He stopped and then asked with a change of voice. 'Or would I?'

'If he's on the Island he will be found,' said Mr Reece coldly. And then to Alleyn: 'You were right to say we should not make too much of this incident. It will probably turn out to be some young hoodlum or another with a camera. But it is a nuisance. Bella has been very much upset by this Strix and his activities. If she hears of it she might well begin to imagine all sorts of things. I suggest we say nothing of it to the guests and performers. You hear that, Marco?'

Marco was all acquiescence.

Alleyn thought that if what was no doubt a completely uncoordinated search was thundering about the premises the chances of keeping the affair secret were extremely slender. But, he reminded himself, for the present the rehearsal should be engaging everybody's attention.

When he had gone, Mr Reece, with a nearer approach to cosiness than Alleyn would have thought within his command, said: 'What do you make of all that? Simply a loutish trespasser or—something else?'

'Impossible to say. Is it pretty widely known in New Zealand that Madame Sommita is your guest?'

'Oh yes. One tries to circumvent the press but one never totally succeeds. It has come out. There have been articles about the Lodge itself and there are pressmen who try to bribe the launchman to bring them over. He is paid a grotesquely high wage and has the sense to refuse. I must say,' Mr Reece confided 'it would be very much in character for one of these persons to skulk about the place, having, by whatever means, swimming perhaps, got himself on the Island. The hangar would be a likely spot, one might think, for him to hide.'

'He would hear the rehearsal from there.'

'Precisely. And await his chance to come out and take a photograph through an open window. It's possible. As long,' Mr Reece said, and actually struck his right fist into his left palm, 'as long as it isn't that filthy Strix at it again. Anything rather than that.'

'Will you tell me something about your staff? You've asked me to do my constabulary stuff and this would be a routine question?'

'Ned Hanley is better qualified than I to answer it. He came over here from Australia and saw to it. An over-ambitious hotel had gone into liquidation. He engaged eight of the staff and a housekeeper for the time we shall be using the Lodge. Marco was not one of these but we had excellent references, I understand. Ned would tell you.'

'An Italian, of course?'

'Oh yes. But a naturalized Australian. He made a great thing, just now, of his story but I would think it was substantially correct. I'm hoping the guests and performers will not, if they do get hold of the story, start jumping to hysterical conclusions. Perhaps we should let it be known quite casually that a boy had swum across and has been sent packing. What do you think?'

Before Alleyn could answer, the door opened and Signor Beppo Lattienzo entered. His immaculate white shorts and silken *matelot* were in disarray and he sweated copiously.

'My dears!' he said. 'Drama! The hunt is up. The Hound

71

of Heaven itself — or should I say Himself? — could not be more diligent.'

He dropped into a chair and fanned himself with an open palm. ' "Over hill, over dale, thorough bush, thorough brier," as the industrious fairy remarks and so do I. What fun to be known as "The Industrious Fairy" ' panted Signor Lattienzo coyly.

'Any luck?' Alleyn asked.

'Not a morsel. The faithful Maria, my dear Monty, is indomitable. Into the underbrush with the best of us. She has left her hairnet as a votive offering on a thorny entanglement known, I am informed, as a Bush Lawyer.'

Signor Lattienzo smiled blandly at Mr Reece and tipped Alleyn a lewdish wink. 'This,' he remarked, 'will not please our diva, no? and if we are to speak of hounds and of persistence, how about the intrepid Strix? What zeal! What devotion! Though she flee to the remotest antipodes, though she, as it were, to go to earth (in, one must add, the greatest possible comfort) upon an enchanted island, there shall he nose her out. One can only applaud. Admit it, my dear Monty.'

Mr Reece said: 'Beppo, there is no reason to suppose that the man Strix has had any part in this incident. The idea is ridiculous and I am most anxious that Bella should not entertain it. It is a trivial matter involving some local lout and must not be blown up into a ridiculous drama. You know very well, none better, how she can over-react and after last night's shock — I really must ask you to use the greatest discretion.'

Signor Lattienzo wiped the sweat away from the area round his left eye. He breathed upon his glass, polished it and with its aid contemplated his host. 'But, of course, my dear Monty,' he said quietly, 'I understand. Perfectly. I dismiss the photographer. Poof! He is gone. And now—'

The door burst open and Ben Ruby strode in. He also showed signs of wear and tear.

'Here! Monty!' he shouted. 'What the hell's the idea?

These servants of yours are all saying bloody Strix is back and you ought to call in the police. What about it?'


IV


Mr Reece, white with annoyance, summoned his entire staff, including the driver and the launchman, into the study. Alleyn, who was asked to remain, admired the manner in which the scene was handled and the absolute authority which Mr Reece seemed to command. He repeated the explanation that had been agreed upon. The theory of the intrusive lout was laid before them and the idea of Strix's recrudescence soundly rubbished. 'You will forget this idiotic notion, if you please,' said Mr Reece and his voice was frigid. He looked pointedly at Maria. 'You understand,' he said, 'You are not to speak of it to Madame.' He added something in Italian—not one of Alleyn's strongest languages but he thought it was a threat of the instant sack if Maria disobeyed orders.

Maria, who had shut her mouth like a trap, glared back at Mr Reece and muttered incomprehensibly. The household was then dismissed.

'I don't like your chances,' said Ben Ruby. 'They'll talk.'

'They will behave themselves. With the possible exception of the woman.'

'She certainly didn't sound co-operative.'

'Jealous.'

'Ah!' said Signor Lattienzo. 'The classic situation: Mistress and Abigail. No doubt Bella confides extensively.'

'No doubt.'

'Well, she can't do so for the moment. The *repetizione* is still in full swing.'

Ben Ruby opened the door. From beyond the back of the hall and the wall of the concert chamber but seeming to come from nowhere in particular there was singing: disembodied as if heard through the wrong end of some auditory telescope.

Above three unremarkable voices there soared an incomparable fourth.

'Yes,' said Signor Lattienzo. 'It is the *repetizione* and they are only at the quartet: a third of the way through. They will break for luncheon at one-thirty and it is now twenty minutes past noon. For the time being we are safe.'

'I wouldn't bet on that one, either,' said Ben Ruby. 'She likes to have Maria on tap at rehearsals.'

'If you don't mind,' Alleyn said, 'I think I'll just take a look at the terrain.'

The three men stared at him and for a moment said nothing. And then Mr Reece stood up. 'You surely cannot for a moment believe — ' he said.

'Oh no, no. But it strikes me that one might find something that would confirm the theory of the naughty boy.'

'Ah.'

'What, for instance?' asked Ben Ruby.

'This or that,' Alleyn said airily. 'You never know. The unexpected has a way of turning up. Sometimes. Like you, I wouldn't bet on it.'

And before any of them had thought of anything else to say he let himself out and gently closed the door.

He went out of the house by the main entrance, turned left and walked along the gravelled front until he came to a path that skirted the western façade. He followed it and as he did so the sound of music and of singing, broken by discussion and the repetition of short passages, grew louder. Presently he came to the windows of the concert chamber and saw that one of them, the first, was still open. It was at the end farthest removed from the stage, which was screened from it by a curtain that operated on a hinged bracket.

He drew nearer. There, quite close, was the spot in the auditorium where the Sommita had stood with her arms folded, directing the singers.

And there, still in her same chair, still crouched over her sketching-block with her short hair tousled and her shoulders hunched, was his wife. She was still hard at work. Her subject was out of sight haranguing the orchestra but her image leapt up under Troy's grubby hand. She was using a conté pencil and the lines she made, sometimes broadly emphatic, sometimes floating into extreme delicacy, made one think of the bowing of an accomplished fiddler.

She put the drawing on the floor pushed it away with her foot, and stared at it, sucking her knuckles and scowling Then she looked up and saw her husband He pulled a face at her, laid a finger across his lips and ducked out of sight.

He had been careful not to tread on the narrow strip of earth that separated the path from the wall and now, squatting, was able to examine it. It had been recently trampled by a number of persons. To hell with the search-party, thought Alleyn.

He moved further along the path, passing a garden seat and keeping as far away as was possible from the windows. The thicket of fern and underbrush on his right was broken here and there by forays, he supposed, of the hunt, successfully ruining any signs there might have been of an intruder taking cover. Presently the path branched away from the house into the bush to emerge, finally, at the hangar.

Inside the hangar there was ample evidence of Marco's proceedings. The earthy short cut he had taken had evidently been damp and Alleyn could trace his progress on the asphalt floor exactly as he had described it.

Alleyn crossed the landing-ground, scorching under the noonday sun. Sounds from the concert chamber had faded. There was no birdsong. He found the path through the bush to the lakeside and followed it: dark green closed about him and the now familiar conservatory smell of wet earth and moss.

It was only a short distance to the lake and soon the bush began to thin out admitting shafts of sunlight. It must have been about here that Marco said he had spotted the protective cap from the camera. Alleyn came out into the open and there, as he remembered them from his morning walk, were the shore and the lake and overhead power-lines reaching away to the far shore.

Alleyn stood for a time out there by the lakeside. The sun that beat down on his head spread a kind of blankness over the landscape, draining it of colour. He absent-mindedly reached into his pocket for his pipe and touched a small hard object. It was the lens cap, wrapped in his handkerchief. He took it out and uncovered it being careful not to touch the surface: a futile precaution, he thought, after Marco's handling of the thing.

It was from a well-known make of Japanese camera and produced self-developing instant results. The trade name 'Koto' was stamped on the top.

He folded it up and returned it to his pocket. In a general way he did not go much for 'inspiration' in detective work, but if ever he had been visited by such a bonus, it was at that moment down by the lake.

*Chapter Four*

PERFORMANCE

I

Early in the morning of the following day there was a change in the weather. A wind came up from the north-west, not a strong wind and not steady but rather it was a matter of occasional brushes of cooler air on the face and a vague stirring among the trees around the house. The sky was invaded by oncoming masses of cloud, turrets and castles that mounted and changed and multiplied The lake was no longer glassy but wrinkled. Wavelets slapped gently at the shore.

At intervals throughout the morning new guests would arrive: some by chartered plane to the nearest airport and thence by helicopter to the Island, others by train and car, and a contingent of indigenous musical intelligentsia by bus. The launch would be very active.

A piano-tuner arrived and could be heard dabbing away at single notes and, to the unmusical ear, affecting no change in their pitch.

Sir David Baumgartner, the distinguished musicologist and critic, was to stay overnight at the Lodge, together with a Dr Carmichael, a celebrated consultant who was also President of the New Zealand Philharmonic Society. The remainder faced many dark hours in launch, bus and cars and in mid-morning would be returned wan and bemused to their homes in Canterbury.

The general idea, as far as the Sommita had concerned herself with their reaction to these formidable exertions, was that the guests would be so enraptured by their entertainment as to be perfectly oblivious of all physical discomfort. In the meantime she issued a command that the entire house-party was to assemble outside the house for Mr Ben Ruby to take a mass photograph. They did so in chilly discomfort under a lowering sky.

'Eyes and teeth to the camera, everybody,' begged Mr Ruby.

The Sommita did not reappear at luncheon and was said to be resting. It was, on the whole, a quiet meal. Even Signor Lattienzo did little to enliven it. Rupert Bartholomew, looking anguished, ate nothing, muttered something to the effect that he was needed in the concert chamber and excused himself. Mr Reece made ponderous small-talk with Troy, while Alleyn, finding himself next to Miss Hilda Dancy, did his best. He asked her if she found opening nights trying and she replied in vibrant contralto: 'When they are important,' clearly indicating that this one was not. After Rupert had left them she said, 'It's a crying shame.'

'A crying shame?' he ventured. 'How?'

'You'll see,' she prophesied. 'Cannibal!' she added, and apart from giving him a dark look which he was unable to interpret, though he thought he could make a fairly good guess, she was disinclined for any further conversation.

After luncheon the Alleyns went up to the studio where he related the story of the interloper and the camera cap. When he had finished and Troy had taken time to think it over, she said: 'Rory, do you think he's still on the Island? The photographer?'

'The photographer? Yes,' he said and something in his voice made her stare at him. 'I think the photographer's here. I'll tell you why.' And he did.

For the rest of the afternoon Troy brooded over her drawings and made some more. Sounds of arrival were heard from time to time. Beyond the great window the prospect steadily darkened and the forest on the far shore moved as if brushed by an invisible hand. 'The arrivals by launch will

78

Alleyn heard her masterful tread. As he had no time to get away, he stepped boldly out of cover and encountered her face to face.

Her own face might have been a mask for one of the Furies. She made a complicated gesture and for a moment he thought that actually she might haul off and hit him, blameless as he was, but she ended up by grasping him by his coat collar, giving him a ferocious précis of their predicament and ordering him to bring Rupert to his senses. When he hesitated she shook him like a cocktail, burst into tears and departed.

Mr Reece, standing with authority on his own hearthrug, had not attempted to stem the tide of his dear one's wrath nor was it possible to guess at his reaction to it. Rupert sat with his head in his hands, raising it momentarily to present a stricken face.

'I'm so sorry,' Alleyn said, 'I've blundered in with what is clearly an inappropriate message.'

'Don't go,' said Mr Reece. 'A message? For me?'

'For Bartholomew. From your secretary.'

'Yes? He had better hear it.'

Alleyn delivered it. Rupert was wanted to set the lights.

Mr Reece asked coldly, 'Will you do this? Or is it going too far to expect it?'

Rupert got to his feet. 'Well,' he asked Alleyn, 'what do you think now? Do you say I should refuse?'

Allen said: 'I'm not sure. It's a case of divided loyalties, isn't it?'

'I would have thought,' said Mr Reece, 'that any question of loyalty was entirely on one side. To whom is he loyal if he betrays his patrons?'

'Oh,' Alleyn said, 'To his art.'

'According to him, he has no "art".'

'I'm not sure,' Alleyn said slowly, 'whether, in making his decision, it really matters. It's a question of aesthetic integrity.'

Rupert was on his feet and walking towards the door.

'Where are you going?' Mr Reece said sharply.

'To set the lights. I've decided,' said Rupert loudly. 'I can't stick this out any longer. I'm sorry I've given so much trouble. I'll see it through.'


## II

When Alleyn went up to their room in search of Troy he found her fast asleep on their enormous bed. At a loose end, and worried about Rupert Bartholomew's sudden capitulation, Alleyn returned downstairs. He could hear voices in the drawing-room and concert chamber. Outside the house, a stronger wind had got up.

Midway down the hall, opposite the dining-room, there was a door which Mr Reece had indicated as opening into the library. Alleyn thought he would find himself something to read and went in.

It might have been created by a meticulous scene-painter for an Edwardian drama. Uniform editions rose in irremovable tiers from floor to ceiling, the result, Alleyn supposed of some mass-ordering process; classics, biographies and travel. There was a section devoted to contemporary novels each a virgin in its unmolested jacket. There was an assembly of 'quality' productions that would have broken the backs of elephantine coffee tables and there were orderly stacks of the most popular weeklies.

He wandered along the ranks at a loss for a good read and high up in an ill-lit corner came upon a book that actually bore signs of usage. It was unjacketed and the spine was rubbed. He drew it out and opened it at the title page.

*Il Mistero di Bianca Rossi* by Pietro Lamparelli. Alleyn didn't read Italian with the complete fluency that alone gives easy pleasure but the title was an intriguing surprise. He allowed the verso to flip over and there on the flyleaf in sharp irregular characters was the owner's name M. V. Rossi.

He settled down to read it.

An hour later he went upstairs and found Troy awake and refreshed.

The opera, a one-acter which lasted only an hour, was to begin at eight o'clock. It would be prefaced by light snacks with drinks and followed by a grand dinner-party.

'Do you suppose,' Troy wondered, as they dressed, 'that a reconciliation has taken place?'

'I've no idea. She may go for a magnificent acceptance of his surrender or she may not be able to do herself out of the passionate rapture bit. My bet would be that she's too professional to allow herself to be upset before a performance.'

'I wish he hadn't given in.'

'He's made the harder choice, darling.'

'I suppose so. But if she does take him back—it's not a pretty thought.'

'I don't think he'll go. I think he'll pack his bags and go back to teaching the piano and playing with his small Sydney group and doing a little typing on the side.'

'Signor Lattienzo did say there were two or three signs of promise in the opera.'

'Did he? If he's right, the more shame on that termagant for what she's done to the boy.'

They were silent for a little while after this and then Troy said: 'Is there a window open? It's turned chilly, hasn't it?'

'I'll look.'

The curtains had been closed for the night. Alleyn parted them, and discovered an open window. It was still light outside. The wind had got up strongly now, there was a great pother of hurrying clouds in the sky and a wide vague sound abroad in the evening.

'It's brewing up out there,' Alleyn said. 'The lake's quite rough.' He shut the window.

'Not much fun for the guests going home,' said Troy, and then: 'I'll be glad, won't you, when this party's over?'

'Devoutly glad.'

'Watching that wretched boy's ordeal, it'll be like sitting out an *auto-da-fé*,' she said.

83

'Would you like to have a migraine? I'd make it sound convincing.'

'No. He'd guess. So, oh Lord, would she.'

'I'm afraid you're right. Should we go down now, darling, to our champagne and snacks?'

'I expect so. Rory, your peculiar mission seems to have got mislaid, doesn't it? I'd almost forgotten about it. Do you by any chance suppose Mr Reece to be a "Godfather" with an infamous Sicilian "Family" background?'

'He's a cold enough fish to be anything, but—' Alleyn hesitated for a moment. 'No,' he said. 'So far there's been nothing to report. I shall continue to accept his hospitality and will no doubt return empty-handed to my blasted boss. I've little stomach for the job, and that's a fact. If it wasn't for you, my particular dish, and your work in hand, I'd have even less. Come on.'

Notwithstanding the absence of Rupert and all the performers, the drawing-room was crowded. About thirty guests had arrived by devious means and were being introduced to each other by Mr Reece and his secretary. There were top people from the Arts Council, various conductors and a selection of indigenous critics, notably a prestigious authority from the *New Zealand Listener*. Conspicuous among the distinguished guests from abroad was a large rubicand man with drooping eyelids and a dictatorial nose: Sir David Baumgartner, the celebrated critic and musicologist. He was in close conversation with Signor Lattienzo who, seeing the Alleyns, gave them one of his exuberant bows, obviously told Sir David who they were and propelled him towards them.

Sir David told Troy that it really was a great honour and a delightful surprise to meet her and asked if it could be true that she was going to paint the Great Lady. He chaffed Alleyn along predictable lines, saying that they would all have to keep their noses clean, wouldn't they? He spoke gravely of the discomforts of his journey. It had come upon him, to put it bluntly, at a most inconvenient time and if it had been anybody else—here he gave them a roguish glance—he wouldn't have dreamt of—he need say no more. The implication clearly was that *The Alien Corn* had better be good.

Lobster sandwiches, pâté, and miniature concoctions of the kind known to Mr Justice Shallow as 'pretty little tiny kickshaws' were handed round and champagne galore. Sir David sipped, raised his eyebrows and was quickly ready for a refill. So were all the new arrivals. Conversation grew noisy.

'Softening up process,' Alleyn muttered.

And indeed by ten minutes to eight all signs of travel fatigue had evaporated and when Marco, who had been much in evidence, tinkled up and down on a little xylophone, he was obliged to do so for some time like a ship's steward walking down corridors with a summons to dinner.

Ben Ruby and Mr Reece began a tactful herding towards the concert chamber.

The doors were open. The audience assembled itself.

The chairs in the front rows were ticketed with the names of the house-guests and some of the new arrivals who evidently qualified as VIPs. Troy and Alleyn were placed on the left of Mr Reece's empty chair, Sir David and Signor Lattienzo on its right with Ben Ruby beyond them. The rest of the élite comprised the conductor of the New Zealand Philharmonic Orchestra and his wife, three professors of music from as many universities, an Australian newspaper magnate and four representatives of the press—which press exactly had not been defined. The remainder of an audience of about fifty chose their own seats while at the back the household staff was feudally accommodated.

The collective voice was loud and animated and the atmosphere of expectancy fully established. 'If only they keep it up,' Troy whispered to Alleyn. She glanced along the row to Signor Lattienzo. His arms were folded and his head inclined towards Sir David who was full of animation and bonhomie. Lattienzo looked up from under his brows, saw Troy and crossed the fingers of his right hand.

The players came in and tuned their instruments, a sound that always caught Troy under the diaphragm. The lights in the auditorium went out. The stage curtain glowed. Mr Reece slipped into his seat beside Troy. Rupert Bartholomew came in from behind the stage so inconspicuously that he had raised his baton before he had been noticed. The overture began.

Troy always wished she knew more about music and could understand why one sound moved her and another left her disengaged. Tonight she was too apprehensive to listen properly. She tried to catch the response of the audience, watched Rupert's back and wondered if he was able to distil any magic from his players, wondered, even, how long the ephemeral good-nature induced by champagne could be expected to last with listeners who knew what music was about. She was so distracted by these speculations that the opening of the curtain caught her by surprise.

She had dreamt up all sorts of awful possibilities: Rupert breaking down and walking out, leaving the show to crawl to disaster; Rupert stopping the proceedings and addressing the audience; or the audience itself growing more and more restless or apathetic and the performance ending on the scantiest show of applause and the audience being harangued by an infuriated Sommita.

None of these things took place. True, as the opera developed the boisterous good humour of the audience seemed to grow tepid but the shock of that Golden Voice, the astonishment it engendered note by note, was so extraordinary that no room was left for criticism. And there was, or so it seemed to Troy, a passage in the duet with Hilda Dancy — 'Whither thou goest' — when suddenly the music came true. She thought: That's one of the bits Signor Lattienzo meant. She looked along the row and he caught her glance and nodded.

Sir David Baumgartner, whose chin was sunk in his shirt frill in what passed for profound absorbtion, raised his head. Mr Reece, sitting bolt upright in his chair, inconspicuously consulted his watch.

The duet came to its end and Troy's attention wandered. The show was well-dressed, the supporting artistes being clad in low-profile biblical gear hired from a New Zealand company who had recently revived the York Cycle. The Sommita's costume, created for the occasion, was white and virginal and if it was designed to make Ruth look like a startling social misfit amidst the alien corn, succeeded wonderfully in achieving this end.

The quartet came and went and left no mark. Sir David looked irritated. The Sommita, alone on stage, sailed into a recitative and thence to her big aria. Troy now saw her purely in terms of paint, fixing her in the memory, translating her into a new idiom. The diva had arrived at the concluding *fioritura*, she moved towards her audience, she lifted her head, she spread her arms and rewarded them with her trump card—A above high C.

No doubt she would have been very cross if they had observed the rule about not applauding until the final curtain. They did not observe it. They broke into a little storm of clapping. She raised a monitory hand. The performance entered into its penultimate phase: a lachrymose parting between Ruth and Signor Romano, plump in kilted smock and leg strappings and looking like a late photograph of Caruso. Enter Boaz, discovering them and ordering the gleaner to be beaten. Ruth and Naomi pleading with Boaz to relent, which he did, and the opera ended with a rather cursory reconciliation of all hands in chorus.

The sense of relief when the curtains closed was so overwhelming that Troy found herself clapping wildly. After all, it had not been so bad. None of the horrors she had imagined had come to pass, it was over and they were in the clear.

Afterwards, she wondered if the obligatory response from the audience could have been evoked by the same emotion.

Three rapid curtain calls were taken. The first by the company, the second by the Sommita who was thinly cheered by back-benchers, and the third again by the Sommita who went through her customary routine of extended arms, kissed hands and deep curtsies.

And then she turned to the orchestra, advanced upon it with outstretched hand and beckoning smile only to find that her quarry had vanished. Rupert Bartholomew was gone. The violinist stood up and said something inaudible but seemed to suggest that Rupert was backstage. The Sommita's smile had become fixed. She swept to an upstage entrance and vanished through it. The audience, nonplussed, kept up a desultory clapping which had all but died out when she re-entered, bringing, almost dragging, Rupert after her.

He was sheet-white and dishevelled. When she exhibited him, retaining her grasp of his hand, he made no acknowledgement of the applause she exacted. It petered out into a dead silence. She whispered something and the sound was caught up in a giant enlargement: the north-west wind sighing round the island.

The discomfeature of the audience was extreme. Someone, a woman, behind Troy said: 'He's not well. He's going to faint,' and there was a murmur of agreement. But Rupert did not faint. He stood bolt upright, looked at nothing, and suddenly freed his hand.

'Ladies and Gentlemen,' he said loudly.

Mr Reece began to clap and was followed by the audience. Rupert shouted: 'Don't do that,' and they stopped. He then made his curtain speech.

'I expect I ought to thank you. Your applause is for a Voice. It's a wonderful Voice, insulted by the stuff it has been given to sing tonight. For that I am responsible. I should have withdrawn it at the beginning when I realized — when I first realized — when I knew —'

He swayed a little and raised his hand to his forehead.

'When I knew,' he said. And then he did faint. The curtains closed.

## III

Mr Reece handled the catastrophe with expertise. He stood up, faced his guests and said that Rupert Bartholomew had been unwell for some days and no doubt the strain of the production had been a little too much for him. He (Mr Reece) knew that they would all appreciate this and he asked them to reassemble in the drawing-room. Dinner would be served as soon as the performers were ready to join them.

So out they all trooped and Mr Reece, followed by Signor Lattienzo, went backstage.

As they passed through the hall the guests became more aware of what was going on outside: irregular onslaughts of wind, rain and, behind these immediate sounds, a vague groundswell of turbulence. Those guests who were to travel through the night by way of launch, bus and car began to exchange glances. One of them, a woman, who was near the windows parted the heavy curtains and looked out releasing the drumming sound of rain against glass and a momentary glimpse of the blinded pane. She let the curtain fall and pulled an anxious grimace. A hearty male voice said loudly. 'Not to worry. She'll be right.'

More champagne in the drawing-room and harder drinks for the asking. The performers began to come in and Hanley with them. He circulated busily. 'Doing his stuff,' said Alleyn.

'Not an easy assignment,' said Troy and then: 'I'd like to know how that boy is.'

'So would I.'

'Might we be able to do anything, do you suppose?'

'Shall we ask?'

Hanley saw them, flashed his winsome smile and joined them. 'We're going in now,' he said. 'The Lady asks us not to wait.'

'How's Rupert?'

'Poor dear! *Wasn't* it a pity? Everything had gone *so* well.

He's in his room. Lying down, you know, but quite all right. Not to be disturbed. He'll be *quite* all right,' Hanley repeated brightly. 'Straight-out case of nervous fatigue. Ah, there's the gong. Will you give a lead? Thank you *so* much.'

On this return passage through the hall, standing inconspicuously just inside the entrance and partly screened by the vast pregnant woman whose elfin leer suggested a clandestine rendezvous, was a figure in dripping oilskins: Les, the launchman. Hanley went to speak to him.

The dining-room had been transformed, two subsidiary tables being introduced to form an E with the middle stroke missing. The three central places at the 'top' table were destined for the Sommita, her host and Rupert Bartholomew, none of whom appeared to occupy them. All the places were named and the Alleyns were again among the VIPs. This time Troy found herself with Mr Reece's chair on her left and Signor Lattienzo on her right. Alleyn was next to the Sommita's empty chair with the wife of the New Zealand conductor on his left.

'This is delightful,' said Signor Lattienzo.

'Yes, indeed,' said Troy who was not in the mood for badinage.

'I arranged it.'

'You, what?' she exclaimed.

'I transposed the cards. You had been given the New Zealand *maestro* and I his wife. She will be enraptured with your husband's company and will pay no attention to her own husband. He will be less enraptured but that cannot be helped.'

'Well,' said Troy, 'for sheer effrontery, I must say—!'

'I take, as you say, the buttery bun? Apropos, I am much in need of refreshment. That was a most painful débâcle, was it not?'

'Is he all right? Is someone doing something? I'm sure I don't know what anybody *can* do,' Troy said, 'but is there someone?'

'I have seen him.'

'You have?'

'I have told him that he took a courageous and honest course. I was also able to say that there was a shining moment — the duet when you and I exchanged signals. He has rewritten it since I saw the score. It is delightful.'

'That will have helped.'

'A little, I think.'

'Yesterday he confided rather alarmingly in us, particularly in Rory. Do you think he might like to see Rory?'

'At the moment I hope he is asleep. A Dr Carmichael has seen him and I have administered a pill. I suffer,' said Signor Lattienzo, 'from insomnia.'

'Is she coming down, do you know?'

'I understand from our good Monty — yes. After the débâcle she appeared to have been in two minds about what sort of temperament it would be appropriate to throw. Obviously an attack upon the still unconscious Rupert was out of the question. There remained the flood of remorse which I fancy she would not care to entertain since it would indicate a flaw in her own behaviour. Finally there could be a demonstration as from a distracted lover. Puzzled by this choice, she burst into a storm of ambiguous tears and Retired, as they say in your Shakespeare, Above. Escorted by Monty. To the ministrations of the baleful Maria and with the intention of making another delayed entrance. We may expect her at any moment, no doubt. In the meantime the grilled trout was delicious and here comes the coq-au-vin.'

But the Sommita did not appear. Instead, Mr Reece arrived to say that she had been greatly upset by poor Rupert Bartholomew's collapse which had no doubt been due to nervous exhaustion, but would rejoin them a little later. He then said that he was sorry indeed to have to tell them that he had been advised by the launchman that the local storm, known as The Rosser, had blown up and would increase in force, probably reaching its peak in about an hour when it would then become inadvisable to make the crossing to the mainland. Loath as he was to break up the party, he felt perhaps . . . He spread his hands.

The response was immediate. The guests, having finished their marrons glacés, professed themselves, with many regrets, ready to leave. There was a general exodus for them to prepare themselves for the journey, Sir David Baumgartner, who had been expected to stay, among them. He had an important appointment looming up, he explained, and dare not risk missing it.

There would be room enough for all the guests and the performers in the bus and cars that waited across the lake. Anyone so inclined could spend the tag-end of the night at the Cornishman's Pass pub on the east side of the Pass and journey down-country by train the next day. The rest would continue through the night, descending to the plains and across them to their ultimate destinations.

The Alleyns agreed that the scene in the hall bore a resemblance to rush-hour on the Underground. There was a sense of urgency and scarcely concealed impatience. The travellers were to leave in two batches of twenty which was the maximum accommodation in the launch. The house-staff fussed about with raincoats and umbrellas. Mr Reece stood near the door repeating validictory remarks of scant originality and shaking hands. Some of the guests, as their anxiety mounted, became perfunctory in their acknowledgements, a few actually neglected him altogether being intent upon manoeuvring themselves into the top twenty. Sir David Baumgartner, in awful isolation and a caped mackintosh, sat in a porter's chair looking very cross indeed.

The entrance doors opened admitting wind, rain and cold all together. The first twenty guests were gone: swallowed up and shut out as if, Troy thought — and disliked herself for so thinking — they were condemned.

Mr Reece explained to the remainder that it would be at least half an hour before the launch returned and advised them to wait in the drawing-room. The servants would keep watch and would report as soon as they sighted the lights of the returning launch.

A few followed this suggestion but most remained in the hall, sitting round the enormous fireplace or in scattered chairs, wandering about, getting themselves behind the window curtains and coming out, scared by their inability to see anything beyond streaming panes.

Eru Johnstone was speaking to the tenor, Rodolfo Romano, and the little band of musicians who listened to him in a huddle of apprehension. Alleyn and Troy joined them. Eru Johnstone was saying: 'It's something one doesn't try to explain. I come from the far north of the North Island and have only heard about the Island indirectly from some of our people down here on the Coast. I had forgotten. When we were engaged for this performance, I didn't connect the two things.'

'But it's tapu?' asked the pianist. 'Is that it?'

'In very early times an important person was buried here,' he said, as it seemed unwillingly. 'Ages afterwards, when the pakehas came, a man named Ross, a prospector, rowed out to the island. The story is that the local storm blew up and he was drowned. I had forgotten,' Eru Johnstone repeated in his deep voice. 'I suggest you do, too. There have been many visitors since those times and many storms —'

'Hence "Rosser"?' Alleyn asked.

'So it seems.'

'How long does it usually last?'

'About twenty-four hours, I'm told. No doubt it varies.'

Alleyn said: 'On my first visit to New Zealand I met one of your people who told me about Maoritanga. We became friends and I learnt a lot from him — Dr Te Pokiha!'

'Rangi Te Pokiha?' Johnstone exclaimed. 'You know him? He is one of our most prominent elders.'

And he settled down to talk at great length of his people. Alleyn led the conversation back to the Island. 'After what you have told me,' he said, 'do you mind my asking if you believe it to be tapu?'

After a long pause Eru Johnstone said: 'Yes.'

'Would you have come,' Troy asked 'if you had known?'

'No,' said Eru Johnstone.

'Are you staying here?' asked Signor Lattienzo, appearing at Troy's elbow, 'or shall we fall back upon our creature comforts in the drawing-room? One can't go on saying goodbye to people who scarcely listen.'

'I've got a letter I want to get off,' said Alleyn. 'I think I'll just scribble it and ask one of these people if they'd mind putting it in the post. What about you, Troy?'

'I rather thought — the studio. I ought to "fix" those drawings.'

'I'll join you there,' he said.

'Yes, darling, do.'

Troy watched him run upstairs.

'Surely you are not going to start painting after all this!' Signor Lattienzo exclaimed.

'Not I!' Troy said. 'It's just that I'm restless and can't settle. It's been a bit of a day, hasn't it? Who's in the drawing-room?'

'Hilda Dancy and the little Parry who are staying on. Also the Dr Carmichael who suffers excruciatingly from seasickness. It is not very gay in the drawing-room although the lissom Hanley weaves in and out. Is it true that you have made drawings this afternoon?'

'One or two preliminary canters.'

'Of Bella?'

'Mostly of her, yes.'

Signor Lattienzo put his head on one side and contrived to look wistful. In spite of herself Troy laughed. 'Would you like to see them?' she said

'Naturally I would like to see them. *May* I see them?'

'Come on, then,' said Troy.

They went upstairs to the studio. Troy propped her drawings, one by one, on the easel, blew fixative through a diffuser over each and laid them side by side on the throne to dry: Signor Lattienzo screwed in his eyeglass, folded his plump hands over his ample stomach and contemplated them.

After a long pause during which vague sounds of activity down in the hall drifted up and somewhere a door slammed, Signor Lattienzo said: 'If you had not made that last one, the one on the right, I would have said you were a merciless lady, Madame Troy.'

It was the slightest of the drawings. The orchestra was merely indicated playing like mad in the background. In the foreground La Sommita, having turned away from them, stared at vacancy and in everything that Troy had set down with such economy there was desolation.

'Look what you've done with her,' Signor Lattienzo said. 'Did she remain for long like that? Did she, for once, face reality? I have never seen her look so and now I feel I have never seen her at all.'

'It only lasted for seconds.'

'Yes? Shall you paint her like that?'

Troy said slowly. 'No, I don't think so.' She pointed to the drawing of La Sommita in full cry, mouth wide open, triumphant. 'I rather thought this—'

'This is the portrait of a Voice.'

'I would have liked to call it "A in alt" because that sounds so nice. I don't know what it means but I understand it would be unsuitable.'

'Highly so. *Mot juste*, by the way.'

' "A in sop" wouldn't have the same charm.'

'No.'

'Perhaps, simply "Top Note". Though why I should fuss about a title when I haven't as yet clapped paint to canvas, I can't imagine.'

'Has she seen the drawings?'

'No.'

'And won't if you can help it?'

'That's right,' said Troy.

They settled down. Signor Lattienzo discoursed cosily, telling Troy of droll occurences in the world of opera and of a celebrated company half-Italian and half-French of which the Sommita had been the star and in which internal feuding ran so high that when people asked at the Box Office what opera was on tonight the manager would intervene and say, 'Wait till the curtain goes up, Madame,' or (Dear Boy!) 'Just wait till the curtain goes up.' With this and further discourse he entertained Troy exceedingly. After some time Alleyn came in and said the launch had been sighted on its return trip and the last batch of travellers were getting ready to leave.

'The wind is almost gale force,' he said. 'The telephone's out of order—probably a branch across the line. Radio and television are cut off.'

'Will they be all right?' Troy asked. 'The passengers?'

'Reece says that Les knows his job and that he wouldn't undertake the passage if he thought there was any risk. Hanley's swanning about telling everyone that the launch is seaworthy, cost the earth and crossed the English Channel in a blizzard.'

'*How* glad I am,' Signor Lattienzo remarked, 'that I am not on board her.'

Alleyn opened the window-curtains. 'She could be just visible from here,' he said, and after a pause, 'Yes, there she is. Down at the jetty.'

Troy joined him. Beyond the half-blinded window lights, having no background, moved across the void, distorted by the runnels of water streaming down the pane. They rose, tilted, sank, rose again, vanished, reappeared and were gone.

'They are going aboard,' said Alleyn. 'I wonder if Eru Johnstone is glad to have left the Island?'

'One would have thought—' Signor Lattienzo began and was cut short by a scream.

It came from within the house and mounted like a siren It broke into a gabble, resumed and increased in volume.

'Oh *no*!' said Signor Lattienzo irritably. 'What now, for pity's sake!' A piercing scream answered him.

And then he was on his feet. 'That is not Bella's voice,' he said loudly.

It was close. On their landing. Outside their door. Alleyn made for the door but before he could reach it, it opened and there was Maria, her mouth wide open, yelling at the top of her voice.

'*Soccorso! Soccorso!*'

Alleyn took her by the upper arms. '*Che succede?*' he demanded. 'Control yourself, Maria. What are you saying?'

She stared at him, broke free, and ran to Signor Lattienzo, beat him with her clenched fists and poured out a stream of Italian.

He held her by the wrists and shook her. '*Taci!*' he shouted, and to Alleyn: 'She is saying that Bella has been murdered.'


IV

The Sommita lay on her back across a red counterpane. The bosom of her Biblical dress had been torn down to the waist and under her left breast, irrelevantly, unbelievably, the haft of a knife stuck out. The wound was not visible, being masked by a piece of glossy coloured paper or card that had been pierced by the knife and transfixed to the body. From beneath this a thin trace of blood had slid down towards naked ribs like a thread of red cotton. The Sommita's face, as seen from the room, was upside down. Its eyes bulged and its mouth was wide open. The tongue protruded as if at the moment of death she had pulled a gargoyle's grimace at her killer. The right arm, rigid as a branch, was raised in the fascist salute. She might have been posed for the jacket on an all-too-predictable shocker.

Alleyn turned to Montague Reece who stood half way between the door and the bed with Beppo Lattienzo holding his arm. The secretary, Hanley, had stopped short just inside the room his hand over his mouth and looking as if he was going to be sick. Beyond the door Maria could be heard to break out afresh in bursts of hysteria. Alleyn said: 'That doctor — Carmichael isn't it? — he stayed behind, didn't he?'

'Yes,' said Mr Reece. 'Of course,' and to Hanley: 'Get him.'

'And shut the door after you,' said Alleyn. 'Whoever's out there on the landing, tell them to go downstairs and wait in the drawing-room.'

'And get rid of that cursed woman,' Mr Reece ordered savagely. 'No! Stop! Tell the housekeeper to take charge of her. I —' he appealed to Alleyn. 'What should we do? You know about these things. I — need a few moments.'

'Monty, my dear! Monty,' Lattienzo begged him, 'don't look. Come away. Leave it to other people. To Alleyn. Come with me.' He turned on Hanley. 'Well. Why do you wait? Do as you're told, imbecile. The doctor!'

'There's no call to be insulting,' Hanley quavered. He looked distractedly about him and his gaze fell upon the Sommita's face. 'God Almighty!' he said and bolted.

When he had gone, Alleyn said to Mr Reece: 'Is your room on this floor? Why not let Signor Lattienzo take you there? Dr Carmichael will come and see you.'

'I would like to see Ben Ruby. I do not require a doctor.'

'We'll find Ben for you,' soothed Lattienzo. 'Come along.'

'I am perfectly all right, Beppo,' Mr Reece stated. He freed himself and actually regained a sort of imitation of his customary manner. He said to Alleyn: 'I will be glad to leave this to you. You will take charge, if you please. I will be available and wish to be kept informed.' And then: 'The police. The police must be notified.'

Alleyn said: 'Of course they must. When it's possible. At the moment it's not. We are shut off.'

Mr Reece stared at him dully. 'I had forgotten,' he conceded. And then astonishingly: 'That is extremely awkward,' he said, and walked out of the room.

'He is in trauma,' said Lattienzo uncertainly. 'He is in shock. Shall I stay with him?'

'If you would. Perhaps when Mr Ruby arrives —'

'Si, sì, sicuro,' said Signor Lattienzo. 'Then I make myself scarce.'

'Only if so desired,' Alleyn rejoined in his respectable Italian.

When he was alone he returned to the bed. Back on the job, he thought, and with no authority.

He thought of Troy: of six scintillating drawings, of a great empty canvas waiting on the brand-new easel and he wished to God he could put them all thirteen thousand miles away in a London studio.

There was a tap on the door. He heard Lattienzo say: 'Yes. In there,' and Dr Carmichael came in.

He was a middle-aged to elderly man with an air of authority. He looked sharply at Alleyn and went straight to the bed. Alleyn watched him make the expected examination and then straighten up.

'I don't need to tell you that nothing can be done,' he said. 'This is a most shocking thing. Who found her?'

'It seems, her maid. Maria. She raised the alarm and was largely incoherent. No doubt you all heard her.'

'Yes.'

'She spoke Italian.' Alleyn explained. 'I understood a certain amount and Lattienzo, of course, much more. But even to him she was sometimes incomprehensible. Apparently after the performance Madame Sommita was escorted to her room by Mr Reece.'

'That's right,' said the doctor. 'I was there. They'd asked me to have a look at the boy. When I arrived they were persuading her to go.'

'Ah yes. Well. Maria was here expecting she would be needed. Her mistress, still upset by young Bartholomew's collapse, ordered them to leave her alone. Maria put out one of her tablets, whatever they are. She also put out her dressing-gown — there it is, that fluffy object still neatly folded over the chair — and she and Reece did leave. As far as I could make out she was anxious about Madame Sommita and after a time returned to the room with a hot drink — there it is untouched —

99

and found her as you see her now. Can you put a time to the death?'

'Not precisely, of course, but I would think not more than an hour ago. Perhaps much less. The body is still warm.'

'What about the raised arm? Rigor mortis? Or cadaveric spasm?'

'The latter, I should think. There doesn't appear to have been a struggle. And that card or paper or whatever it is?' said Dr Carmichael.

'I'll tell you what that is,' said Alleyn, 'it's a photograph.'


V

Dr Carmichael, after an incredulous stare at Alleyn, stooped over the body.

'It'd be as well not to touch the paper,' said Alleyn, 'but look at it.'

He took a ball-point pen from his pocket and used it to open out the creases. 'You can see for yourself,' he said.

Dr Carmichael looked. 'Good God!' he exclaimed. 'You're right. It's a photograph of her. With her mouth open. Singing.'

'And the knife has been pushed through the photograph at the appropriate place—the heart.'

'It's—grotesque. When—where could it have been taken?'

'This afternoon, in the concert chamber,' said Alleyn. 'Those are the clothes she wore. She stood in a shaft of sunlight. My wife made a drawing of her standing as she is here. The photograph must have been taken from outside a window. One of those instant self-developing jobs.'

Dr Carmichael said: 'What should we do? I feel helpless.'

'So, believe me, do I! Reece tells me I am to "take charge", which is all very well but I have no real authority.'

'Oh—surely!'

'I can only assume it until the local police take over. And

when that will be depends on this blasted "Rosser" and the telephone breakdown.'

'I heard the young man who seems to be more or less in charge — I don't know his name —'

'Hanley.'

'— say that if the lake got rougher the launchman would stay on the mainland and sleep on board or in the boatshed. He was going to flash a lamp when they got there from the second trip to show they were all right. I think Hanley said something about him ringing a bell, though how they could expect anyone to hear it through the storm I can't imagine.'

'Eru Johnstone said the "Rosser" usually lasts about twenty-four hours.'

'In the meantime — ?' Dr Carmichael motioned with his head, indicating the bed and its occupant. 'What should be the drill? Usually?'

'An exhaustive examination of the scene. Nothing moved until the crime squad have gone over the ground: photographer, dabs — fingerprints — pathologist's first report. See any self-respecting whodunit,' said Alleyn.

'So we cover her up and maintain a masterly inactivity?'

Alleyn waited for a moment or two. 'As it happens,' he said, 'I have got my working camera with me. My wife has a wide camel-hair water-colour brush. Talc-powder would work all right. It's a hell of a time since I did this sort of field work but I think I can manage. When it's done the body can be covered.'

'Can I be of help?'

Alleyn hesitated for a very brief moment and then said: 'I'd be very glad of your company and of your help. You will of course be asked to give evidence at the inquest and I'd like to have a witness to my possibly irregular activities.'

'Right.'

'So if you don't mind I'll leave you here while I collect what I need and see my wife. And I suppose I'd better have a word with Hanley and the hangovers in the drawing-room. I won't be long.'

'Good.'

An onslaught of wind shook the window frames.

'Not much letting-up out there,' Alleyn said. He parted the heavy curtains. 'By George!' he exclaimed. 'He's signalling! Have a look.'

Dr Carmichael joined him. Out in the blackness a pinpoint of light appeared, held for a good second and went out. It did this three times. A pause followed. The light reappeared for a full second, was followed by a momentary flash and then a long one. A pause and the performance was repeated.

'Is that Morse?' asked the doctor.

'Yes, it reads "OK" ' said Alleyn. 'Somewhat ironically, under the circumstances. It was to let us know they'd made it in the launch.'

The signals were repeated.

'Here!' Alleyn said. 'Before he goes. Quick. Open up.'

They opened the curtain wide. Alleyn ran to the group of light switches on the wall and threw them all on.

The Sommita, gaping on her bed, was as she had always demanded she should be, fully lit.

Alleyn blacked out. 'Don't say anything,' he begged the doctor, 'or I'll muck it up. Do you know Morse?'

'No.'

'Oh, for a tiny boy scout. Here goes, then.'

Using both hands on the switches, he began to signal. The Sommita flashed up and out, up and out. The storm lashed the windows, the switches clicked: '*Dot-dot-dot. Dash-dash-dash* and *Dot-dot-dot.*'

He waited. 'If he's still watching,' he said. 'He'll reply.'

And after a daunting interval, he did. The point of light reappeared and vanished.

Alleyn began again: slowly, laboriously. '*SOS. Urgent. Contact. Police. Murder.*' And again: '*SOS. Urgent. Contact. Police. Murder.*'

He did it three times and waited an eternity.

And at last the acknowledgment: '*Roger.*'

Alleyn said: 'Let's hope it works. I'll be off. If you'd rather leave the room, get her key from the housekeeper. Lock it from the outside and wait for me on the landing. There's a chair behind a screen. Half a minute. I'd better just look round here before I go.'

There was another door in the Sommita's enormous bedroom: it opened into her bathroom, an extraordinarily exotic apartment carpeted in crimson with a built-in dressing-table and a glass surrounded by lights and flanked by shelves thronged with flasks, atomizers, jars, boxes and an arrangement of crystal flowers in a Venetian vase.

Alleyn looked at the hand basin. It was spotless but damp, and the soap wet. Of the array of scarlet towels on heated rails, one was wet but unstained.

He returned to the bedroom and had a quick look round. On the bedside table was a full cup of some milky concoction. It was still faintly warm and a skin had formed on top. Beside this was a glass of water and a bottle of sleeping tablets of a well-known proprietary brand. One had been laid out beside the water. Dr Carmichael waited with his back to the bed.

They left the room together. At Dr Carmicheal's suggestion Alleyn took charge of the key.

'If it's all right,' said the doctor, 'I thought I'd have a look at the young chap. He was rather under the weather after that faint.'

'Yes,' said Alleyn. 'So I gathered. Did you look after him?'

'Reece asked me to. The secretary came round to the front in a great taking-on. I went backstage with him.'

'Good. What did you find?'

'I found Bartholomew coming to, Madame Sommita shaking him like a rabbit and that Italian singing master of hers—Lattienzo—ordering her to stop. She burst out crying and left. Reece followed her. I suppose it was then that she came upstairs. The ingenue—little Miss Parry—had the good sense to bring a glass of water for the boy. We got him to a seat and from there, when he was ready for it, to his room. Lattienzo offered to give him one of his own sleeping pills and put him to bed, but he wanted to be left to himself. I returned to the drawing-room. If it's OK by you I think I'll take a look-see at him.'

'Certainly. I'd like to come with you.'

'Would you?' said Dr Carmichael, surprised. And then: 'I see. Or do I? You're checking up. Right?'

'Well — sort of. Hold on a jiffy, will you?'

Below in the hall a door had shut and he caught the sound of a bolt being pushed home. He went to the head of the stairs and looked down. There was the unmistakable, greatly foreshortened figure of their driver: short ginger hair and heavy shoulders. He was coming away from the front door and had evidently been looking up. What was his name? Ah yes. Bert.

Alleyn gave a not too loud whistle between his teeth. 'Hi! Bert!' he said. The head tilted back and the dependable face was presented. Alleyn beckoned and Bert came upstairs.

'G'day,' he said. 'This is no good. Murder eh?'

Alleyn said: 'Look, do you feel like lending a hand? Dr Carmichael and I have got a call to make but I don't want to leave this landing unguarded. Would you be a good chap and stay here? We won't be too long. I hope.'

'She'll be right,' said Bert. And then, with a motion of his head towards the bedroom door: 'Would that be where it is?'

'Yes. The door's locked.'

'But you reckon somebody might get nosey?'

'Something like that. How about it?'

'I don't mind,' said Bert. 'Got it all on your own, eh?'

'With Dr Carmichael. I *would* be grateful. Nobody, no matter who, is to go in.'

'Good as gold,' said Bert.

So they left him there, lounging in the chair behind the screen.

'Come on,' Alleyn said to Dr Carmichael. 'Where's his room?'

'This way.'

They were passing the studio door. Alleyn said: 'Half a second, will you?' and went in. Troy was sitting on the edge of the throne looking desolate. She jumped to her feet.

He said. 'You know about it?'

'Signor Lattienzo came and told me. Rory, how terrible!'

'I know. Wait here. All right? Or would you rather go to bed?'

'I'm all right. I don't think I really believe it has happened.'

'I won't be long, I promise.'

'Don't give it another thought. I'm OK. Rory, Signor Lattienzo seems to think it was Strix — the photographer. Is that possible?'

'Remotely, I suppose.'

'I don't quite believe in the photographer.'

'If you want to talk about it, we will. In the meantime could you look me out my camera, a big sable brush and a squirt-thing of talc powder?'

'Certainly. There are at least three of the latter in our bathroom. Why,' asked Troy, rallying, 'do people perpetually give each other talc powder and never use it themselves?'

'We must work it out when we've the leisure,' said Alleyn. 'I'll come back for the things.'

He kissed her and rejoined the doctor.

Rupert Bartholomew's room was two doors along the passage. Dr Carmichael stopped. 'He doesn't know,' he said. 'Unless, of course, someone has come up and told him.'

'If he's taken Lattienzo's pill he'll be asleep.'

'Should be. But it's one of the mildest sort.'

Dr Carmichael opened the door and Alleyn followed him.

Rupert was not asleep. Nor had he undressed. He was sitting upright on his bed with his arms clasped round his knees. He looked very young.

'Hello!' said Dr Carmichael, 'what's all this? You ought to be sound asleep.' He looked at the bedside table with its switched-on lamp, glass of water and the tablet lying beside it. 'So you haven't taken your Lattienzo pill,' he said. 'Why's that?'

'I didn't want it. I want to know what's happening. All that screaming and rushing about.' He looked at Alleyn. 'Was it her? Bella? Was it because of me? I want to know. What have I done?'

Dr Carmichael slid his fingers over Rupert's wrist. 'You haven't done anything,' he said. 'Calm down.'

'Then what—?'

'The rumpus,' Alleyn said, 'was nothing to do with you. As far as we know. Nothing. It was Maria who screamed.'

An expression that in less dramatic circumstances might almost have been described as 'huffy' appeared and faded: Rupert looked at them out of the corners of his eyes. 'Then why *did* Maria scream?' he asked.

Alleyn exchanged a glance with the doctor who slightly nodded his head.

'Well?' Rupert demanded.

'Because,' Alleyn said, 'there has been a disaster. A tragedy. A death. It will be a shock to you but, as far as we can see, which admittedly is not very far, there is no reason to link it with what happened after the performance. You will have to know of it and there would be no point in holding it back.'

'A *death*? Do you mean—? You can't mean—? Bella?'

'I'm afraid—yes.'

'Bella?' Rupert said and sounded incredulous. 'Bella? *Dead*?'

'It's hard to believe, isn't it?'

There was a long silence, broken by Rupert.

'But—why? What was it? Was it heart-failure?'

'You could say,' Dr Carmichael observed with a macabre touch of the professional whimsy sometimes employed by doctors, 'that all deaths are due to heart-failure.'

'Do you know if she had any heart-trouble at all?' Alleyn asked Rupert.

'She had high blood-pressure. She saw a specialist in Sydney.'

'Do you know who?'

'I've forgotten. Monty will know. So will Ned Hanley.'

'Was it a serious condition, did you gather?'

'She was told to—to slow down. Not get, over-excited. That sort of thing.' He looked at them with what seemed to be apprehension.

'Should I see her?' he mumbled.

'No,' they both said quickly. He breathed out a sigh.

'I can't get hold of this,' he said, and shook his head slowly. 'I can't get hold of it at all. I can't sort of seem to believe it.'

'The best thing you can do,' said Dr Carmichael, 'is to take this tablet and settle down. There's absolutely nothing else you *can* do.'

'Oh. Oh, I see. Well; all right, then,' he replied with a strange air of speaking at random. 'But I'll put myself to bed if you don't mind.'

He took the tablet, drank the water and leant back, staring in front of him. 'Extraordinary!' he said and closed his eyes.

Alleyn and Carmichael waited for a minute or two. Rupert opened his eyes and turned off the bedside lamp. Disconcerted, they moved to the door.

'Thank you,' said Rupert in the dark. 'Good night.'

When they were in the passage Carmichael said: 'That was a very odd little conversation.'

'It was, rather.'

'You'd have almost said—well, I mean—'

'What?'

'That he was relieved. Don't get me wrong. He's had a shock—I mean, that extraordinary apology for his opera which I must say I didn't find very impressive and his faint. His pulse is still a bit erratic. But the reaction,' Carmichael repeated, '*was* odd, didn't you think?'

'People do tend to behave oddly when they hear of death. I'm sure you've found that, haven't you? In this case I rather

107

think there *has* actually been a sense of release.'

'A *release*? From what?'

'Oh,' said Alleyn, 'from a tricky situation. From extreme anxiety. High tension. Didn't somebody say—was it Shaw?—that after the death of even one's closest and dearest, there is always a sensation of release. And relief.'

Carmichael made the noise that is written 'Humph.' He gave Alleyn a speculative look. 'You didn't' he said, 'tell him it was murder.'

'No. Time enough in the morning. He may as well enjoy the benefit of the Lattienzo pill.'

Dr Carmichael said 'Humph,' again.

Alleyn returned to Troy who had the camera, brush and talc powder ready for him.

'How is that boy?' she asked. 'How has he taken it?'

'On the whole, very well. Remarkably well.'

'Perhaps he's run out of emotional reactions,' said Troy. 'He's been fully extended in that department.'

'Perhaps he has. You're the wisest of downy owls and had better go to roost. I'm off, and it looks like being one of those nights.'

'Oh, for Brer Fox and Thompson and Baily?'

'You can say that again. And oh, for you to be in your London nest thirteen thousand miles away, which sounds like the burden of a ballad,' said Alleyn. 'But as you're here you'd better turn the key in your lock when you go to bed.'

'*Me*!' said Troy incredulously, 'Why?'

'So that I'll be obliged to wake you up,' said Alleyn and left her.

He asked Bert to continue his vigil, while he himself and Dr Carmichael went down to the drawing-room.

Dr Carmichael said: 'But I don't quite see—I mean you've got the key.'

'There may be other keys and other people may have them. Maria, for instance. If Bert sits behind that screen he can see anyone who tries to effect an entry.'

'I can't imagine anyone wanting to go back. Not even the murderer.'

'Can't you?' said Alleyn. 'I can.'

He and Dr Carmichael went downstairs to the drawing-room.

A wan little trio of left-overs was there: Hilda Dancy, Sylvia Parry, Lattienzo. Mr Reece, Alleyn gathered, was closeted with Ben Ruby and Hanley in the study. The drawing-room had only been half-tidied of its pre-prandial litter when the news broke. It was tarnished with used champagne glasses, full ashtrays and buckets of melted ice. The fire had burnt down to embers and when Alleyn came in Signor Lattienzo was gingerly dropping a small log on them.

Miss Dancy at once tackled Alleyn. Was it, she boomed, true that he was in charge? If so, would he tell them exactly what had happened? Had the Sommita really been done away with? Did this mean there was a murderer at large in the house? *How* had she been done away with?

Signor Lattienzo had by this time stationed himself behind Miss Dancy in order to make deprecating faces at Alleyn.

'We have a right to be told,' said the masterful Miss Dancy.

'And told you shall be,' Alleyn replied. 'Between one and two hours ago Madame Sommita was murdered in her bedroom. That is all that any of us knows. I have been asked by Mr Reece to take charge until such time as the local police can be informed. I'm going to organize a search of the premises. There are routine questions that should be asked of everybody who was in the house after the last launch trip. If you would prefer to go to your rooms, please do so but with the knowledge that I may be obliged to knock you up when the search is completed. I'm sure Signor Lattienzo will be pleased to escort you to your rooms.'

Signor Lattienzo gave slightly incoherent assurances that he was theirs, dear ladies, to command.

'I'm staying where I am,' Miss Dancy decided. 'What about you, dear?'

'Yes. Yes, so am I,' Sylvia Parry decided: and to Alleyn: 'Does Rupert know? About Madame Sommita?'

'Dr Carmichael and I told him.'

Dr Carmichael made diffident noises.

'It will have been a terrible shock for Rupert,' said Sylvia. 'For everybody, of course, but specially for Rupert. After—what happened.' And with an air of defiance she added: 'I think Rupert did a very brave thing. It took an awful lot of guts.'

'We all know that, dear,' said Miss Dancy with a kind of gloomy cosiness.

Alleyn said, 'Before I go I wonder if you'd tell me exactly what happened after Bartholomew fainted.'

Their account was put together like a sort of unrehearsed duet with occasional stoppages when they disagreed about details and called upon Signor Lattienzo. It seemed that as soon as Rupert fell, Hanley, who was standing by, said 'Curtains' and closed them himself. Sylvia Parry knelt down by Rupert and loosened his collar and tie. Rodolfo Romano said something about fresh air and fanned Rupert with his biblical skirt. The Sommita, it appeared, after letting out an abortive shriek, stifled herself with her own hand, looked frantically round the assembly and then flung herself upon the still unconscious Rupert with such abandon that it was impossible to decide whether she was moved by remorse or fury. It was at this point that Signor Lattienzo arrived, followed in turn by Mr Reece and Ben Ruby.

As far as Alleyn could make out these three men lost no time in tackling the diva in a very businesslike manner, detaching her from Rupert and suggesting strongly that she go to her room. From here the narrative followed, more or less, the accounts already given by Signor Lattienzo and the doctor. Mr Reece accompanied the Sommita out of the concert hall, which was by this time emptied of its audience and was understood to conduct her to her room. Hanley fetched Dr Carmichael and Sylvia Parry fetched water. Rupert when sufficiently recovered was removed to his room by the doctor and Signor Lattienzo, who fetched the sleeping tablet and placed it on the bedside table. Rupert refused all offers to help him undress and get into bed so they left him and went down to dinner. The ladies and the rest of the cast were already at table.

'After Hanley had fetched Dr Carmichael, what did he do?' Alleyn asked.

Nobody had noticed. Miss Dancy said that he 'seemed to be all over the shop' and Sylvia thought it had been he who urged them into the dining-room.

On this vague note Alleyn left them.

In the hall he ran into the ubiquitous Hanley, who said that the entire staff was assembled in their sitting-room awaiting instructions. Alleyn gathered that Maria had, so to put it, 'stolen the show'. The New Zealand members of the staff — they of the recently bankrupt luxury hotel, including the chef and housekeeper — had grown restive under recurrent onsets of Maria's hysteria, modelled, Alleyn guessed, upon those of her late employer.

The staff sitting-room, which in less democratic days would have been called the servants' hall, was large, modern in design, gaily furnished and equipped with colour television, a ping-pong table and any number of functional armchairs. The housekeeper, who turned out to be called, with Congrevian explicitness, Mrs Bacon, sat apart from her staff but adjacent to Mr Reece. She was a well-dressed, personable lady of capable appearance. Behind her was a subdued bevy of two men and three girls, the ex-hotel staff, Alleyn assumed, that she had brought with her to the Lodge.

Hanley continued in his role of restless dogsbody and hovered, apparently in readiness for something unexpected to turn up, near the door.

Alleyn spoke briefly. He said he knew how shocked and horrified they all must be and assured them that he would make as few demands upon them as possible.

'I'm sure,' he said, 'that you all wonder if there is a connection between this appalling crime and the recent

111

activities of the elusive cameraman.' (And he wondered if Maria had noticed the photograph pinned to the body.) 'You will, I dare say, be asking yourselves if yesterday's intruder whom we failed to hunt down could be the criminal. I'm sure your search,' Alleyn said and managed to avoid a sardonic tone, 'was extremely thorough. But in a case like this every possibility, however remote, should be explored. For that reason I am going to ask the men of the household to sort themselves into pairs and to search the whole of the indoor premises. I want the pairs to remain strictly together throughout the exercise. You will not go into Madame Sommita's bedroom which is now locked. Mr Bartholomew has already gone to bed and you need not disturb him. Just look in quietly and make sure he is there. I must ask you simply to assure yourselves that there is no intruder in the house. Open any doors behind which someone might be hiding, look under beds and behind curtains, but don't handle anything else. I am going to ask Mrs Bacon and Mr Hanley to supervise this operation.'

He turned to Mrs Bacon. 'Perhaps we might just have a word?' he suggested.

'Certainly,' she said. 'In my office.'

'Good.' He looked round the assembled staff.

'I want you all to remain here,' he said. 'We won't keep you long. I'll leave Dr Carmichael in charge.'

Mrs Bacon conducted Alleyn and Hanley to her office, which turned out to be a sitting-room with a large desk in it.

She said: 'I don't know whether you gentlemen would care for a drink but I do know I would,' and went to a cupboard from which she produced a bottle of whisky and three glasses. Alleyn didn't want a drink but thought it politic to accept. Hanley said: 'Oh yes. Oh *yes. Please!*'

Alleyn said: 'I see no point in pretending that I think the perpetrator of this crime has contrived to leave the island and nor do I think he is somewhere out there in the storm or skulking in the hangar. Mrs Bacon, is the entire staff collected in there? Nobody missing?'

'No. I made sure of that.'

'Good. I think it will be best to pair the members of the household with the guests and for you two, if you will, to apportion the various areas so that all are covered without overlapping. I'm not familiar enough with the topography of the Lodge to do this. I'll cruise.'

Mrs Bacon had watched him very steadily. He thought that this had probably been her manner in her hotel days when listening to complaints.

She said: 'Am I wrong in understanding that you don't believe the murderer was on the Island yesterday? That the trespasser was not the murderer, in fact?'

Alleyn hesitated and then said: 'I don't think the murderer was a trespasser, no.'

Hanley said loudly: 'Oh *no*! But you can't — I mean — that would mean — I mean — oh *no*!'

'It would mean,' said Mrs Bacon, still looking at Alleyn, 'that Mr Alleyn thinks Madame Sommita was murdered either by a guest or by a member of the household. That's correct, Mr Alleyn, isn't it? By, if I can put it that way — one of us?'

'That is perfectly correct, Mrs Bacon.' said Alleyn.

*Chapter Five*

NOCTURNE

I

The hunt turned out as Alleyn had expected it would, to be a perfectly useless exercise. The couples were carefully assorted. Marco was paired with Mrs Bacon, Ben Ruby with Dr Carmichael and Hanley with the chef for whom he seemed to have an affinity. Alleyn dodged from one pair to another, turning up where he was least expected, sometimes checking a room that had already been searched, sometimes watching the reluctant activities of the investigators, always registering in detail their reactions to the exercise.

These did not vary much. Hanley was all eyes and teeth and inclined to get up little intimate arguments with the chef. Ben Ruby, smoking a cigar, instructed his partner, Dr Carmichael, where to search, but did nothing in particular himself. Alleyn thought he seemed to be preoccupied as if confronted by a difficult crossword puzzle. Signor Lattienzo looked as if he thought the exercise was futile.

When the search was over they all returned to the staff sitting-room where, on Alleyn's request, Hilda Dancy and Sylvia Parry joined them. Nobody had anything to report. The New Zealanders, Alleyn noticed, collected in a huddle. Mrs Bacon and the ex-hotel staff showed a joint tendency to eye the Italians. Marco attached himself to Signor Lattienzo. Maria entered weeping but in a subdued manner, having been chastened, Alleyn fancied, by Mrs Bacon. Hanley detached himself from his chef and joined Ben Ruby.

When they were all assembled, the door opened and Mr Reece walked in. He might have arrived to take the chair at a shareholders' meeting. Hanley was assiduous with offers of a seat and was disregarded.

Mr Reece said to Alleyn: 'Please don't let me interrupt. Do carry on.'

'Thank you,' Alleyn said. He told Mr Reece of the search and its non-result and was listened to with stony attention. He then addressed the company. He said he was grateful to them for having carried out a disagreeable job and asked that if any of them, on afterthought, should remember something that could be of significance, however remotely, he would at once speak of it. There was no response. He then asked how many of them possessed cameras.

The question was received with concern. Glances were exchanged. There was a general shuffling of feet.

'Come on,' Alleyn said. 'There's no need to show the whites of your eyes over a harmless enquiry. I'll give you a lead.' He raised his hand, 'I've got a camera and I don't mind betting most of you have. Hands up.' Mr Reece, in the manner of seconding the motion, raised his. Seven more followed suit, one after another, until only six had not responded: Three New Zealand housemen with Maria, Marco and Hilda Dancy.

'Good,' Alleyn said. 'Now. I'm going to ask those of you who *do* possess a camera to tell me what the make is and if you've used it at any time during the last week and if so what you took. Mrs Bacon?'

'Old-fashioned Simplex. I used it yesterday. I snapped the people round the bathing pool from my sitting-room window.'

'Miss Parry?'

'It's a Pixie. I used it yesterday.' She turned pink. 'I took Rupert. By the landing-stage.'

'Signor Lattienzo?'

'Oh, my dear Mr Alleyn!' he said, spreading his hands. 'Yes, I have a camera. It was presented to me by—forgive my conscious looks and mantling cheeks—a grateful pupil. Isabella, in fact. I cannot remember its name and have been unable to master its ridiculously complicated mechanism. I

115

carry it about with me, in order to show keen.'

'And you haven't used it?'

'Well,' said Signor Lattienzo, 'in a sense I *have* used it. Yesterday. It upsets me to remember. Isabella proposed that I take photographs of her at the bathing pool. Rather than confess my incompetence I aimed it at her and pressed a little button. It gave a persuasive click. I repeated the performance several times. As to the results, one has grave misgivings. If there are any they rest in a pre-natal state in the womb of the camera. You shall play the midwife,' offered Signor Lattienzo.

'Thank you. What about you, Mr Ruby? There's that magnificent German job, isn't there?'

Mr Ruby's camera was a very sophisticated and expensive version of instantaneous self-development. He had used it that very morning when he had lined up the entire house-party with the Lodge for a background. He actually had the 'picture' as he consistently called the photograph, on him and showed it to Alleyn. There was Troy between Mr Reece, who as usual conveyed nothing, and Signor Lattienzo who playfully ogled her. And there, at the centre, of course, the Sommita with her arm laid in tigerish possession across the shoulders of a haunted Rupert while Sylvia Parry on his other side, looked straight ahead. A closer examination showed that she had taken his hand.

Alleyn himself, head and shoulders taller than his neighbours, was, he now saw with stoic distaste, being winsomely contemplated by the ubiquitous Hanley, three places removed in the back row.

The round of camera owners was completed, the net result being that Mr Reece, Ben Ruby, Hanley and Signor Lattienzo (if he had known how to use it) all possessed cameras that could have achieved the photograph now pinned under the breast of the murdered Sommita.

To these proceedings Maria had listened with a sort of smouldering resentment. At one point she flared up and reminded Marco in vituperative Italian that he had a

116

camera and had not declared it. He responded with equal animosity that his camera had disappeared during the Australian tour and hinted darkly that Maria herself knew more than she was prepared to let on in that connection. As neither of them could remember the make of the camera their dialogue was unfruitful.

Alleyn asked if Rupert Bartholomew possessed a camera. Hanley said he did and had taken photographs of the Island from the lake shore and of the lake shore from the Island. Nobody knew anything at all about his camera.

Alleyn wound up the proceedings, which had taken less time in performance than in description. He said that if this had been a police enquiry they would all have been asked to show their hands and roll up their sleeves and if they didn't object he would be obliged if—?

Only Maria objected but on being called to order in no uncertain terms by Mr Reece, offered her clawlike extremities as if she expected to be stripped to the buff.

This daunting but fruitless formality completed, Alleyn told them they could all go to bed and it might be as well to lock their doors. He then returned to the landing where Bert sustained his vigil behind a large screen across whose surface ultra-modern nudes frisked busily. He had been able to keep a watch on the Sommita's bedroom door through hinged gaps between panels. The searchers in this part of the house had been Ben Ruby and Dr Carmichael. They had not tried the bedroom door but stood outside it for a moment or two, whispering, for all the world as if they were afraid the Sommita might overhear them.

Alleyn told Bert to remain unseen and inactive for the time being. He then unlocked the door and he and Dr Carmichael returned to the room.

In cases of homicide when the body has been left undisturbed, and particularly when there is an element of the grotesque or of extreme violence in its posture, there can be a strange reaction before returning to it. Might it have moved? There is something shocking about finding it just as

117

it was, like the Sommita, still agape, still with her gargoyle tongue, still staring, still rigidly pointing. He photographed it from just inside the door.

Soon the room smelt horridly of synthetic violets as Alleyn made use of the talc powder. He then photographed the haft of the knife, a slender, vertically grooved affair with an ornate silver knob. Dr Carmichael held the bedside lamp close to it.

'I suppose you don't know where it came from?' he asked.

'I think so. One of a pair on the wall behind the pregnant woman.'

'What pregnant woman?' exclaimed the startled doctor.

'In the hall.'

'Oh. That.'

'There were two, crossed and held by brackets. Only one now.' And after a pause during which Alleyn took three more shots. 'You wouldn't know when it was removed?' Dr Carmichael said.

'Only that it was there before the general exodus this evening.'

'You're trained to notice details, of course.'

Using Troy's camel hair brush, he spread the violet powder round the mouth, turning the silent scream into the grimace of a painted clown.

'By God, you're a cool hand,' the doctor remarked.

Alleyn looked up at him and something in the look caused Dr Carmichael to say in a hurry: 'Sorry, I didn't mean—'

'I'm sure you didn't,' Alleyn said. 'Do you see this? Above the corners of the mouth? Under the cheekbones?'

Carmichael stooped. 'Bruising,' he said.

'Not hypostasis?'

'I wouldn't think so. I'm not a pathologist, Alleyn.'

'No. But there are well defined differences, aren't there?'

'Precisely.'

'She used very heavy make-up. Heavier than usual, of course, for the performance and she hadn't removed it. Some sort of basic stuff topped up with a finishing cream.

118

The colouring. And then a final powdering. Don't those bruises, if bruises they are, look as if the make-up under the cheekbones has been disturbed? Pushed up, as it were.'

After a considerable pause, Dr Carmichael said: 'Could be. Certainly could be.'

'And look at the area below the lower lip. It's not very marked but don't you think it may become more so? What does that suggest to you?'

'Again bruising.'

'Pressure against the lower teeth?'

'Yes. That. It's possible.'

Alleyn went to the Sommita's dressing-table where there was an inevitable gold-mounted manicure box. He selected a slender nail file, returned to the bed, slid it between the tongue and the lower lip, exposing the inner surface.

'Bitten,' he said. He extended his left hand to within half an inch of the terrible face with his thumb below one cheekbone, his fingers below the other and the heel of his hand over the chin and mouth. He did not touch the face.

'Somebody with a larger hand than mine, I fancy,' he said, 'But not much. I could almost cover it.'

'You're talking about asphyxia, aren't you?'

'I'm wondering about it. Yes. There are those pinpoint spots.'

'Asphyxial haemorrhages. On the eyeballs.'

'Yes,' said Alleyn and closed his own eyes momentarily. 'Can you come any nearer to a positive answer?'

'An autopsy would settle it.'

'Of course,' Alleyn agreed.

He had again stooped over his subject and was about to take another photograph when he checked, stooped lower, sniffed, and then straightened up.

'Will you?' he said. 'It's very faint.'

Dr Carmichael stooped. 'Chloroform,' he said. 'Faint, as you say, but unmistakable. And look here, Alleyn. There's a bruise on the throat to the right of the voice-box.'

'And have you noticed the wrists?'

119

Dr Carmichael looked at them—at the left wrist on the end of the rigid upraised arm and at the right one on the counterpane. 'Bruising,' he said.

'Caused by—would you say?'

'Hands. So now what?' asked Dr Carmichael.

'Does a tentative pattern emerge?' Alleyn suggested. 'Chloroform. Asphyxia. Death. Ripping the dress. Two persons—one holding the wrists. The other using the chloroform. The stabbing coming later. If it's right it would account for there being so little blood, wouldn't it?'

'Certainly would,' Dr Carmichael said. 'And there's very, very little. I'd say that tells us there was a considerable gap between death and the stabbing. The blood had had time to sink.'

'How long?'

'Don't make too much of my guesswork, will you? Perhaps as much as twenty minutes—longer even. But what a picture!' said Dr Carmichael. 'You know? Cutting the dress, ripping it open, placing the photograph over the heart and then using the knife. I mean—it's so—so far-fetched. *Why?*'

'As far-fetched as a vengeful killing in a Jacobean play,' Alleyn said, and then: 'Yes. A vengeful killing.'

'Are you—are we,' Carmichael asked 'not going to withdraw the weapon?'

'I'm afraid not. I've blown my top often enough when some well-meaning fool has interfered with the body. In this case I'd be the well-meaning fool.'

'Oh, come. But I see your point,' Carmichael said. 'I suppose I'm in the same boat myself. I should go no further than making sure she's dead. And, by God, it doesn't need a professional man to do that.'

'The law, in respect of bodies, is a bit odd. They belong to nobody. They are not the legal property of anyone. This can lead to muddles.'

'I can imagine.'

'It's all jolly fine for the lordly Reece to order me to take charge. I've no right to do so and the local police would have *every* right to cut up rough if I did.'

'So would the pathologist if I butted in.'

'I imagine,' Alleyn said 'they won't boggle at the photographs. After all there will be—changes.'

'There will indeed. This house is central-heated.'

'There may be a local switch in this room. Yes. Over there where it could be reached from the bed. Off with it.'

'I will,' said Carmichael and switched it off.

'I wonder if we can open the windows a crack without wreaking havoc,' Alleyn said. He pulled back the heavy curtains and there was the black and streaming glass. They were sash windows. He opened one and then others half an inch at the top, admitting blades of cold air and the voice of the storm.

'At least, if we can find something appropriate, we can cover her,' he said and looked about the room. There was a sandalwood chest against the wall. He opened it and lifted out a folded bulk of black material. 'This will do,' he said. He and Carmichael opened it out, and spread it over the body. It was scented and heavy and it shone dully. The rigid arm jutted up underneath it.

'What on earth is it *for*?' Carmichael wondered.

'It's one of her black satin sheets. There are pillow cases to match in the box.'

'Good God!'

'I know.'

Alleyn locked the door into the bathroom, wrapped the key in his handkerchief and pocketed it.

He and the doctor stood in the middle of the room. Already it was colder. Slivers of wind from outside stirred the marabou trimming on the Sommita's dressing-gown and even fiddled with her black satin pall so that she might have been thought to move stealthily underneath it.'

'No sign of the wind dropping,' said Carmichael. 'Or is there?'

'It's not raining quite so hard, I fancy. I wonder if the

launchman's got through. Where would the nearest police station be?'

'Rivermouth, I should think. Down on the coast. About sixty miles, at a guess.'

'And as, presumably, the cars are all miles away returning guests to their homes east of the ranges, and the telephone at the boathouse will be out of order, we can only hope that the unfortunate Les has set out on foot for the nearest sign of habitation. I remember that on coming here we stopped to collect the mailbag at a railway station some two miles back along the line. A very small station called Kai-kai, I think.'

'That's right. With about three *whares*[1] and a pub. He may wait till first light,' said Dr Carmichael, 'before he goes anywhere.'

'He *did* signal "Roger", which of course may only have meant "Message received and understood." Let's leave this bloody room, shall we?'

They turned, and took two steps. Alleyn put his hand on Carmichael's arm. Something had clicked.

The door handle was turning, this way and that. Alleyn unlocked and opened it and Maria strode into the room.


II


This time Maria did not launch into histrionics. When she saw the two men she stopped, drew herself up, looked beyond them to the shrouded figure on the bed and said in English that she had come to be of service to her mistress.

'I perform the last rites,' said Maria. 'This is my duty. Nobody else. It is for me.'

Alleyn said: 'Maria, certainly it would be for you if circumstances had been different, but this is murder and she must not be touched until permission has been given by the authorities. Neither Dr Carmichael nor I have touched her.

[1] *whare* — small dwelling

We have examined but we have not touched. We have covered her for dignity's sake but that is all and so it must remain until permission is given. We can understand your wish and are sorry to prevent you. Do you understand?'

She neither replied nor looked at him. She went to a window and reached for the cord that operated it.

'No,' Alleyn said. 'Nothing must be touched.' She made for the heavier, ornate cord belonging to the curtains. 'Not that either,' Alleyn said. 'Nothing must be touched. And I'm afraid I must ask you to come away from the room, Maria.'

'I wait. I keep *veglia*.'

'It is not permitted. I am sorry.'

She said in Italian, 'It is necessary for me to pray for her soul.'

'You can do so. But not here.'

Now she did look at him, directly and for an uncomfortably long time. Dr Carmichael cleared his throat.

She walked towards the door. Alleyn reached it first. He opened it, removed the key and stood aside.

'*Sozzume*,' Maria said and spat inaccurately at him. She looked and sounded like a snake. He motioned with his head to Dr Carmichael who followed Maria quickly to the landing. Alleyn turned off the lights in the room, left it, and locked the door. He put Maria's key in his pocket. He now had two keys to the room.

'I remain,' Maria said. 'All night. Here.'

'That is as you wish,' Alleyn said.

Beside the frisky nude-embellished screen behind which Bert still kept his vigil there were chairs and a clever occasional table with a lamp carved in wood — an abstract with unmistakable phallic implications, the creation, Alleyn guessed, of the master whose pregnant lady dominated the hall.

'Sit down, Maria,' Alleyn said. 'I have something to say to you.'

He moved a chair towards her. 'Please,' he said.

At first he thought she would refuse but after two seconds

or so of stony immobility she did sit, poker-backed, on the edge of the offered chair.

'You have seen Madame Sommita and you know she has been murdered,' he said. 'You wish that her murderer will be found, don't you?'

Her mouth set in a tight line and her eyes flashed. She did not speak but if she had delivered herself of a tirade it could not have been more eloquent.

'Very well,' Alleyn said. 'Now then: when the storm is over and the lake is calmer the New Zealand police will come and they will ask many questions. Until they come Mr Reece has put me in charge and anything you tell me, I will tell them. Anything I ask you, I will ask for one reason only: because I hope your answer may help us to find the criminal. If your reply is of no help it will be forgotten—it will be as if you had not made it. Do you understand?'

He thought: I shall pretend she has answered. And he said: 'Good. Well, now. First question. Do you know what time it was when Madame Sommita came upstairs with Mr Reece and found you waiting for her? No? It doesn't matter. The opera began at eight and they will know how long it runs.'

He had a pocket diary on him and produced it. He made quite a business of opening it and flattening it on the table. He wrote in it, almost under her nose.

'Maria. Time of S's arrival in bedroom. No answer.'

When he looked up he found that Maria was glaring at his notebook. He pushed it nearer and turned it towards her. 'Can you see?' he asked politely.

She unclamped her mouth.

'Twenty past nine. By her clock,' she said.

'Splendid. And now, Maria—by the way I haven't got your surname, have I? Your *cognome*.'

'Bennini.'

'Thank you.' He added it to his note. 'I see you wear a wedding-ring,' he said. 'What was your maiden name, please?'

124

'Why do you ask me such questions? You are impertinent.'

'You prefer not to answer?' Alleyn inquired politely.

Silence.

'Ah well,' he said. 'When you are more composed and I hope a little recovered from the terrible shock you have sustained, will you tell me exactly what happened after she arrived with Signor Reece?'

And astonishingly, with no further ado, this creature of surprises who a few seconds ago had called him 'filth' and spat at him, embarked upon a coherent and lucid account. Maria had gone straight upstairs as soon as the curtain fell on the opera. She had performed her usual duties, putting out the glass of water and the sleeping pill that the Sommita always took after an opening night, folding her negligée and nightdress over the back of a chair and turning down the crimson counterpane. The Sommita arrived with Signor Reece. She was much displeased, Maria said, which Alleyn thought was probably the understatement of the year, and ordered Maria to leave the room. This, he gathered was a not unusual occurrence. She also ordered Mr Reece to leave, which *was*. He tried to soothe her but she became enraged.

'About what?' Alleyn asked.

About something that happened after the opera Maria had already left the audience. The Signor Bartholomew, she gathered, had insulted the diva. Signor Reece tried to calm her, Maria herself offered to massage her shoulders but was flung off. In the upshot he and Maria left and went downstairs together, Mr Reece suggesting that Maria give the diva time to calm down and go to bed and then take her a hot drink, which had been known on similar occasions to produce a favourable reaction.

Maria had followed this advice.

How long between the time when they had left the room and Maria returned to it?

About twenty minutes, she thought.

Where was she during that time?

In the servants' quarters where she made the hot drink. Mrs

Bacon and Bert the chauffeur were there most of the time and others of the staff came to and fro from their duties in the dining-room where the guests were now at table. Mr Reece had joined them. Maria made the hot drink, returned to the bedroom, found her mistress murdered and raised the alarm.

'When Madame Sommita dismissed you, did she lock the door after you?'

Yes, it appeared. Maria heard the lock click. She had her own key and used it on her return.

Had anybody else a key to the room?

For the first time she boggled. Her mouth worked but she did not speak.

'Signor Reece, for instance?' Alleyn prompted.

She made the Italian negative sign with her finger.

'Who, then?'

A sly look appeared. Her eyes slid round in the direction of the passage to the right of the landing. Her hand moved to her breast.

'Do you mean Signor Bartholomew?' Alleyn asked.

'Perhaps,' she said, and he saw that, very furtively, she crossed herself.

He made a note about keys in his book.

She watched him avidly.

'Maria,' he said when he had finished writing, 'how long have you been with Madame Sommita?'

Five years, it appeared. She had come to Australia as wardrobe mistress with an Italian opera company, and had stayed on as sewing-maid at the Italian Embassy. The Signora's personal maid had displeased her and been dismissed and Signor Reece had enquired of an aide-de-camp who was a friend of his if they could tell him of anyone suitable. The Ambassador had come to the end of his term and the household staff was to be reorganized. Maria had been engaged as personal dresser and lady's maid to Isabella Sommita.

'Who do you think committed this crime?' Alleyn asked suddenly.

'The young man,' she answered venomously and at once,

126

as if that was a foolish question. And then with another of her abrupt changes of key she urged, begged, demanded that she go back into the room and perform the last services for her mistress — lay her out with decency and close her eyes and pray it would not be held in wrath against her that she had died in a state of sin. 'I must go. I insist,' said Maria.

'That is still impossible,' said Alleyn. 'I'm sorry.'

He saw that she was on the edge of another outburst and hoped that if she was again moved to spit at him her aim would not have improved.

'You must pull yourself together,' he said. 'Otherwise I shall be obliged to ask Mr Reece to have you locked up in your own room. Be a good girl, Maria. Grieve for her. Pray for her soul but do not make scenes. They won't get you anywhere, you know.'

Dr Carmichael who had contemplated Maria dubiously throughout now said with professional authority: 'Come along like a sensible woman. You'll make yourself unwell if you go on like this. I'll take you down and we'll see if we can find the housekeeper. Mrs Bacon, isn't it? You'd much better go to bed, you know. Take an aspirin.'

'And a hot drink?' Alleyn mildly suggested.

She looked furies at him but with the abruptness that was no longer unexpected stood up, crossed the landing and walked quickly downstairs.

'Shall I see if I can find Mrs Bacon and hand her over?' Dr Carmichael offered.

'Do, like a good chap,' said Alleyn. 'And if Mrs B. has vanished, take her to bed yourself.'

'Choose your words,' said Dr Carmichael and set off in pursuit.

Alleyn caught him up at the head of the stairs. 'I'm going back in there,' he said. 'I may be a little time. Join me if you will when you've brought home the Bacon. Actually I hope they're all tucked up for the night but I'd like to know.'

Dr Carmichael ran nimbly downstairs and Alleyn returned once more to the bedroom.

He began a search. The bedroom was much more ornate than the rest of the house. No doubt, Alleyn thought, this reflected the Sommita's taste more than that of the clever young architect. The wardrobe doors, for instance, were carved with elegant festoons and swags of flowers in deep relief each depending from the central motif of a conventionalized sunflower with a sunken black centre: the whole concoction being rather loudly painted and reminiscent of art nouveau.

Alleyn made a thorough search of the surfaces under the bed, of the top of her dressing-table, of an escritoire, on which he found the Sommita's jewel-box. This was unlocked and the contents were startling in their magnificence. The bedside table. The crimson coverlet. Nothing. Could it be under the body? Possible, he supposed, but he must not move the body.

The bathroom: all along the glass shelves, the floor, everywhere.

And yet Maria, if she was to be believed, had heard the key turned in the lock after she and Mr Reece were kicked out. And when she returned she had used her own key. He tried to picture the Sommita, at the height, it seemed, of one of her rages, turning the key in the lock, withdrawing it and then putting it—where? Hiding it? But why? There was no accommodation for it in the bosom of her Hebraic gown which was now slashed down in ribbons. He uncovered the horror that was the Sommita, and with infinite caution, scarcely touching it, examined the surface of the counterpane round the body. He even slid his hand under the body. Nothing. He re-covered the body.

'When all likely places have been fruitlessly explored, begin on the unlikely and carry on into the preposterous.' This was the standard practice. He attacked the drawers of the dressing-table. They were kept, by Maria, no doubt, in perfect order. He patted, lifted and replaced lacy undergarments, stockings, gloves. Finally, in the bottom drawer on the left he arrived at the Sommita's collection of handbags. On the top was a gold mesh, bejewelled affair that he remembered her carrying on the evening of their arrival.

Using his handkerchief he gingerly opened it and found her key to the room lying on top of an unused handkerchief.

The bag would have to be fingerprinted but for the moment it would be best to leave it undisturbed.

So what was to be concluded? If she had taken her bag downstairs and left it in her dressing-room, then she must have taken it back to the bedroom. Mr Reece was with her. There would have been no call for the key for Maria was already in the room, waiting for her. She was, it must never be forgotten, in a passion, and the Sommita's passions he would have thought, did not admit of methodical tidying away of handbags into drawers. She would have been more likely to chuck the bag at Mr Reece's or Maria's head, but Maria had made no mention of any such gesture. She had merely repeated that when they beat their retreat they heard the key turn in the lock and that when she came back with the hot drink she used her own key.

Was it then to be supposed that, having locked herself in, the Sommita stopped raging and methodically replaced her key in the bag and the bag in the drawer? Unlikely, because she must have used the key to admit her killer and was not likely to replace it. Being, presumably, dead.

Unless, of course, Maria was her killer. This conjured up a strange picture. The fanatically devoted Maria, hot drink in hand, re-enters the bedroom, places the brimming cup in its saucer on the bedside table and chloroforms her tigerish mistress who offers no resistence; she then produces the dagger and photograph and having completed the job, sets up her own brand of hullabaloo and rushes downstairs proclaiming the murder? No.

Back to the Sommita, then. What had she done after she had locked herself in? She had not undressed. She had not taken her pill. How had she spent her last minutes before she was murdered?

And what, oh what, about Rupert Bartholomew?

At this point there was a tap on the door and Dr Carmichael returned.

' "Safely stowed",' he said. 'At least, I hope so. Mrs Bacon was still up and ready to cope. We escorted that tiresome woman to her room, she offering no resistance. I waited outside. Mrs B. saw her undressed, be-nightied and in bed. She gave her a couple of aspirins, made sure she took them and came out. We didn't lock her up, by the way.'

'We've really no authority to do that,' said Alleyn. 'I was making an idle threat.'

' 'It seemed to work.'

'I really am very grateful indeed for your help, Carmichael. I don't know how I'd manage without you.'

'To tell you the truth, in a macabre sort of way, I'm enjoying myself. It's a change from general practice. What now?' asked Dr Carmichael.

'Look here. This is important. When you went backstage to succour the wretched Bartholomew the Sommita was still on deck, wasn't she?'

'She was indeed. Trying to manhandle the boy.'

'Still in her Old Testament gear, of course?'

'Of course.'

'When they persuaded her to go upstairs — Reece and Lattienzo, wasn't it? — did she take a gold handbag with her? Or did Reece take it?'

'I can't remember. I don't think so.'

'It would have looked pretty silly,' Alleyn said. 'It wouldn't exactly team up with the white samite number. I'd have thought you'd have noticed it.' He opened the drawer and showed Dr Carmichael the bag.

'She was threshing about with her arms quite a bit,' the doctor said. 'No, I'm sure she hadn't got that thing in her hand. Why?' Alleyn explained.

Dr Carmichael closed his eyes for some seconds. 'No,' he

said at last, 'I can't reconcile the available data with any plausible theory. Unless—'

'Well?'

'Well, it's a most unpleasant thought, but—unless the young man—'

'There is that, of course.'

'Maria is already making strong suggestions along those lines.'

'Is she, by George,' said Alleyn, and after a pause: 'But it's the Sommita's behaviour and her bloody key that won't fit in. Did you see anything of our host downstairs?'

'There's a light under what I believe is his study door and voices beyond.'

'Come on, then. It's high time I reported. He may be able to clear things up a bit.'

'I suppose so.'

'Either confirm or refute la bella Maria, at least,' said Alleyn. 'Would you rather go to bed?'

Dr Carmichael looked at his watch. 'Good Lord,' he exclaimed, 'it's a quarter to twelve.'

'As Iago said, "Pleasure and action make the hours seem short." '

'Who? Oh. Oh yes. No, I don't want to go to bed.'

'Come on, then.'

Again they turned off the lights and left the room. Alleyn locked the door with Maria's key.

Bert was on the landing.

'Was you still wanting a watch kept up?' he said. 'I'll take it on if you like. Only a suggestion.'

'You *are* a good chap,' Alleyn said. 'But—'

'I appreciate you got to be careful. The way things are. But seeing you suggested it yourself before and seeing I never set eyes on one of this mob until I took the job on, I don't look much like a suspect. Please yourself.'

'I accept with very many thanks. But—'

'If you was thinking I might drop off, I'd thought of that. I might, too. I could put a couple of them chairs in front of

the door and doss down for the night. Just an idea,' said
Bert.

'It's the answer,' Alleyn said warmly. 'Thank you,
Bert.'

And he and Dr Carmichael went downstairs to the study.

Here they found, not only Mr Reece but Signor Lattienzo,
Ben Ruby and Hanley, the secretary.

Mr Reece, perhaps a trifle paler than usual but he was
always rather wan, sat at his trendy desk — his swivel chair
turned towards the room as if he had interrupted his work to
give an interview. Hanley drooped by the window curtains
and had probably been looking out at the night. The other
two men sat by the fire and seemed to be relieved at Alleyn's
appearance. Signor Lattienzo did in fact, exclaim: '*Ecco*! At
last!' Hanley, reverting to his customary solicitude, pushed
chairs forward.

'I am very glad to see you, Mr Alleyn,' said Mr Reece in
his pallid way. 'Doctor,' he added with an inclination of his
head towards Carmichael.

'I'm afraid we've little to report,' Alleyn said. 'Dr
Carmichael is very kindly helping me but so far we haven't
got beyond the preliminary stages. I'm hoping that you, sir,
will be able to put us right on some points, particularly in
respect of the order of events from the time Rupert
Bartholomew fainted until Maria raised the alarm.'

He had hoped for some differences: something that could
give him a hint of a pattern or explain the seeming dis-
crepancies in Maria's narrative. Particularly, something
about keys. But no, on all points the account corresponded
with Maria's.

Alleyn asked if the Sommita made much use of her bedroom key.

'Yes; I think she did, I recommended it. She has —
had — there was always — a considerable amount of jewellery
in her bedroom. You may say very valuable pieces. I tried to
persuade her to keep it in my safe in this room but she
wouldn't do that. It was the same thing in hotels. After all,

132

we have got a considerable staff here and it would be a temptation.'

'Her jewel-case is in the escritoire — unlocked.'

Mr Reece clicked his tongue. 'She's — she was incorrigible. The artistic temperament, I am told, though I never, I'm afraid, have known precisely what that means.'

'One is never quite sure of its manifestations,' said Alleyn, surprised by this unexpected turn in the conversation. Mr Reece seemed actually to have offered something remotely suggesting a rueful twinkle.

'Well,' he said, 'you, no doubt have had first-hand experience.' And with a return to his elaborately cumbersome social manner. 'Delightful, in your case, may I hasten to say.'

'Thank you. While I think of it,' Alleyn said, 'do you, by any chance remember if Madame Sommita carried a gold mesh handbag when you took her up to her room?'

'No,' said Mr Reece, after considering it. 'No, I'm sure she didn't.'

'Right. About these jewels. No doubt the police will ask you later to check the contents of the box.'

'Certainly. But I am not familiar with all her jewels.'

Only, Alleyn thought, with the ones he gave her, I dare say.

'They are insured,' Mr Reece offered. 'And Maria would be able to check them.'

'Is Maria completely to be trusted?'

'Oh, certainly. Completely. Like many of her class and origin she has an uncertain temper and she can be rather a nuisance, but she was devoted to her mistress, you might say fanatically so. She has been upset,' Mr Reece added with one of his own essays in understatement.

'Oh, my dear Monty,' Signor Lattienzo murmured, 'Upset! So have we all been upset. Shattered would be a more appropriate word.' He made an uncertain gesture and took out his cigarette case.

And indeed he looked quite unlike himself, being white

and, as Alleyn noticed, tremulous. 'Monty, my dear,' he said. 'I should like a little more of your superb cognac. Is it permitted?'

'Of course, Beppo. Mr Alleyn? Doctor? Ben?'

The secretary with a sort of ghostly reminder of his customary readiness, hurried into action. Dr Carmichael had a large whisky and soda and Alleyn nothing.

Ben Ruby, whose face was puffed and blotched and his eyes bloodshot, hurriedly knocked back his cognac and pushed his glass forward. 'What say it's one of that mob?' he demanded insecurely. 'Eh? What say one of those buggers stayed behind?'

'Nonsense,' said Mr Reece.

'S'all very fine, say "nonsense".'

'They were carefully chosen guests of known distinction.'

'All ver' well. But what say,' repeated Mr Ruby, building to an unsteady climax, 'one of your sodding guestserknownstinction was not what he bloody seemed. Eh? *What say* he was Six.'

'Six?' Signor Lattienzo asked mildly. 'Did you say six?'

'I said nothing of sort. I said,' shouted Mr Ruby, '*Strix*.'

'Oh *no*!' Hanley cried out, and to Mr Reece: 'I'm sorry, but honestly! There *was* the guest list. I gave one to the launch person and he was to tick off all the names as they came aboard in case anybody had been left behind. In the loo or something. I thought you couldn't be too careful in case of accidents. Well, you know, it was — I mean *is* — *such* a night.'

'Yes, yes,' Mr Reece said wearily. 'Give it a rest. You acted very properly.' He turned to Alleyn. 'I really can't see why it should be supposed that Strix, if he is on the premises, could have any motive for committing this crime. On the contrary, he had every reason for wishing Bella to remain alive. She was a fortune to him.'

'All ver' well,' Mr Ruby sulked. 'If it wasn't, then who was it? Thass the point. D'you think you know who it was? Beppo? Monty? Ned? Come on. No, you don't. See what I mean?'

'Ben,' said Mr Reece quite gently, 'don't you think you'd better go to bed?'

'You may be right. I mean to say,' said Mr Ruby, appealing to Alleyn, 'I've got a hell of a lot to do. Cables. Letters. There's the US concert tour. She's booked out twelve months ahead: booked solid. All those managements.'

'They'll know about it soon enough,' said Mr Reece bitterly. 'Once this storm dies down and the police arrive it'll be world news. Go to bed, boy. If you can use him, Ned will give you some time tomorrow.' He glanced at Hanley. 'See to that,' he said.

'Yes, of *course*,' Hanley effused, smiling palely upon Mr Ruby who acknowledged the offer without enthusiasm. 'Well, ta,' he said, 'Won't be necessary, I dare say. I can type.'

He seemed to pull himself together. He finished his brandy, rose, advanced successfully upon Mr Reece and took his hand. 'Monty,' he said, 'Dear old boy. You know me. Anything I can do? Say the word.'

'Yes, Benny,' Mr Reece said, shaking his hand. 'I know. Thank you.'

'There've been good times, haven't there?' Mr Ruby said wistfully. 'It wasn't all fireworks, was it? And now . . .'

For the first time Mr Reece seemed to be on the edge of losing his composure. 'And now,' he surprised Alleyn by saying, 'she no longer casts a shadow.' He clapped Mr Ruby on the shoulder and turned away. Mr Ruby gazed mournfully at his back for a moment or two and then moved to the door.

'Good night, all,' he said. He blew his nose like a trumpet and left them.

He was heard to fall rather heavily on his way upstairs.

'He is fortunate,' said Signor Lattienzo who was swinging his untouched cognac around in the glass. 'Now, for my part, the only occasions on which I take no consolation from alcohol are those of disaster. This is my third libation. The cognac is superb. Yet I know it will leave me stone-cold

135

sober. It is very provoking.'

Mr Reece, without turning to face Alleyn, said: 'Have you anything further to tell me, Mr Alleyn?' and his voice was elderly and tired.

Alleyn told him about the Morse signals and he said dully that it was good news. 'But I meant,' he said, 'about the crime itself. You will appreciate, I'm sure, how—confused and shocked—to find her—like that. It was—' He made a singular and uncharacteristic gesture as if warding off some menace. 'It was so dreadful,' he said.

'Of course it was. One can't imagine anything worse. Forgive me,' Alleyn said, 'but I don't know exactly how you learned about it. Were you prepared in any way? Did Maria—?'

'You must have heard her. I was in the drawing-room and came out and she was there on the stairs, screaming. I went straight up with her. I think I made out before we went into the room and without really taking it in, that Bella was dead. Was murdered. But not—how. Beppo, here, and Ned—arrived almost at the same moment. It may sound strange but the whole thing, at the time, seemed unreal: a nightmare, you might say. It still does.'

Alleyn said: 'You've asked me to take over until the police come. I'm very sorry indeed to trouble you—'

'No. Please,' Mr Reece interrupted with a shaky return to his customary formality. 'Please, do as you would under any other circumstances.'

'You make it easy for me. First of all, you are sure, sir, are you, that after Madame Sommita ordered you and Maria to leave the bedroom you heard her turn the key in the lock?'

'Absolutely certain. May I ask why?'

'And Maria used her own key when she returned?'

'She must have done so, I presume. The door was not locked when Maria and I returned after she raised the alarm.'

'And there are—how many keys to the room?'

If atmosphere can be said to tighten without a word being

uttered it did so then in Mr Reece's study. The silence was absolute, nobody spoke, nobody moved.

'Four?' Alleyn at last suggested.

'If you know, why do you ask?' Hanley threw out.

Mr Reece said: 'That will do, Ned.'

'I'm sorry,' he said, cringing a little yet with a disreputable suggestion of blandishment. 'Truly.'

'Who has the fourth key?' Alleyn asked.

'If there is one I don't imagine it is used,' said Mr Reece.

'I think the police will want to know.'

'In that case we must find out. Maria will probably know.'

'Yes,' Alleyn agreed. 'I expect she will.' He hesitated for a moment and then said, 'Forgive me. The circumstances I know are almost unbelievably grotesque, but did you look closely? At what had been done? And how it had been done?'

'Oh, really, Alleyn—' Signor Lattienzo protested but Mr Reece held up his hand.

'No, Beppo,' he said and cracked a dismal joke. 'As you yourself would say: I asked for it, and now I'm getting it.' And to Alleyn. 'There's something under the knife. I didn't go—near. I couldn't. What is it?'

'It is a photograph. Of Madame Sommita.'

Mr Reece's lips formed the word 'photograph' but no sound came from them.

'This is a madman,' Signor Lattienzo broke out. 'A homicidal maniac. It cannot be otherwise.'

Hanley said: 'Oh yes, *yes!*' as if there was some sort of comfort in the thought. 'A madman. Of course. A lunatic.'

Mr Reece cried out so loudly that they were all startled. 'No! What you tell me alters the whole picture. I have been wrong. From the beginning I have been wrong. The photograph proves it. If he had left a signed acknowledgment it couldn't be clearer.'

There was a long silence before Lattienzo said flatly: 'I think you may be right.'

'Right! Of course I am right.'

'And if you are, Monty, my dear, this Strix was on the

Island yesterday and unless he managed to escape by the launch is still on this Island tonight. And in spite of all our zealous searching may actually be in the house. In which case we shall indeed do wisely to lock our doors.' He turned to Alleyn. 'And what does the professional say to all this?' he asked.

'I think you are probably correct in every respect, Signor Lattienzo,' said Alleyn. 'Or rather, in every respect but one.'

'And what may that be?' Lattienzo asked sharply.

'You are proposing, aren't you, that Strix is the murderer. I'm inclined to think you may be mistaken there.'

'And I would be interested to hear why?'

'Oh,' said Alleyn, 'just one of those things, you know. I would find it hard to say why. Call it a hunch.'

'But my dear sir — the photograph.'

'Ah yes,' said Alleyn. 'Quite so. There always the photograph, isn't there?'

'You choose to be mysterious.'

'Do I? Not really. What I really came in for was to ask you all if you happened to notice that the Italian stiletto, if that is what it is, was missing from its bracket on the wall behind the nude sculpture. And if you did notice, when.'

They stared at him. After a long pause Mr Reece said: 'You will find this extraordinary but nevertheless it is a fact. I had not realized that was the weapon.'

'Had you not?'

'I am, I think I may say, an observant man but I did not notice that the stiletto was missing and I did not recognize it — ' he covered his eyes with his hands — 'when I — saw it.'

Hanley said: 'Oh God! Oh, how terrible.'

And Lattienzo: 'They were hers. You knew that, of course, Monty, didn't you? Family possessions, I always understood. I remember her showing them to me and saying she would like to use one of them in *Tosca*. I said it would be much too dangerous, however cleverly she faked it. And I may add that the Scarpia wouldn't entertain the suggestion for a second. Remembering her temperament, poor darling,

138

t was not surprising.'

Mr Reece looked up at Alleyn. His face was deadly tired and he seemed an old man.

'If you don't mind,' he said, 'I think I must go to my room. Unless of course there is anything else.'

'Of course not.' Alleyn glanced at Dr Carmichael, who went to Mr Reece.

'You've had about as much as you can take,' he said. 'Will you let me see you to your room?'

'You are very kind. No, thank you, doctor. I am perfectly all right. Only tired.'

He stood up, straightened himself and walked composedly out of the room.

When he had gone Alleyn turned to the secretary.

'Mr Hanley,' he said. 'Did you notice one of the stilettos was missing?'

'I'd have said so, wouldn't I, if I had?' Hanley pointed out in an aggrieved voice. 'As a matter of fact, I simply loathe the things. I'm like that over knives. They make me feel sick. I expect Freud would have had something to say about it.'

'No doubt,' said Signor Lattienzo.

'It was her idea,' Hanley went on. 'She had them hung on the wall. She thought they teamed up with that marvellous pregnant female. In a way, one could see why.'

'Could one?' said Signor Lattienzo and cast up his eyes.

'I would like again to ask you all,' said Alleyn, 'if on consideration you can think of anyone—but *anyone*, however unlikely—who might have had some cause, however outrageous, to wish for Madame Sommita's death. Yes, Signor Lattienzo?'

'I feel impelled to say that while my answer is no, I can *not* think of anyone, I believe that this is a crime of passion and impulse and not a coldly calculated affair. The outrageous *grotesquerie*, the use of the photograph and of her own weapon—everything points to some—I feel inclined to say strindbergian love-hatred of lunatic force. Strix or not, I believe you are looking for a madman, Mr Alleyn.'

## IV

After that the interview began to languish and Alleyn sense[d]
the unlikelihood of anything to the point emerging from it.
He suggested that they went to bed.

'I am going to the studio,' he said. 'I shall be there for th[e]
next half-hour or so and if anything crops up, howeve[r]
slight, that seems to be of interest, I would be glad if yo[u]
would report to me there. I do remind you all,' he said, 'tha[t]
what I am trying to do is a sort of caretaker's job for th[e]
police: to see, if possible, that nothing is done inadvertentl[y]
or with intention, to muddle the case for them before the[y]
arrive. Even if it were proper for me to attempt a routin[e]
police investigation, it wouldn't be possible to do so single[-]
handed. Is that clear?'

They muttered weary assents and got to their feet.

'Good night,' said Dr Carmichael. It was the second an[d]
last time he had spoken.

He followed Alleyn into the hall and up the stairs.

When they reached the first landing they found that Ber[t]
had put two chairs together face to face, hard against th[e]
door to the Sommita's room and was lying very comfortab[ly]
on this improvised couch, gently snoring.

'I'm along there,' said Dr Carmichael, pointing to the left[-]
hand passage.

'Unless you're asleep on your feet,' said Alleyn, 'will yo[u]
come into the studio for a moment or two? No need, if yo[u]
can't bear the thought.'

'I'm well-trained to eccentric hours.'

'Good.'

They crossed the landing and went into the studio. Th[e]
great empty canvas still stood on its easel but Troy had pu[t]
away her drawings. Alleyn's dispatch case had been remove[d]
from their bedroom and placed conspicuously on th[e]
model's throne with an electric torch on top of it. Good fo[r]
Troy, he thought.

Yesterday, sometime after Troy had been settled in th[e]

studio, a supply of drinks had been brought in and stored in a wall-side unit. Alleyn wondered if this was common practice at the Lodge wherever a room was inhabited.

He said: 'I didn't have a drink down there: could you do with another?'

'I believe I could. A small one, though.'

They had their drinks and lit their pipes. 'I haven't dared do this before,' said the doctor.

'Nor I,' said Alleyn. He performed what had now become a routine exercise and drew back the curtains. The voice of the wind, which he was always to remember as a kind of *leitmotif* to the action, invaded their room. The window-pane was no longer masked with water but was a black nothing with vague suggestions of violence beyond. When he leant forward his ghost-face, cadaverous with shadows, moved towards him. He closed the curtains.

'It's not raining,' he said, 'but blowing great guns.'

'What's called "blowing itself out" perhaps?'

'Hope so. But that doesn't mean the lake will automatically go calmer.'

'Unfortunately no. Everything else apart, it's bloody inconvenient,' said the doctor. 'I've got a medical conference opening in Auckland tomorrow. Eru Johnstone said he'd ring them up. I hope he remembers.'

'Why did you stay?'

'Not from choice. I'm a travel sickness subject. Ten minutes in that launch topped up by mile after mile in a closed bus would have been absolute hell for me and everyone else. Reece was insistent that I should stay. He wanted me to take on the Great Lady as a patient. Some notion that she was heading for a nervous crisis, it seemed.'

'One would have thought it was a chronic condition,' said Alleyn. 'All the same, I got the impression that even when she peaked, temperamentally speaking, she never went completely over the top. I'd risk a guess that she always knew jolly well what she was up to. Perhaps with one exception.'

'That wretched boy?'

'Exactly.'

'You'd say she'd gone overboard for him?' asked the doctor.

'I certainly got that impression,' Alleyn said.

'So did I, I must say. In Sydney—'

'You'd met them before?' Alleyn exclaimed. 'In Sydney?'

'Oh yes. I went over there for her season. Marvellous it was, too. I was asked to meet her at a dinner-party and then to a supper Reece gave after the performance. He—they—were hospitable and kind to me for the rest of the season. Young Bartholomew was very much in evidence and she made no bones about it. I got the impression that she was—I feel inclined to say "savagely" devoted.'

'And he?'

'Oh, besotted and completely out of his depth.'

'And Reece?'

'If he objected he didn't show it. I think his might be a case of collector's satisfaction. You know? He'd acquired the biggest star in the firmament.'

'And was satisfied with the *fait accompli*? So that was that?'

'Quite. He may even have been a bit sick of her tantrums, though I must say he gave no sign of it.'

'No.'

By the way, Alleyn, I suppose it's occurred to you that I'm a candidate for your list of suspects.'

'In common with everyone else in the house. Oh yes. But you don't come very high on the list. Of course, I didn't know you'd had a previous acquaintance with her,' Alleyn said coolly.

'Well, I must say!' Dr Carmichael exclaimed.

'I felt I really needed somebody I could call upon. You and Bert seemed my safest bets. Having had, as I then supposed, no previous connection with her and no conceivable motive.'

Dr Carmichael looked fixedly at him. Alleyn pulled a long face.

'I am a lowland Scot,' said the doctor, 'and consequently a bit heavy-handed when it comes to jokes.'

'I'll tell you when I mean to be funny.'

'Thank you.'

'Although, God knows, there's not much jokey material going in this business.'

'No, indeed.'

'I suppose,' said Dr Carmichael after a companionable silence. 'That you've noticed my tact? Another lowland Scottish characteristic is commonly thought to be curiosity.'

'So I've always understood. Yes. I noticed. You didn't ask me if I know who dunnit.'

'Do you?'

'No.'

'Do you hae you suspeesions?'

'Yes. You're allowed one more.'

'Am I? What shall I choose? Do you think the photographer — Strix — is on the Island?'

'Yes.'

'And took — that photograph?'

'You've exceeded your allowance. But, yes. Of course. Who else?' said Alleyn.

'And murdered Isabella Sommita?'

'No.'

And after that they wished each other good-night. It was now thirteen minutes past one in the morning.

When Dr Carmichael had gone Alleyn opened a note that lay on top of his dispatch case — took out an all too familiar file and settled down to read it for the seventh time.

Isabella Pepitone known as Isabella Sommita. Born 1940, reputedly in Palermo, Sicily. Family subsequently settled in USA.

*Father* Alfredo Pepitone, successful businessman USA, suspected of Mafia activities but never arrested. Suspect in Rossi homicide case 1965. Victim: Bianca Rossi, female. Pepitone subsequently killed in car accident. Homicide suspected. No arrest.

Alleyn had brought his library book upstairs. There it lay near to hand—*Il Mistero di Bianca Rossi*.

Subject trained as singer. First in New York and later for three years under Beppo Lattienzo in Milan. Subject's debut 1968 La Scala. Became celebrated. 1970-79 Associated socially with Hoffman-Beilstein group.

1977 May 10th. Self-styled 'Baron' Hoffman-Beilstein since believed to be Mr Big behind large scale heroin chain cruised his yacht *Black Star* round the Bermudas. Subject was one of his guests. Visited Miami via Fort Lauderdale. First meeting with Montague F. Reece, fellow passenger.

1977 May 11th: Subject and Hoffman-Beilstein lunched at Palm Beach with Earl J. Ogden now known to be background figure in heroin trade. He dined aboard yacht same night. Subsequently a marked increase in street sales and socially high-class markets Florida and, later, New York. FBI suspects heroin brought ashore from *Black Star* at Fort Lauderdale. Interpol interested.

1977: Relations with Hoffman-Beilstein became less frequent.

1978: Relations H-B apparently terminated. Close relationship developed with Reece. Subject's circle now consists of top impeccable socialites and musical celebrities.

Written underneath these notes in the spiky, irritable hand of Alleyn's Assistant Commissioner:

For Ch. Sup. Alleyn's attn. Not much joy. Any items however insignificant will be appreciated.

Alleyn locked the file back in the case. He began to walk about the room as if he kept an obligatory watch. It would be so easy, he thought, to concoct a theory based on the meagre document. How would it go?

The Sommita, born Bella Pepitone which he thought he'd heard or read somewhere, was a common Sicilian name, was reared in the United States. He remembered the unresolved Rossi case quite well. It was of the sort that turns up in books

144

about actual crimes. The feud was said to be generations deep: a hangover from some initial murder in Sicily. It offered good material for 'true crimes' collections being particularly bloody and having a peculiar twist: in the long succession of murders the victims had always been women and the style of their putting-off grisly.

The original crime which took place in 1910 in Sicily and triggered off the feud, was said to have been the killing of a Pepitone woman in circumstances of extreme cruelty. Ever since, hideous idiocies had been perpetrated on both sides at irregular intervals in the name of this vendetta.

The macabre nature of the Sommita's demise and her family connections would certainly qualify her as a likely candidate and it must be supposed would notch up several points on the Rossi score.

Accepting, for the moment, this outrageous proposition, what, he speculated, about the MO? How was it all laid on? Could Strix be slotted into the pattern? Very readily, if you let your imagination off the chain. Suppose Strix was in the Rossi interest and had been hired, no doubt at an exorbitant price, to torment the victim, but not necessarily to dispatch her? Perhaps Strix was himself a member of the Rossi Family? In this mixed stew of concoctions there was one outstanding ingredient: the identity of Strix. For Alleyn it was hardly in doubt but if he was right it followed that Strix was not the assassin. (And how readily that melodramatic word surfaced in this preposterous case.) From the conclusion of the opera until Alleyn went upstairs to write his letter this 'Strix' had been much in evidence downstairs. He had played the ubiquitous busybody. He had been present all through dinner and in the hall when the guests were milling about waiting to embark

He had made repeated trips from house to jetty full of consoling chat, sheltering departing guests under a gigantic umbrella. He had been here, there and everywhere but he certainly had not had time to push his way through the crowd, go upstairs, knock on the Sommita's door, be admitted, administer chloroform, asphyxiate her wait twenty minutes and then implant the stiletto and the photograph. And return to his duties, unruffled, in his natty evening get-up.

For, in Alleyn's mind, at this juncture there were no two ways about the identity of Strix.

## Chapter Six

## STORM CONTINUED

I

Alleyn wrote up his notes. He sat at the brand-new paint-table Troy would never use and worked for an hour, taking great pains to be comprehensive, detailed, succinct and lucid, bearing in mind that the notes were destined for the New Zealand police. And the sooner he handed them over and he and Troy packed their bags, the better he would like it.

The small hours came and went and with them that drained sensation accompanied by the wakefulness that replaces an unsatisfied desire for sleep. The room, the passage outside, the landing and the silent house beyond seemed to change their character and lead a stealthy night life of their own.

It was raining again. Giant handfuls of rice seemed to be thrown across the window panes. The Lodge, new as it was, jolted under the onslaught. Alleyn thought of the bathing pool below the studio windows, and almost fancied he could hear its risen waters slapping at the house.

At a few minutes short of two o'clock he was visited by an experience Troy, ever since the early days of their marriage when he had first confided in her, called his 'Familiar', though truly a more accurate name might be 'Unfamiliar' or perhaps 'Alter Ego'. He understood that people interested in such matters were well acquainted with this state of being and that it was not at all unusual. Perhaps the ESP buffs had it taped. He had never cared to ask.

The nearest he could get to it was to say that without

warning he would feel as if he had moved away from his own identity and looked at himself as if at a complete stranger. He felt that if he held on outside himself something new and very remarkable would come out of it. But he never did hang on and as suddenly as normality had gone it would return. The slightest disturbance clicked it back and he was within himself again.

As now, when he caught a faint movement that had not been there before — the sense rather than the sound — of someone in the passage outside the room.

He went to the door and opened it and was face to face with the ubiquitous and serviceable Hanley.

'Oh,' said Hanley, '*so* sorry. I was just going to knock. One saw the light under your door and wondered if — you know — one might be of use.'

'You're up late. Come in.'

He came in, embellishing his entrance with thanks and apologies. He wore a dressing-gown of Noel Coward vintage and Moroccan slippers. His hair was fluffed up into a little crest like a baby's. In the uncompromising lights of the studio it could be seen that he was not very young.

'I think,' he said, 'it's absolutely fantastic of you to take on all this beastliness. Honestly!'

'Oh,' Alleyn said, 'I'm only treading water, you know, until the proper authorities arrive.'

'A prospect that doesn't exactly fill one with rapture.'

'Why are you abroad so late, Mr Hanley?'

'Couldn't you settle for "Ned"? Mr Hanley makes one feel like an undergraduate getting gated. I'm abroad in the night because I can't sleep. I can't help seeing — everything — her. Whenever I close my eyes — there it is. If I do doze — it's there. Like those crumby old horror films. An awful face suddenly rushing at one. It might as well be one of Dracula's ladies after the full treatment.' He gave a miserable giggle and then looked appalled. 'I shouldn't be like this,' he said. 'Even though, as a matter of fact, it's no more than the truth. But I mustn't bore you with my woes.'

'Where is your room?'

'One flight up. Why? Oh, I see. You're wondering what brought me down here, aren't you? You'll think it very peculiar and it's not easy to explain but actually it was that thing about being drawn towards something that gives one the horrors like edges of precipices and spiders. You know? After trying to sleep and getting nightmares I began to think I had to make myself come down to this floor and cross the landing outside—that room. When I went to bed I actually used the staff stairs to avoid doing that very thing and here I was under this beastly compulsion. So I did it. I hated it and I did it. And in the event there was our rather good-looking chauffeur, Bert, snoring on chairs. He must have very acute hearing, because when I crossed the landing he opened his eyes and stared at me. It was disconcerting because he didn't utter. I lost my head and said: "Oh, hullo, Bert, it's perfectly all right. Don't get up," and made a bolt of it into this passage and saw the light under your door. I seem to be cold. Would you think it too bold if I asked you if I might have a brandy? I didn't downstairs because I make it a rule never to unless the Boss-Man offers and anyway I don't really like the stuff. But I think— tonight—'

'Yes, of course. Help yourself.'

'Terrific,' Hanley said. Alleyn saw him half fill a small tumbler, take a pull at it, shudder violently and close his eyes.

'Would you mind awfully if I turned on that radiator?' he asked. 'Our central heating goes off between twelve and seven.'

Alleyn turned it on. Hanley sat close to it on the edge of the throne and nursed his brandy. 'That's better,' he said. 'I feel much better. Sweet of you to understand.'

Alleyn, as far as he knew, had given no sign of having understood anything. He had been thinking that Hanley was the second distraught visitor to the studio over the past forty-eight hours and that in a way he was a sort of unconvincing parody of Rupert Bartholomew. It struck him that Hanley

149

was making the most of his distress, almost relishing it.

'As you're feeling better,' he suggested, 'perhaps you won't mind putting me straight on one or two domestic matters — especially concerning the servants.'

'If I can,' Hanley said readily enough.

'I hope you can. You've been with Mr Reece for some years, haven't you?'

'Since January 1977. I was a senior secretary with the Hoffman-Beilstein Group in New York. Transferred from their Sydney offices. The Boss-Man was chums with them in those days and I saw quite a lot of him. And he of me. His secretary had died and in the upshot,' said Hanley, a little too casually, 'I got the job.' He finished his brandy. 'It was all quite amicable and took place during a cruise on the Caribbean in the Hoffman yacht. I was on duty. The Boss-Man was a guest. I think it was then that he found out about the Hoffman-Beilstein organization being naughty. He's absolutely Caesar's Wife himself. Well, you know what I mean. Pure as the driven snow. Incidentally, that was when he first encountered The Lady,' said Hanley and his mouth tightened. 'But without any noticeable reaction. He wasn't really a lady's man.'

'No?'

'Oh no. She made all the running. And, face it, she *was* a collector's piece. It was like pulling off a big deal. As a matter of fact, in my opinion, it was — well — far from being a *grande passion*. Oh dear, there I go again. But it was, as you might say, a very aseptic relationship.'

This chimed, Alleyn thought, with Dr Carmichael's speculation.

'Yes, I see,' he said lightly. 'Has Mr Reece any business relationships with Hoffman-Beilstein?'

'He pulled out. Like I said, he didn't fancy the way things shaped up. There were very funny rumours. He broke everything off after the cruise. Actually he rescued Madame — and me — at the same time. That's how it all started.'

'I see. And now — about the servants.'

'I suppose you mean Marco and Maria, don't you? Straight out of grand opera the two of them. Without the voice for it, of course.'

'Did they come into the household before your time?'

'Maria came with Madame, of course, at the same time as I made my paltry entrance. I understand the Boss-Man produced her. From the Italian Embassy or somewhere rather smooth. But Marco arrived after me.'

'When was that?'

'Three years ago. The Boss-Man wanted a personal servant. I advertised and Marco was easily the best bet. He had marvellous references. We thought that being Italian he might understand Maria and The Lady.'

'Would that be about the time when Strix began to operate?'

'About then, yes.' Hanley agreed and then stared at Alleyn. 'Oh *no*!' he said. 'You're not suggesting? Or are you?'

'I'm not suggesting anything. Naturally I would like to hear more about Strix. Can you give me any idea of how many times the offensive photographs appeared?'

Hanley eyed him warily. 'Not precisely,' he said. 'There had been some on her European tour, before I joined the circus. About six I think. I've filed them and could let you know.'

'Thank you. And afterwards? After you and Marco had both arrived on the scene?'

'Now you'll be making *me* feel awkward. No, of course you won't. I don't mean that. Let me think. There was the one in Double Bay when he bounced round a corner in dark glasses with a scarf over his mouth. And the stage-door débâcle when he was in drag, and the one in Melbourne when he came alongside in a car and shot off before they could see what he was like. *And* of course the *really* awful one on the Opera House steps. There was a rumour then that he was a blond. That's only *four*!' Hanley exclaimed. 'With all the hullabaloo it seemed more like the round dozen. It certainly did the trick with Madame. The *scenes*!'

He finished his brandy.

'Did Madame Sommita keep in touch with her family, do you know?'

'I don't think there is any family in Australia. I think I've heard they're all in the States. I don't know what they're called or anything, really, about them. The origins, one understood, were of the earth, earthy.'

'In her circle of acquaintances, are there many—or any—Italians?'

'Well—'. Hanley said, warming slightly to the task, 'let's see. There are the ambassadorial ones. We always make VIP noises about them, of course. And I understand there was a big Italian fan mail in Australia. We've a considerable immigrant population over there, you know.'

'Did you ever hear of anybody called Rossi?'

Hanley shook his head slowly. 'Not to remember.'

'Or Pepitone?'

'No. What an enchanting fun-name. Is he a fan? But, honestly, I don't have anything to do with The Lady's acquaintances or correspondents or on-goings of any sort. If you want to dig into *her* affairs,' said Hanley, and now a sneer was clearly to be heard, 'you'd better ask the infant phenomenon, hadn't you?'

'Bartholomew?'

'Who else? He's supposed to be her secretary. Secretary! My God!'

'You don't approve of Bartholomew?'

'He's marvellous to *look* at, of course.'

'Looks apart?'

'One doesn't want to be catty,' said Hanley, succeeding in being so pretty well, nevertheless, 'but what else is there? The opera? You heard that for yourself. And all that carry-on at the curtain call! I'm afraid I think he's a complete phoney. *And* spiteful with it.'

'Really? Spiteful? You surprise me.'

'Well, look at him. Take, take, take. Everything she could give. But *everything*. All caught up with the opera nonsense and then when it flopped, turning round and making a public fool of himself. *And* her. I could see *right* through the high tragedy bit, don't you worry: it was an act. He blamed her for the disaster. For egging him on. He was getting back on her.' Hanley had spoken rapidly in a high voice. He stopped short, swung round and stared at Alleyn.

'I suppose,' he said, 'I shouldn't say these things to you. For Christ's sake don't go reading something awful into it all. It's just that I got *so* bored with the way everyone fell for the boy-beautiful. *Everyone*. Even the Boss-Man. Until he chickened out and said he wouldn't go on with the show. That put a different complexion on the *affaire*, didn't it? Well, on everything, really. The Boss-Man was livid. Such a change!'

He stood up and carefully replaced his glass on the tray. 'I'm a trifle tiddly,' he said, 'but quite clear in the head. Is it true or did I dream it that the British press used to call you the Handsome Sleuth? Or something like that?'

'You dreamt it,' said Alleyn. 'Good night.'


## II

At twenty to three Alleyn had finished his notes. He locked them away in his dispatch case, looked round the studio, turned out the lights and, carrying the case, went out into the passage, locking the door behind him.

And now how quiet was the Lodge. It smelt of new carpets, of dying fires and of the aftermath of food, champagne and cigarettes. It was not altogether silent. There were minuscule sounds suggestive of its adjusting to the storm. As he approached the landing there were Bert's snores to be heard, rhythmic but not very loud.

Alleyn had, by now, a pretty accurate knowledge, acquired on the earlier search, of the Lodge and its sleeping quarters. The principal bedrooms, and the studio were all on this floor and opened on to two passages that led off, right and left, from the landing, each taking a right-angled turn after three rooms had been passed. The guests' names were inserted in neat little slots on their doors: a la Versailles, thought Alleyn; they might as well have gone the whole hog while they were about it and used the discriminating *pour*. It would be *Pour Signor Lattienzo*. But he suspected merely *Dr Carmichael*.

He crossed the landing. Bert had left the shaded table lamp on and it softly illuminated his innocent face. As Alleyn passed him he stopped snoring and opened his eyes. They looked at each other for a second or two. Bert said 'Gidday' and went back to sleep.

Alleyn entered the now dark passage on the right of the landing, passed his own bedroom door and thought how strange it was that Troy should be in there and that soon he would be able to join her. He paused for a moment and as he did so heard a door open somewhere beyond the turn of the passage.

The floor, like all floors in this padded house, was thickly carpeted; nevertheless he felt rather than heard somebody walking towards him.

Realizing that he might be silhouetted against the dimly glowing landing, he flattened himself against the wall and slid back to where he remembered seeing a switch for the passage lights. After some groping his hand found it. He turned it on and there, almost within touching distance, was Rupert Bartholomew.

For a moment he though Rupert would bolt. He had jerked up his hands as if to guard his face. He looked quickly behind him, hesitated, and then seemed to pull himself together.

'It's you,' he whispered. 'You gave me a shock.'

'Wasn't Signor Lattienzo's pill any good?'

'No. I've got to get to the lavatory. I can't wait.'

'There isn't one along here, you must know that.'

'Oh God!' said Rupert loudly. 'Lay off me, can't you?'

'Don't start anything here, you silly chap. Keep your voice down and come to the studio.'

'No.'

'Oh yes you will. Come on.'

He took him by the arm.

Down the passage, back across the landing, back past Bert Smith, back into the studio, will this night never end? Alleyn wondered, putting down his dispatch case.

'If you really want the Usual Offices,' he said, 'there's one next door which you know as well as I do and I don't mind betting there's one in your own communicating bathroom. But you *don't* want it, do you?'

'Not now.'

'Where were you bound for?'

'I've told you.'

'Oh, come *on*.'

'Does it matter?'

'Of course it matters, you ass. Ask yourself.'

Silence.

'Well?'

'I left something. Downstairs.'

'What?'

'The score.'

'Of *The Alien Corn*?'

'Yes.'

'Couldn't it wait till daylight? Which is not far off.'

'No.'

'Why?'

'I want to burn it. The score. All the parts. Everything. I woke up and kept thinking of it. There, on the hall fire, burn it, I thought.'

'The fire will probably be out.'

'I'll blow it together,' said Rupert.

'You're making this up as you go along. Aren't you?'

'No. No. Honestly. I swear not. I want to burn it.'

'And anything else?'

He caught back his breath and shook his head.

'Are you *sure* you want to burn it?'

'How many times do I have to say!'

'Very well,' said Alleyn.

'Thank God.'

'I'll come with you.'

'*No*. I mean there's no need. I won't,' said Rupert with a wan attempt at lightness, 'get up to any funny business.'

'Such as?'

'Anything. Nothing I just don't want an audience. I've had enough of audiences,' said Rupert and contrived a laugh.

'I'll be unobtrusive '

'You suspect me Don't you?'

'I suspect a round half-dozen of you. Come on.'

Alleyn took him by the arm.

'I've changed my mind,' Rupert said and broke away. 'If you're thinking I'll go to bed and then you'll pop down by yourself, you couldn't be more mistaken. I'll sit you out.'

Rupert bit his finger and stared at Alleyn. A sudden battering by the gale sent some metal object clattering across the patio down below. Still blowing great guns, thought Alleyn.

'Come along,' he said. 'I'm sorry I've got to be bloody-minded but you might as well take it gracefully. We don't want to do a cinematic roll down the stairs in each other's arms, do we?'

Rupert turned on his heel and walked out of the room. They went together, quickly, to the stairs and down them to the hall.

It was a descent into almost total darkness. A red glow at the far end must come from the embers of the fire and there was a vague, scarcely perceptible luminosity filtered down from the lamp on the landing. Alleyn had put Troy's torch in his pocket and used it. Its beam dodged down the stairs ahead of them.

'There's your fire,' he said. 'Now, I suppose, for the sacrifice.'

He guided Rupert to the back of the hall and through the double doors that opened into the concert chamber. When

156

they were there he shut the doors and turned on the wall lamps. They stood blinking at a litter of discarded programmes, the blank face of the stage curtain, the piano and the players' chairs and music stands with their sheets of manuscript. How long, Alleyn wondered, had it taken Rupert to write them out! And then on the piano, the full score. On the cover *The Alien Corn* painstakingly lettered, 'by Rupert Bartholomew'. And underneath: 'Dedicated to Isabella Sommita.'

'Never mind,' Alleyn said. 'This was only a beginning. Lattienzo thinks you will do better things.'

'Did he say so?'

'He did indeed.'

'The duet, I suppose. He did say something about the duet,' Rupert admitted.

'The duet it was.'

'I re-wrote it.'

'So he said. Greatly to its advantage.'

'All the same,' Rupert muttered after a pause, 'I shall burn it.'

'Sure?'

'Absolutely. I'm just going behind. There's a spare copy, I won't be a moment.'

'Hold on,' Alleyn said. 'I'll light you.'

'*No!* Don't bother. Please. I know where the switch is.'

He made for a door in the back wall, stumbled over a music stand and fell. While he was clambering to his feet, Alleyn ran up the apron steps and slipped through the curtains. He crossed upstage and went out by the rear exit arriving in a back passage that ran parallel with the stage and had four doors opening off it.

Rupert was before him. The passage lights were on and a door with a silver star fixed to it was open. The reek of cosmetics flowed out of the room.

Alleyn reached the door. Rupert was in there, too late with the envelope he was trying to stuff into his pocket.

The picture he presented was stagey in the extreme. He looked like an early illustration for a Sherlock Holmes story—the young delinquent caught red-handed with the incriminating document. His eyes even started in the approved manner.

He straightened up, achieved an awful little laugh, and pushed the envelope down in his pocket.

'That doesn't look much like a spare copy of an opera,' Alleyn remarked.

'It's a good luck card I left for her. I—it seemed so ghastly, sitting there. Among the others. *Good Luck*! You know?'

'I'm afraid I don't Let me see it.'

'No. I can't. It's private '

'When someone has been murdered,' Alleyn said, 'nothing is private '

'You can'† make me '

'I could very easily ' he answered and thought: And how the hell would *that* look in subsequent proceedings?

'You don't understand. It's got nothing to do with what happened. You wouldn't understand.'

'Try me,' Alleyn suggested and sat down.

'No.'

'You know you're doing yourself no good by this,' Alleyn said. 'If whatever's in that envelope has no relevance it will not be brought into the picture. By behaving like this you suggest that it has. You make me wonder if your real object in coming down here was not to destroy your work but to regain possession of this card, if that's what it is.'

'No. *No*. I *am* going to burn the script. I'd made up my mind.'

'Both copies?'

'What? Yes. Yes, of course. I've said so. Both.'

'And where is the second copy, exactly? Not in here?'

'Another room.'

'Come now,' Alleyn said, not unkindly. 'There is no second copy is there? Show me what you have in your pocket.'

'You'd read—all sorts of things—into it.'

'I haven't got that kind of imagination. You might ask

yourself, with more cause, what I am likely to read into a persistent refusal to let me see it.'

He spared a thought for what he would in fact be able to do if Rupert *did* persist. With no authority to take possession forcibly, he saw himself spending the fag end of the night in Rupert's room and the coming day until such time as the police might arrive, keeping him under ludicrous surveillance. No. His best bet was to keep the whole thing in as low a key as possible and trust to luck.

'I do wish,' he said, 'that you'd just think sensibly about this. Weigh it up. Ask yourself what a refusal is bound to mean to you and for God's sake cough up with the bloody thing and let's go to bed for what's left of this interminable night.'

He could see the hand working in the pocket and hear paper crumple. He wondered if Rupert tried, foolishly, to tear it. He sat out the silence, read messages of good-will pinned round the Sommita's looking-glass and smelt the age old incense of the make-up bench. He even found himself, after a fashion, at home.

And there, abruptly, was Rupert, holding out the envelope. Alleyn took it. It was addressed tidily to the Sommita in what looked to be a feminine hand and Alleyn thought had probably enclosed one of the greeting cards. It was unsealed. He drew out the enclosure: a crumpled corner, torn from a sheet of music.

He opened it. The message had been scrawled in pencil and the writing was irregular as if the paper had rested on an uneven surface.

> Soon it will all be over. If I were a Rossi I
> would make a better job of it. R.

Alleyn looked at the message for much longer than it took to read it. Then he returned it to the envelope and put it in his pocket.

'When did you write this?' he asked.

'After the curtain came down. I tore the paper off the score.'

'And wrote it here, in her room?'

159

'Yes.'

'Did she find you in here when she came for you?'

'I was in the doorway. I'd finished—that.'

'And you allowed yourself to be dragged on?'

'Yes. I'd made up my mind what I'd say. She asked for it,' said Rupert through his teeth, 'and she got it.'

' "Soon it will be all over",' Alleyn quoted. 'What would be over?'

'Everything. The opera. Us. What I was going to do. You heard me, for God's sake. I told them the truth.' Rupert caught his breath back and said, 'I was not planning to kill her, Mr Alleyn. And I did not kill her.'

'I didn't think that even you would have informed her in writing, however ambiguously, of your intention. Would you care to elaborate on the Rossi bit?'

'I wrote that to frighten her. She'd told me about it. One of those Italian family feuds. Mafia sort of stuff. A series of murders and the victim always a woman. She said she was in the direct line to be murdered. She really believed that. She even thought the Strix man might be one of them—the Rossis. She said she'd never spoken about it to anyone else. Something about silence.'

'*Omertà?*'

'Yes. That was it.'

'Why did she tell *you*, then?'

Rupert stamped his feet and threw up his hands. 'Why! Why! Because she wanted me to pity her. It was when I first told her that thing was no good and I couldn't go on with the performance: She—I think she saw that I'd changed. Seen her for what she was. It was awful. I was trapped. From then on I—well, you know, don't you, what it was like. She could still whip up—'

'Yes. All right.'

'Tonight—last night—it all came to a head. I hated her for singing my opera so beautifully. Can you understand that? It was a kind of insult. As if she deliberately showed how worthless it was. She was a vulgar woman, you know.

160

That was why she degraded me. That was what I felt after the curtain fell—degraded—and it was then I knew I hated her.'

'And this was written on the spur of the moment?'

'Of course. I suppose you could say I was sort of beside myself. I can't tell you what it did to me. Standing there. Conducting, for Christ's sake. It was indecent exposure.'

Alleyn said carefully: 'You will realize that I must keep the paper for the time being, at least. I will write you a receipt for it.'

'Do you believe what I've said?'

'That's the sort of question we're not supposed to answer. By and large—yes.'

'Have you finished with me?'

'I think so. For the present.'

'It's an extraordinary thing,' said Rupert. 'And there's no sense in it but I feel better. Horribly tired but—yes—better.'

'You'll sleep now,' Alleyn said.

'I still want to get rid of that abortion.'

Alleyn thought wearily that he supposed he ought to prevent this but said he would look at the score. They switched off the backstage lights and went to the front-of-house. Alleyn sat on the apron steps and turned through the score, forcing himself to look closely at each page. All those busy little black marks that had seemed so eloquent, he supposed, until the moment of truth came to Rupert and all the strangely unreal dialogue that librettists put in the mouths of their singers. Remarks like: 'What a comedy!' and 'Do I dream?' and 'If she were mine.'

He came to the last page and found that, sure enough, the corner had been torn off. He looked at Rupert and found he was sound asleep in one of the VIP chairs.

Alleyn gathered the score and separate parts together, put them beside Rupert and touched his shoulder. He woke with a start as if tweaked by a puppeteer.

'If you are still of the same mind,' Alleyn said, 'it's all yours.'

So Rupert went to the fireplace in the hall where the embers glowed. Papers bound solidly together are slow to burn. *The Alien Corn* merely smouldered, blackened and curled. Rupert used an oversized pair of bellows and flames crawled round the edges. He threw on loose sheets from the individual parts and these burst at once into flame and flew up the chimney. There was a basket of kindling by the hearth. He began to heap it on the fire in haphazard industry as if to put his opera out of its misery. Soon firelight and shadows leapt about the hall. The pregnant woman looked like a smirking candidate for martyrdom. At one moment the solitary dagger on the wall flashed red. At another the doors into the concert chamber appeared momentarily and once the stairs were caught by an erratic flare.

It was then that Alleyn caught sight of a figure on the landing. It stood with its hands on the balustrade and its head bent, looking down into the hall. Its appearance was as brief as a thought, a fraction of a fraction of a second. The flare expired and when it fitfully reappeared whoever it was up there had gone.

Bert? Alleyn didn't think so. It had, he felt sure, worn a dressing-gown or overcoat but beyond that there had been no impression of an individual among the seven men, any one of whom might have been abroad in the night.

At its end *The Alien Corn* achieved dramatic value. The wind howled in the chimney, blazing logs fell apart and what was left of the score flew up and away. The last they saw of it was a floating ghost of black thread-paper with 'dedicated to Isabella Sommita' in white showing for a fraction of a second before it too disintegrated and was gone up the chimney.

Without a word Rupert turned away and walked quickly upstairs. Alleyn put a fireguard across the hearth. When he turned away he noticed, on a table inside the front entrance, a heavy canvas bag with a padlock and chain: the mailbag. Evidently it should have gone off with the launch and in the confusion had been overlooked.

Alleyn followed Rupert upstairs. The house was now very quiet. He fancied there were longer intervals between the buffets of the storm.

When he reached the landing he was surprised to find Rupert still there and staring at the sleeping Bert.

Alleyn murmured: 'You've got a key to that door, haven't you?'

'Didn't you get it?' Rupert whispered.

'I? Get it? What do you mean?'

'She said you wanted it.'

'Who did?'

'Maria.'

'When?'

'After you and doctor left my room. After I'd gone to bed. She came and asked for the key.'

'Did you give it to her?'

'Yes, of course. For you.' Alleyn drew in his breath. 'I didn't want it,' Rupert whispered. 'My God! Go into that room! See her! *Like that.*'

Alleyn waited for several seconds before he asked: 'Like what?'

'Are you mad?' Rupert asked. 'You've seen her. A nightmare.'

'So *you've* seen her too?'

And then Rupert realized what he had said. He broke into a jumble of whispered expostulations and denials. Of course he hadn't seen her. Maria had told him what it was like. Maria had described it. Maria had said Alleyn had sent her for the key.

He ran out of words, made a violent gesture of dismissal and bolted. Alleyn heard his door slam.

And at last Alleyn himself went to bed. The clock on the landing struck four as he walked down the passage to their room. When he parted the window curtains there was a faint greyness in the world outside. Troy was fast asleep.

Marco brought their breakfast at eight o'clock. Troy had been awake for an hour. She had woken when Alleyn came to bed and had lain quiet and waited to see if he wanted to talk but he had touched her head lightly and in a matter of seconds was dead to the world.

It was not his habit to use a half-way interval between sleep and wake. He woke like a cat, fully and instantly and gave Marco good-morning. Marco drew the curtains and the room was flooded with pallid light. There was no rain on the window-panes and no sound of wind.

'Clearing is it?' Alleyn asked.

'Yes, sir. Slowly. The lake is still very rough.'

'Too rough for the launch?'

'Too much rough, sir, certainly.'

He placed elaborate trays across them both and brought them extra pillows. His dark rather handsome head came close to theirs.

'It must be quite a sight — the lake and the mountains?' Alleyn said lightly.

'Very impressive, sir.'

'Your mysterious photographer should be there again with his camera.'

A little muscle jumped under Marco's olive cheek.

'It is certain he has gone, sir. But of course you re joking.'

'Do you know exactly how Madame Sommita was murdered, Marco? The details?'

'Maria is talking last night but she is excitable. When she is excitable she is not reasonable. Or possible to understand. It is all,' said Marco, 'very dreadful, sir.'

'They forgot to take the mailbag to the launch last night. Had you noticed?'

Marco knocked over the marmalade pot on Troy's tray.

'I am very sorry, madame,' he said. 'I am clumsy.'

'It's all right,' Troy said. 'It hasn't spilt.'

'Do you know what I think, Marco?' said Alleyn. 'I think there never was a strange photographer on the Island.'

'Do you, sir? Thank you, sir. Will that be all?'

'Do you have a key to the postbag?'

'It is kept in the study, sir.'

'And is the bag unlocked during the time it is in the house?'

'There is a posting-box in the entrance, sir. Mr Hanley empties it into the bag when it is time for the launchman to take it.'

'Too bad he overlooked it last night.'

Marco, sheet-white, bowed and left the room.

'And I suppose,' Troy ventured, 'I pretend I didn't notice you've terrified the pants off that poor little man.'

'Not such a poor little man.'

'Not?'

'I'm afraid not.'

'Rory,' said his wife. 'Under ordinary circumstances I never, *never* ask about cases. Admit.'

'My darling, you are perfection in that as in all other respects. You never do.'

'Very well. These circumstances are *not* ordinary and if you wish me to give my customary imitation of a violet by a mossy stone half hidden *from* the view you must also be prepared for me to spontaneously combust.'

'Upon my word, love, I can't remember how much you do or do not know of our continuing soap opera. Let us eat our breakfasts and you ask questions the while. When, by the way, did we last meet? Not counting bed.'

'When I gave you the powder and brush in the studio. Remember?'

'Ah yes. Oh, and thank you for the dispatch case. Just what I wanted, like a Christmas present. You don't know *how* she was killed, do you?'

'Signor Lattienzo told me. Remember?'

'Ah yes. He came up to the studio, didn't he?'

'Yes. To see if I was all right. It was kind of him, really.'

165

'Very,' said Alleyn drily.

'Don't you like him?'

'Did he tell you in detail?'

'Just that she was stabbed. At first it seemed unreal. Like more bad opera. You know his flowery way of saying things. And then, of course, when it got real—quite appalling. It's rather awful to be wallowing between silken sheets, crunching toast while we talk about it,' said Troy, 'but I happen to be hungry.'

'You wouldn't help matters if you suddenly decided to diet.'

'True.'

'I think I'd better tell you the events of the night in order of occurrence. Or, no,' said Alleyn. 'You can read my file. While you're doing that I'll get up and see if Bert is still on duty, poor chap.'

'Bert? The chauffeur?'

'That's right. I won't be long.'

He gave her the file, put on his dressing-gown and slippers and went out to the landing. Bert was up and slightly dishevelled. The chairs still barricaded the door.

'Gidday,' he said. 'Glad to see you.'

'I'm sorry I've left it so late. Did you have a beastly night of it?'

'Naow. She was good. Wee bit draughty but we mustn't grumble.'

'Anything to report?'

'Maria. At four-twenty. I'm right out to it but I reckon she must of touched me because I open my eyes and there she bloody is, hanging over me with a key in her hand looking as if she's trying to nut it out how to get the door open. Brainless. I say: "What's the big idea?" and she lets out a screech and drops the key. On me. Plonk. No trouble.'

'And did you—?'

'Grab it. Kind of reflex action, really.'

'You didn't give it back to her, Bert?'

Bert assumed a patient, quizzical expression and produced

the key from his trouser pocket.

'Good *on* you, boy,' said Alleyn, displaying what he hoped was the correct idiom and the proper show of enthusiasm. He clapped Bert on the shoulder. 'What was her reaction?' he asked and wondered if he too ought to adopt the present tense.

'She's moanin',' said Bert.

'Moaning?'

'This is right. Complainin'. Reckonin' she'll put my pot on with the boss. Clawin' at me to get it back. Reckonin' she wants to lay out the deceased and say prayers and that lot. But never raising her voice, mind. Never once. When she sees it's no dice and when I tell her I'll hand the key over to you she spits in my face, no trouble, and beats it downstairs.'

'That seems to be the Maria form. I'll take the key, Bert, and thank you very much indeed. Do you happen to know how many keys there are to the room? Four, is it?'

'That's right. To all the rooms. Weird idea.'

Alleyn thought: This one, which was Rupert Bartholomew's. The one already in my pocket which was Maria's, the housekeeper's key, and the Sommita's in her evening bag at the bottom of her dressing-table drawer.

He said: 'While I think of it. On the way over here you said something about a vet putting down Madame Sommita's dog. You said he chloroformed it before giving it the injection.'

'That's correct,' said Bert looking surprised.

'Do you remember by any chance what happened to the bottle?'

Bert stared at him. 'That's a hairy one,' he said. 'What happened to the bottle, eh?' He scratched his head and pulled a face. 'Hold on,' he said. 'Yeah! That's right. He put it on a shelf in the hangar and forgot to take it away.'

'And would you,' said Alleyn, 'know what became of it. Is it still there?'

'No, it is not. Maria come out to see if it was all OK about the dog. She'd been sent by the Lady. She seen the bottle. It was, you know, labelled. She reckoned it wasn't safe having it lying around. She took it off.'

'Did she indeed?' said Alleyn. 'Thank you, Bert.'

'Be my guest.'

Alleyn said: 'Well, you'd better get something to eat, hadn't you?'

'I don't mind if I do,' said Bert. 'Seeing you,' and went, in a leisurely manner, downstairs.

Alleyn returned to their bedroom. Troy was deep in the file and continued to read it while he shaved, bathed and dressed. Occasionally she shouted an inquiry or a comment. She had just finished it and was about to get up when there was a tap on the door. Alleyn opened it and there was Mrs Bacon, trim and competent: the very epitome of the five-star housekeeper.

'Good morning, Mr Alleyn,' said Mrs Bacon. 'I've just come up to see if Mrs Alleyn has everything she wants. I'm afraid, in all this disturbance, she may have been neglected and we can't have that, can we?'

Alleyn said we couldn't and Troy called out for her to come in.

When she had been assured of Troy's well-being, Mrs Bacon told Alleyn she was glad of the opportunity to have a word with him. 'There are difficulties. It's very inconvenient,' she said as if the plumbing had failed them.

'I'm sure it is,' he said. 'If there's anything I can do—'

'It's Maria.'

'Is she still cutting up rough?'

'Indeed she is.' Mrs Bacon turned to Troy. 'This is all so unpleasant, Mrs Alleyn,' she apologized. 'I'm sorry to bring it up!'

The Alleyns made appropriate noises.

'Of course she *is* upset,' Mrs Bacon conceded. 'We understand that, don't we? But really!'

'What form is it taking now?' Alleyn asked.

'She wants to go—in there.'

'Still on that lay, is she? Well, she can't.'

'She—being a Catholic, of course, one should make allowances,' Mrs Bacon herself astonishingly allowed. 'I hope you're not—?' she hurriedly added, turning pink. 'And, of course, being a foreigner should be taken into consideration. But it's getting more than a joke. She wants to lay Madame out. I was wondering if—just to satisfy her?'

'I'm afraid not, Mrs Bacon,' Alleyn said, 'the body must be left as it is until the police have seen it.'

'That's what they always say in the thrillers, of course. I know that, but I thought it might be an exaggeration.'

'Not in this instance at any rate.'

'She's worrying Mr Reece about it. He's spoken to me. He's very much shocked, you can sense that, although he doesn't allow himself to show it. He told me everything must be referred to you. I think he would like to see you.'

'Where is he?'

'In the study. That Italian gentleman, Mr Lattienzo, and Mr Ruby are with him. And then,' Mrs Bacon went on, 'there are the two ladies, the singers, who stayed last night, I must say what I can to them. They'll be wondering. Really, it's almost more than one can be expected to cope with.'

'Maddening for you,' said Troy.

'Well, it *is*. And the staff! The two housemaids are talking themselves into hysterics and refusing to come up to this landing and the men are not much better. I thought I could depend on Marco but he's suddenly gone peculiar and doesn't seem to hear when he's spoken to. Upon my word,' said Mrs Bacon, 'I'll be glad to see the police on the premises and I never thought to say *that* in my occupation.'

'Can't Hanley help out?' asked Alleyn.

'Not really. They all giggle at him, or did when they had a giggle left in them. I told them they were making a mistake. It's obvious what he is, of course, but that doesn't mean he's not competent. Far from it. He's very shrewd and very capable and he and I get on quite well. I really don't know,' Mrs Bacon exclaimed, 'why I'm boring you like this! I must be going off at the deep end, myself.'

'Small wonder if you did,' said Troy. 'Look, don't worry about the rooms. How about you and me whipping round when they're all out of them.'

'Oh!' cried Mrs Bacon, 'I couldn't dream of it.'

'Yes, you could. Or, I tell you what. I'll talk to Miss Dancy and Miss Parry and see how they feel about a bit of bedmaking. Do us all good instead of sitting round giving each other the jim-jams. Wouldn't it, Rory?'

'Certainly,' said Alleyn and put his arm round her.

'Are they in their rooms? I'll ring them up,' Troy offered.

'If you don't mind my saying so, Mrs Alleyn, you're a darling. Their breakfasts went up at eight-thirty. They'll still be in bed, eating it.'

'One of them isn't,' said Alleyn who had gone to the window. 'Look.'

Mrs Bacon joined him.

The prospect from their windows commanded the swimming-pool on the extreme left and the hangar on the right. In the centre, Lake Waihoe swept turbulently away into nothing. The mountains that rose from its far shore had been shut off by a curtain of ashen cloud. The fringes of trees that ran out into the lake were intermittently wind-whipped. The waters tumbled about the shore, washed over the patio and reared and collapsed into the brimming pool which still overflowed its borders.

And down below on the bricked terrace, just clear of the water stood Rupert and a figure in a heavy mackintosh and sou'wester so much too big that it was difficult to identify as Miss Sylvia Parry.

Mrs Bacon joined Alleyn at the window. 'Well,' she said after a pause. 'If that's what it seems to be it's a pity it didn't develop when he was going away for days at a time for all those rehearsals.'

'Where was that?'

'On the other side — at a Canterbury seaside resort. The chopper used to take him over and he stayed the night. Mr Reece had them all put up at the Carisbrook. Luxury. Seven star,' said Mrs Bacon. 'They rehearsed in a local hall and gave concerts.'

Down below Rupert was speaking. The girl touched his arm and he took her hand in his. They remained like that for some moments. It had begun fitfully to rain again. He led her out of sight, presumably into the house.

'Nice girl,' said Mrs Bacon crisply. 'Pity. Oh well, you never know, do you?'

She made for the door.

Alleyn said: 'Wait a second, Mrs Bacon. Listen. Troy, listen.'

They listened. As always when an imposed silence takes over, the background of household sounds that had passed unnoticed and the voice of the wind outside to which they had grown inattentive, declared themselves. Behind them, very distant but thinly clear, was the sound of a bell.

'Les, by Heaven!' said Alleyn. 'Here! Mrs Bacon, have you got a bell in the house? A big bell?'

'No,' she said, startled.

'A gong?'

'Yes. We don't use it.'

'Bring it out on the terrace, please. Or get the men to bring it. And field-glasses. I saw a pair in the hall, didn't I? But quick.'

He pulled the slips off two of their pillows and ran down the hall and out on the terrace to a point from which the jetty and boathouse could be seen across the lake. Out here the sound of the bell was louder and echoed in the unseen hills.

It was ringing irregularly: long-spaced notes mixed with quick short-spaced ones.

'Bless his heart he's signalling again,' said Alleyn. He got out his notebook and pen and set himself to read the code. It was a shortish sequence confused by its echo and repeated after a considerable pause. The second time round he got it. *Police informed*, Les signalled.

Alleyn, hoping he was a fairly conspicuous figure from the

boatshed, had begun a laborious attempt at semaphoring with pillow cases when Bert and Marco piloted by Mrs Bacon staggered out of the house bearing an enormous Burmese gong on a carved stand. They set it up on the terrace. Alleyn discarded his pillowcases and whacked out a booming acknowledgement. This too set up an echo.

*Received and understood thanks.*

It struck him that he had created a picture worthy of Salvador Dali—a Burmese gong on an island in New Zealand, a figure beating it—pillowslips on a wet shore and on the far shore another figure, waving. And in the foreground a string of unrelated persons strung out at intervals. For, in addition to trim Mrs Bacon, Dr Carmichael, Hanley, Ben Ruby, Signor Lattienzo and Mr Reece, in that order, had come out of the house.

Mrs Bacon gave Alleyn the binoculars. He focused them and Les, the launchman, jumped up before him. He was wearing a red woollen cap and oilskins. He wiped his nose with a mittened hand and pointed in the direction of the rustic belfry. He was going to signal again. He gesticulated, as much as to say 'Hold on' and went into the belfry.

'*Doyng*!' said the bell. ' '*onyg, 'onyg, 'onyg,*' said the echo.

This time Alleyn got it first time. *Launch engine crook* it read and was repeated. *Launch engine crook.*

'Hell!' said Alleyn and took it out on the gong.

Mr Reece, wearing an American sporting raincoat and hogskin gloves, was at this elbow. 'What's the message?' he asked.

'Shut up,' said Alleyn. 'Sorry. He's at it again.'

Les signalled: '*Hope temporary.*'

'*Bang*!' Alleyn acknowledged. ' '*ang, 'ang, 'ang*' said the echo.

'*Over and out,*' signalled Les.

'Bang.'

Alleyn followed Les through the binoculars down to the jetty which was swept at intervals by waves. He saw Les dodge the waves, board the launch, jouncing at its moor-

172

ings, and disappear into the engine-room.

He gave Mr Reece a full account of the exchange.

'I must apologize for my incivility,' he said.

Mr Reece waved it aside. 'So if the lake becomes navigable,' he said, 'we are still cut off.'

'He did say he hopes the trouble's temporary. And by the time he's fixed it, surely the wind will have dropped and the helicopter will become a possibility.'

'The helicopter is in Canterbury. It took the piano-tuner back yesterday afternoon and remained on the other side.'

'Nobody loves us,' said Alleyn. 'Could I have a word with you, indoors?'

'Certainly. Alone?'

'It might be as well, I think.'

When they went indoors Alleyn was given an illustration of Mr Reece's gift of authority. Signor Lattienzo and Ben Ruby clearly expected to return with him to the study. Hanley hovered. Without saying a word to any of them but with something in his manner that was perfectly explicit Mr Reece gave them to understand that this was not to be.

Signor Lattienzo who was rigged out in a shepherd's cape and a Tyrolean hat said: 'My dear Ben, it is not raining. Should we perhaps, for the good of our digestions, venture a modest step or two abroad? To the landing and back? What do you say?'

Mr Ruby agreed without enthusiasm.

Mr Reece said to Hanley: 'I think the ladies have come down. Find out if there is anything we can do for them, will you? I shan't need you at present.'

'Certainly, sir,' said Hanley.

Dr Carmichael returned from outside. Alleyn suggested to their host that perhaps he might join them in the study.

When they were once more seated in the huge soft leather chairs of that singularly negative apartment, Alleyn said he thought that Mr Reece would probably like to know about the events of the previous night.

He went over them in some detail, making very little of

Rupert's bonfire and quite a lot of Maria's on-goings and Bert's vigil. Mr Reece listened with his habitual passivity. Alleyn thought it quite possible that he had gone his own rounds during the night and wondered if it was he who had looked down from the landing. It would somehow be in character for Mr Reece not to mention his prowl but to allow Alleyn to give his own account of the bonfire without interruption.

Alleyn said: 'I hope you managed to get some sleep last night.'

'Not very much, I confess. I am not a heavy sleeper at normal times. You wanted to see me?'

'I'd better explain. I seem to be forever raising the cry that I am really, as indeed we all are, treading water until the police arrive. It's difficult to decide how far I can, with propriety, probe. The important thing has been to make sure, as far as possible, that there has been no interference at the scene of the crime. I thought perhaps you might be prepared to give me some account of Madame Sommita's background and of any events that might, however remotely, have some bearing on this appalling crime.'

'I will tell you anything I can, of course.'

'Please don't feel you are under any obligation to do so. Of course you are not. And if my questions are impertinent we'll make it a case of "No comment" and, I hope, no bones broken.'

Mr Reece smiled faintly. 'Very well,' he said, 'agreed.'

'You see, it's like this. I've been wondering, as of course we all have, if the crime ties up in any way with the Strix business and if it does whether the motive could be a long-standing affair. Based, perhaps, on some sort of enmity. Like the Macdonalds and the Campbells, for instance. Not that in this day and age they have recourse to enormities of that kind. Better perhaps to instance the Montagues and Capulets.'

Mr Reece's faint smile deepened.

He said, "You are really thinking more of the Lucianos

and Costellos, aren't you?'

Alleyn thought: he's rumbled that one pretty smartly, and he said: 'Yes, in a way, I am. It's the Italian background that put it into my head. The whole thing is so shockingly outlandish and — well — theatrical. I believe Madame Sommita was born a Pepitone: a Sicilian.'

'You are very well-informed.'

'Oh,' Alleyn said, 'when we got your letter, asking me to come out with Troy and take a look at the Strix business, the Yard did a bit of research. It did seem a remote possibility that Strix might be acting as an agent of sorts. I was going to ask you if such an idea, or something at all like it, had ever occurred to you.'

With more animation than one might have supposed him to be capable of, Mr Reece gave a dismal little laugh and brought the palms of his hands down on the arms of his chair. He actually raised his voice.

'*Occurred to me!*' he exclaimed. 'You've got, as they say, to be joking, Mr Alleyn. How could it not have occurred to me when she herself brought it to my notice day in, day out, ever since this wretched photographer came on the scene.'

He paused and looked very hard at Alleyn who merely replied: 'She did?'

'She most certainly did. It was an obsession with her. Some family feud that had started generations ago in Sicily. She persuaded herself that it had cropped up again in Australia of all places. She really believed she was next in line for — elimination. It was no good telling her that this guy Strix was in it for the money. She would listen, say nothing, calm down and then when you thought you'd got somewhere simply say she *knew*. I made inquiries. I talked to the police in Australia and the USA. There was not a shred of evidence to support the idea. But she couldn't be moved.'

'Last night you said you were certain Strix was her murderer.'

'Because of what you told me about — the photograph.

175

That seemed to be—still seems to be—so much in character with the sort of thing she said these people do. It was as if the man had signed his work and wanted to make sure it was recognized. As if I had been wrong and she had been right—right to be terrified. That we should have had her fully guarded. That I am responsible. And this,' said Mr Reece, 'is a very, very dreadful thought, Mr Alleyn.'

'It may turn out to be a mistaken thought. Tell me, how much do you know about Madame Sommita's background—her early life? Her recent associates?'

Mr Reece clasped his large well-kept hands and tapped them against his lower teeth. He frowned and seemed to be at a loss. At last he said: 'That is difficult to answer. How much do I know? In some ways a lot, in others very little. Her mother died in childbirth. She was educated at convent schools in USA, the last being in New York where her voice was first trained. I got the impression that she saw next to nothing of her father, who lived in Chicago and died when Bella was twelve years old. She was brought up by an aunt of sorts who accompanied her to Italy and is now deceased. There used to be confused allusions to this reputed feud but in a way they were reticent—generalizations, nothing specific. Only these—these expressions of fear. I am afraid I thought they were little more than fairytales. I knew how she exaggerated and dramatized everything.'

'Did she ever mention the name Rossi?'

'Rossi? It sounds familiar. Yes, I believe she may have but she didn't, as a matter of fact, mention names—Italian names—when she talked about this threat. She would seem as if she was going to but if I asked her point blank to be specific in order that I could make inquiries, she merely crossed herself and wouldn't utter. I'm afraid I found that exasperating. It confirmed me in the opinion that the whole thing was imaginary.'

'Yes, I see.' Alleyn put his hand in his overcoat pocket, drew out the book from the library and handed it to Mr Reece. 'Have you ever seen this?' he asked.

He took it and turned it over distastfully.

'Not that I remember,' he said. He opened it and read the title, translating it. '*The Mystery of Bianca Rossi*. Oh, I see—Rossi. What is all this, Mr Alleyn?'

'I don't know. I hoped you might throw some light on it.'

'Where did you find it? In her room?' he asked.

'In the library. Have you noticed the name on the fly-leaf?'

Mr Reece looked at it. 'M. V. Rossi,' he said. And then: 'I can't make any sense out of this. Do we assume it was hers?'

'It will be fingerprinted, of course.'

'Ah yes. Oh, I see. I shouldn't have handled it, should I?'

'I don't think you've done any damage,' Alleyn said, and took it from him.

'If it was Bella's she may have left it lying about somewhere and one of the servants put it in the library. We can ask.'

'So we can. Leaving it for the moment: did you ever hear of her association with the Hoffman-Beilstein group?'

It was curious to see how immediate was Mr Reece's return to his own world of financial expertise. He at once became solemn, disapproving and grand.

'I certainly did,' he said shortly and shot an appraising glance at Alleyn. 'Again,' he said, 'you seem to be well-informed.'

'I thought I remembered,' Alleyn improvised, 'seeing press photographs of her in a group of guests aboard Hoffman's yacht.'

'I see. It was not a desirable association. I broke it off '

'He came to grief, didn't he?'

'Deservedly so,' said Mr Reece, pursing his mouth rather in the manner of a disapproving governess. Perhaps he felt he could not quite leave it at that because he added, stuffily, as if he was humouring an inquisitive child: 'Hoffman had approached me with a view to interesting me in an enterprise he hoped to float. Actually, he invited me to join the cruise you allude to. I did so and was confirmed in my opinion of his activities.' Mr Reece waited for a moment. 'As a matter of fact,' he said, 'it was then that I met one of his executives — young Ned Hanley. I considered he might well come to grief in that company and as I required a private secretary, offered him the position.' He looked much more fixedly at Alleyn. 'Has he been prattling?' he asked and Alleyn thought: he's formidable, all right.

'No, no,' he said. 'Not indiscreetly, I promise you. I asked him how long he'd been in your employ and he simply arrived at the answer by recalling the date of the cruise.'

'He talks too much,' said Mr Reece, dismissing him, but with an air of — what? Indulgence? Tolerance? Proprietorship? He turned to Dr Carmichael. 'I wanted to speak to you, doctor,' he said. 'I want to hear from you exactly how my friend was killed. I do not wish, if it can be spared me, to see her again as she was last night and I presume still is. But I must know how it was done. I must *know*.'

Dr Carmichael glanced at Alleyn who nodded very slightly.

'Madame Sommita,' said Dr Carmichael, 'was almost certainly anaesthetized, probably asphyxiated, when she had become unconscious and, after death, stabbed. There will be an autopsy, of course, which will tell us more.'

'Did she suffer?'

'I think, most unlikely.'

'Anaesthetized? With what? How?'

'I suspect, chloroform.'

'But — chloroform? Do you mean somebody came here prepared to commit this crime? Provided?'

'It looks like it. Unless there was chloroform somewhere on the premises.'

'Not to my knowledge. I can't imagine it.'

Alleyn suddenly remembered the gossip of Bert the chauffeur. 'Did you by any chance have a vet come to the house?' he asked.

'Ah! Yes. Yes, we did. To see Isabella's Afghan hound. She was very — distressed. The vet examined the dog under an anaesthetic and found it had a malignant growth. He

178

advised that it be put down immediately and it was done '"

'You wouldn't of course, know if by any chance the vet forgot to take the chloroform away with him?'

'No. Ned might know. He superintended the whole thing.'

'I'll ask him,' said Alleyn.

'Or perhaps Marco,' speculated Mr Reece 'I seem to remember he was involved.'

'Ah yes. Marco,' said Alleyn. 'You have told me, haven't you, that Marco is completely dependable.'

'Certainly. I have no reason to suppose anything else.'

'In the very nature of the circumstances and the development of events as we hear about them, we must all have been asking ourselves disturbing questions about each other, mustn't we? Have you not asked yourself disturbing questions about Marco?'

'Well, of course I have,' Mr Reece said at once. 'About him, and, as you say, about all of them. But there is no earthly reason, no conceivable motive for Marco to do anything — wrong.'

'Not if Marco should happen to be Strix?' Alleyn asked.

## Chapter Seven

## STRIX

### I

When Alleyn and Dr Carmichael joined Troy in the studio rifts had appeared in the rampart of clouds and at intervals, shafts of sunlight played fitfully across Lake Waihoe and struck up patches of livid green on mountain flanks that had begun to reappear through the mist.

The landing-stage was still under turbulent water. No one could have used it. There were now no signs of Les on the mainland.

'You gave Mr Reece a bit of a shake-up,' said Dr Carmichael. 'Do you think he was right when he said the idea had never entered his head?'

'What, that Marco was Strix? Who can tell? I imagine Marco has been conspicuously zealous in the anti-Strix cause. His reporting an intruder on the Island topped up with his production of the lens-cap was highly convincing. Remember how you all plunged about in the undergrowth? I suppose you assisted in the search for nobody, didn't you?'

'Blast!' said Dr Carmichael.

'Incidentally the cap was a mistake, a fancy touch too many. It's off a mass-produced camera, probably his own, as it were, official toy and not at all the sort of job that Strix must use to get his results. Perhaps he didn't want to part with the Strix cap and hadn't quite got the nerve to produce it or perhaps it hasn't got a cap.'

'Why,' asked Troy, 'did he embark on all that nonsense about an intruder?'

'Well, darling, don't you think because he intended to

180

take a "Strix" photograph of the Sommita—his *bonne bouche*—and it seemed advisable to plant the idea that a visiting Strix was lurking in the underbrush. But the whole story of the intruder was fishy. The search-party was a shocking-awful carry-on but by virtue of sheer numbers some one would have floundered into an intruder if he'd been there.'

'And you are certain,' said Dr Carmichael, 'that he is not your man?'

'He couldn't be. He was waiting in the dining-room and busy in the hall until the guests left and trotting to and from the launch with an umbrella while they were leaving.'

'And incidentally in the porch, with me, watching the launch after they had gone. Yes. That's right,' agreed Dr Carmichael.

'Is Mr Reece going to tackle him about Strix?' Troy asked.

'Not yet. He says he's not fully persuaded. He prefers to leave it with me.'

'And you?'

'I'm trying to make up my mind. On the whole I think it may be best to settle Strix before the police get here.'

'Now?'

'Why not?'

Troy said: 'Of course he knows you're on to it. After your breakfast-tray remarks.'

'He's got a pretty good idea of it, at least,' said Alleyn and put his thumb on the bell.

'Perhaps he won't come.'

'I think he will. What's the alternative? Fling himself into the billowy wave and do a Leander for the main-land?'

'Shall I disappear?' offered Dr Carmichael.

'And I?' said Troy.

'Not unless you'd rather. After all, I'm not going to arrest him.'

'Oh? Not?' they said.

'Why would I do that? For being Strix? I've no authority. Or do you think we might borrow him for being a public nuisance or perhaps for false pretences? On my information he's never actually conned anybody. He's just dressed himself up funny-like and taken unflattering photographs. There's the forged letter in *The Watchman*, of course. That might come within the meaning of some act: I'd have to look it up. Oh yes, and makes himself out to be a gentleman's gent, with forged references, I dare say.'

'Little beast,' said Troy. 'Cruel little pig, tormenting her like that. And everybody thinking it a jolly joke. And the shaming thing is, it *was* rather funny.'

'That's the worst of ill-doing, isn't it? It so often has its funny side. Come to think of it, I don't believe I could have stuck my job out if it wasn't so. The earliest playwrights knew all about that: their devils more often than not were clowns and their clowns were always cruel. Here we go.'

There had been a tap at the door. It opened and Marco came in.

He was an unattractive shade of yellow but otherwise looked much as usual.

He said: 'You rang, sir?'

'Yes,' Alleyn agreed. 'I rang. I've one or two questions to ask you. First, about the photograph you took yesterday afternoon through the window of the concert chamber. Did you put the print in the letter-bag?'

'I don't know what you mean, sir.'

'Yes, you do. You are Strix. You got yourself into your present job with the intention of following up your activities with the camera. Stop me if I'm wrong. But on second thoughts you're more likely to stop me if I'm right, aren't you? Did you see the advertisement for a personal servant for Mr Reece in the paper? Did it occur to you that as a member of Mr Reece's entourage you would be able to learn a lot more about Madame Sommita's programmes for the day? On some occasion when she was accompanied by Mr Reece or when Mr Reece was not at home and you were not required, you would be able to pop out to a room you kept for the purpose, dress yourself up like a sore thumb, startle her and photograph her with her mouth open looking ridiculous. You would hand the result in to the press and notch up another win. It was an impudently bold decision and it worked. You gave satisfaction as a valet and came here with your employer.'

Marco had assumed an air of casual insolence.

'Isn't it marvellous?' he asked of nobody in particular and shrugged elaborately.

'You took yesterday's photograph with the intention of sending it back to *The Watchman* and through them to the chain of newspapers with whom you've syndicated your productions. I know you did this. Your footprints are underneath the window. I fancy this was to be your final impertinence and that having knocked it off you would have given in your notice, claimed your money, retired to some inconspicuous retreat and written your autobiography.'

'No comment,' said Marco.

'I didn't really suppose there would be. Do you know where that photograph is now? Do you, Marco?'

'I don't know anything about any . . . .ing photograph,' said Marco, whose Italian accent had become less conspicuous and his English a good deal more idiomatic.

'It is skewered by a dagger to your victim's dead body.'

'My victim! She was not my victim. Not —' he stopped.

'Not in the sense of your having murdered her, were you going to say?'

'Not in any sense. I don't,' said Marco, 'know what you're talking about.'

'And I don't expect there'll be much trouble about finding your fingerprints on the glossy surface.'

Marco's hand went to his mouth.

'Come,' Alleyn said, 'don't you think you're being unwise? What would you say if I told you your room will be searched?'

'Nothing!' said Marco loudly. 'I would say nothing. You're welcome to search my room.'

'Do you carry the camera — is it a Strassman, by the way? — on you? How about searching *you*?'

'You have no authority.'

'That is unfortunately correct. See here, Marco. Just take a look at yourself. I shall tell the police what I believe to be the facts: that you are Strix, that you took the photograph now transfixed over Madame Sommita's heart, that it probably carries your fingerprints. If it does not, it is no great matter. Faced by police investigation, the newspapers that bought your photographs will identify you.'

'They've never seen me,' Marco said quickly and then looked as if he could have killed himself.

'It was all done by correspondence, was it?'

'They've never seen me because I'm not — I've never had anything to do with them. You're putting words in my mouth.'

'Your Strix activities have come to any end. The woman you tormented is dead, you've made a packet and will make more if you write a book. With illustrations. The only thing that is likely to bother you is the question of how the photograph got from your camera to the body. The best thing you can do if you're not the murderer of Isabella Sommita is help us find out who *is*. If you refuse, you remain a prime suspect.'

Marco looked from Troy to Dr Carmichael and back to Troy again. It was as if he asked for their advice. Troy turned away to the studio window.

Dr Carmichael said: 'You'd much better come across, you know. You'll do yourself no good by holding back.'

There was a long silence.

'Well,' said Marco at last and stopped.

'Well?' said Alleyn.

'I'm not admitting anything.'

'But suppose — ?' Alleyn prompted.

'Suppose, for the sake of argument, Strix took the shot you talk about. What *would* he do with it? he'd post if off to *The Watchman* at once, wouldn't he? He'd put it in the mail-box to be taken away in the bag.'

'Or,' Alleyn suggested, 'to avoid Mr Hanley noticing it when he cleared the box he might slip it directly into the mailbag while it was still unlocked and waiting in the study.'

'He might do that.'

'Is that what you'd say he did?'

'I don't say what he did. I don't know what he did.'

'Did you know the mailbag was forgotten last night and is still on the premises?'

Marco began to look very scary. 'No,' he said. 'Is it?'

'So if our speculation should turn out to be the truth: if you put the photograph, addressed to *The Watchman*, in the mailbag, the question is: who removed it. Who impaled it on the body? If, of course, you didn't.'

'It is idiotic to persist in this lie. Why do you do it? Where for me is the motive? Suppose I were Strix? So. I kill the goose that lays the golden egg? Does it make sense? So: after all, the man who takes the photograph does not post it. He is the murderer and he leaves it on the body.'

'What is your surname?'

'Smith.'

'I see.'

'It is *Smith*,' Marco shouted. 'Why do you look like that? Why should it not be Smith? Is there a law against Smith? My father was an American.'

'And your mother?'

'A Calabrian. Her name was Croce. I am Marco Croce Smith. Why?'

'Have you any Rossis in your family?'

'None. Again, why?'

'There is an enmity between the Rossis and Madame Sommita's family.'

'I know nothing of it,' said Marco and then burst out. 'How could I have done it? When was it done? I don't even know when it was done but all the time from when the opera is ended until Maria found her I am on duty. You saw me. Everybody saw me. I wait at table I attend in the hall. I go to and from the launch. I have alibis.'

'That may be true. But you may also have had a collaborator.'

'You are mad.'

'I am telling you how the police will think.'

'It is a trap. You try to trap me.'

'If you choose to put it like that. I want, if you didn't do it, to satisfy myself that you didn't. I want to get you out of the way. I believe you to be Strix and as Strix I think your activities were despicable but I do not accuse you of murder. I simply want you to tell me if you put the photograph in the postbag. In an envelope addressed to *The Watchman*.'

There followed a silence. The sun now shone in at the studio windows on the blank canvas and the empty model's throne. Outside a tui sang: a deep lucid phrase, uncivilized as snow-water and ending in a consequential clatter as if it cleared its throat. You darling, thought Troy, standing by the window, and knew that she could not endure to stay much longer inside this clever house with its arid perfections and its killed woman in the room on the landing.

Marco said: 'I surmise it was in the postbag. I do not know. I do not say I put it there.'

'And the bag was in the study?'

'That is where it is kept.'

'When was the letter put in it? Immediately after the photograph was taken? Or perhaps only just before the post-box was emptied into it and it was locked.'

Marco shrugged.

'And finally—crucially—when was the photograph removed, and by whom, and stabbed on to the body?'

'Of that I know nothing. Nothing, I tell you,' said Marco, and then with sudden venom. 'But I can guess.'

'Yes?'

'It is simple. Who clears the post-box always? Always! Who? I have seen him. He puts his arms into the bag and rounds it with his hands to receive the box and then he opens the box and holds it inside the bag to empty itself. Who?'

'Mr Hanley?'

'Ah. The secretary. *Il favorito*,' said Marco and achieved an angry smirk. He bowed in Troy's direction. 'Excuse me, madam,' he said. 'It is not a suitable topic.'

'Did you actually see Mr Hanley do this, last evening?'

'No, sir.'

'Very well,' said Alleyn. 'You may go.'

He went out with a kind of mean flourish and did not quite bang the door.

'He's a horrible little man,' said Troy, 'but I don't think he did it.'

'Nor I,' Dr Carmichael agreed.

'His next move,' said Alleyn, 'will be to hand in his notice and wait for the waters to subside.'

'Sling his hook?'

'Yes.'

'Will you let him?'

'I can't stop him. The police may try to or I suppose Reece could simply deny him transport.'

'Do you think Reece believes Marco is Strix?'

'If ever there was a clam its middle name was Reece but I think he does.'

'Are you any further on?' asked the doctor.

'A bit. I wish I'd found out whether Marco knows who took his bloody snapshot out of the bag. If ever it was in the bloody bag, which is conjectural. It's so boring of him not to admit he put it in. If he did.'

'He almost admitted *something*, didn't he?' said Troy.

'He's trying to work it out whether it would do him more good or harm to come clean.'

'I suppose,' hazarded Dr Carmichael, 'that whoever it was, Hanley or anyone else, who removed the photograph, it doesn't follow he was the killer.'

'Not as the night the day. No.'

Troy suddenly said: 'Having offered to make beds, I suppose I'd better make them. Do you think Miss Dancy would be outraged if I asked her to bear a hand? I imagine the little Sylvia is otherwise engaged.'

'Determined to maintain the house-party tone against all hazards, are you, darling?' said her husband.

'That's right. The dinner-jacket-in-the-jungle spirit.'

Dr Carmichael gazed at Troy in admiration and surprise. 'I must say, Mrs Alleyn, you set us all an example. How many beds do you plan to make?'

'I haven't counted.'

'The round dozen or more,' teased Alleyn, 'and God help all those who sleep in them.'

'He's being beastly,' Troy remarked. 'I'm not all that good at bedmaking. I'll just give Miss Dancy a call, I think.'

She consulted the list of room numbers by the telephone. Dr Carmichael joined Alleyn at the windows. 'It really is clearing,' he said. 'The wind's dropping. And I do believe the lake's settling.'

'Yes, it really is.'

'What do you suppose will happen first: the telephone be reconnected, or the launch engine be got going, or the police appear on the far bank, or the chopper turn up?'

'Lord knows.'

Troy said into the telephone. 'Of *course* I understand. Don't give it another thought. We'll meet at lunch-time. Oh. Oh, I see. I'm so sorry. Yes, I think you're very wise. No, no news. Awful, isn't it?'

She hung up. 'Miss Dancy has got a migraine,' she said. 'She sounds very Wagnerian. Well, I'd better make the best I can of the beds.'

'You're not going round on your own, Troy.'

'Aren't I? But why?'

'It's inadvisable.'

'But Rory, I promised Mrs Bacon.'

'To hell with Mrs Bacon. I'll tell her it's not on. They can make their own bloody beds. I've made ours,' said Alleyn. 'I'd go round with you but I don't think that'd do either.'

'I'll make beds with you, Mrs Alleyn,' offered Dr Carmichael in a sprightly manner.

'That's big of you, Carmichael,' said Alleyn. 'I dare say all the rooms will be locked. Mrs Bacon will have spare keys.'

'I'll find out.'

Troy said: 'You can pretend it's a hospital. You're the

188

matron and I'm a hamfisted probationer. I'll just go along to our palatial suite for a moment. Rejoin you here.'

When she had gone Alleyn said: 'She's hating this. You can always tell if she goes all jokey. I'll be glad to get her out of it.'

'If I may say so, you're a lucky man.'

'You may indeed say so.'

'Perhaps a brisk walk round the Island when we've done our chores.'

'A splendid idea. In a way,' Alleyn said, 'this bedmaking nonsense might turn out to be handy. I've no authority to search, of course, but you two might just keep your eyes skinned.'

'Anything in particular?'

'Not a thing. But you never know. The skinned eye and a few minor liberties.'

'I'll see about the keys,' said Dr Carmichael happily and bustled off.


II


Alleyn wondered if he was about to take the most dangerous decision of his investigative career. If he took this decision and failed, not only would he make an egregious ass of himself before the New Zealand police but he would effectively queer the pitch for their subsequent investigations and probably muck up any chance of an arrest. Or would he? In the event of failure, was there no chance of a new move, a strategy in reserve, a surprise attack? If there was, he was damned if he knew what it could be.

He went over the arguments again: The time factor. The riddle of the keys. The photograph. The conjectural motive. The appalling conclusion. He searched for possible alternatives to each of these and could find none.

He resurrected the dusty old bit of investigative folklore: If all explanations except one fail, then that one, however outrageous, will be the answer.

And, God knew, they were dealing with the outrageous.

So he made up his mind and having done that went downstairs and out into the watery sunshine for a breather.

All the guests had evidently been moved by the same impulse. They were abroad on the Island in pairs and singly. Whereas earlier in the morning Alleyn had likened those of them who had come out into the landscape to surrealistic details; now, while still wildly anachronistic, as was the house itself, in their primordial setting, they made him think of persons in a poem by Verlaine or perhaps by Edith Sitwell. Signor Lattienzo in his Tyrolean hat and his gleaming eyeglass, stylishly strolled beside Mr Ben Ruby who smoked a cigar and was rigged out for the country in a brand new Harris tweed suit. Rupert Bartholomew, wan in corduroy, his hair romantically disordered, his shoulders hunched, stood by the tumbled shore and stared over the lake. And was himself stared at, from a discreet distance, by the little Sylvia Parry with a scarlet handkerchief round her head. Even the stricken Miss Dancy had braved the elements. Wrapped up, scarfed and felt-hatted, she paced alone up and down a gravel path in front of the house as if it were the deck of a cruiser.

To her from indoors came Mr Reece in his custom-built outfit straight from pages headed 'Rugged Elegance: For Him' in the glossiest of periodicals. He wore a peaked cap which he raised ceremoniously to Miss Dancy, who immediately engaged him in conversation, clearly of an emotional kind. But he's used to that, thought Alleyn, and noticed how Mr Reece balanced Miss Dancy's elbow in his dogskin grasp as he squired her on her promenade.

He had thought they completed the number of persons in the landscape until he caught sight out of the corner of his eye, of some movement near one of the great trees near the lake. Ned Hanley was standing there. He wore a dark green coat and sweater and merged with his background. He seemed to survey the other figures in the picture.

One thing they all had in common and that was a tend
ency to halt and stare across the lake or shade their eyes, tip
back their heads and look eastward into the fast-thinning
clouds. He had been doing this himself.

Mr Ben Ruby spied him, waved his cigar energetically
and made towards him. Alleyn advanced and at close
quarters found Mr Ruby looking the worse for wear and self-
conscious.

' 'Morning, old man,' said Mr Ruby. 'Glad to see you.
Brightening up, isn't it? Won't be long now. We hope.'

'We do indeed.'

'*You* hope, anyway, I don't mind betting. Don't envy you
your job. Responsibility without the proper backing, eh?'

'Something like that,' said Alleyn.

'I owe you an apology, old man. Last evening. I'd had one
or two drinks. You know that?'

'Well . . .'

'What with one thing and another — the shock and that. I
was all to pieces. Know what I mean?'

'Of course.'

'All the same — bad show. Very bad show,' said Mr Ruby,
shaking his head and then wincing.

'Don't give it another thought.'

'Christ, I feel awful,' confided Mr Ruby and threw away
his cigar. 'It was good brandy, too. The best. Special
cognac. Wonder if this guy Marco could rustle up a corpse-
reviver.'

'I dare say. Or Hanley might.'

Mr Ruby made the sound that is usually written: 'T'ss'
and after a brief pause said in a deep voice and with
enormous expression: 'Bella! Bella Sommita! You can't
credit it, can you? The most beautiful woman with the most
gorgeous voice God ever put breath into. Gone! And how!
And what the hell we're going to do about the funeral's
nobody's business. I don't know of any relatives. It'd be
thoroughly in character if she's left detailed instructions and
bloody awkward ones at that. Pardon me, it slipped out. But

it might mean cold storage to anywhere she fancied or ashes in the Adriatic.' He caught himself up and gave Alleyn a hard if bloodshot stare. 'I suppose it's out of order to ask if you've formed an idea?'

'It is, really. At this stage,' Alleyn said. 'We must wait for the police.'

'Yeah? Well, here's hoping they know their stuff.' He reverted to his elegiac mood. 'Bella!' he apostrophized. 'After all these years of taking the rough with the smooth, if you can understand me. Hell, it hurts!'

'How long an association has it been?'

'You don't measure grief by months and years,' Mr Ruby said reproachfully. 'How long? Let me see? It was on her first tour of Aussie That would be in '72. Under the Bel Canto management in association with my firm—Ben Ruby Associates. There was a disagreement with Bel Canto and we took over.'

Here Mr Ruby embarked on a long parenthesis explaining that he was a self-made man, a Sydneysider who had pulled himself up by his own boot-strings and was proud of it and how the Sommita had understood this and had herself evolved from peasant stock.

'And,' said Alleyn when an opportunity presented itself, 'a close personal friendship had developed with the business association?'

'This is right, old man. I reckon I understood her as well as anybody ever could. There was the famous temperament, mind, and it was a snorter while it lasted but it never lasted long. She always sends—sent—for Maria to massage her shoulders and that would do the trick. Back into the honied-kindness bit and everybody loving everybody.'

'Mr Ruby, have you anything to tell me that might, in however far-fetched or remote a degree, help to throw light on this tragedy?

Mr Ruby opened his arms wide and let them fall in the classic gesture of defeat

'Nothing?' Alleyn said.

'This is what I've been asking myself ever since I woke up. When I got round, that is, to asking myself anything other than why the hell I had to down those cognacs.'

'And how do you answer yourself?'

Again the gesture. 'I don't,' Mr Ruby confessed. 'I can't. Except—' he stopped, provokingly, and stared at Signor Lattienzo who by now had arrived at the lakeside and contemplated the water rather, in his Tyrolean outfit, like some poet of the post-Romantic era.

'Except?' Alleyn prompted.

'Look!' Mr Ruby invited. 'Look at what's been done and *how* it's been done. Look at that. If you had to say—you, with your experience—what it reminded you of, what would it be? Come on.'

'Grand opera,' Alleyn said promptly.

Mr Ruby let out a strangulated yelp and clapped him heavily on the back. 'Good on you!' he cried. 'Got it in one! Good on you, mate. And the Italian sort of grand opera, what's more. That funny business with the dagger and the picture! Verdi would have loved it. Particularly the picture. Can you see any of *us*, supposing he was a murderer, doing it that way? That poor kid Rupert? Ned Hanley, never mind if he's one of those? Monty? *Me*? *You*? Even if you'd draw the line at the props and the business. "No" you'd say "No". Not that way. It's not in character, it's impossible, it's not—it's not—' and Mr Ruby appeared to hunt excitedly for the *mot juste* of his argument. 'It's not British,' he finally pronounced, and added: 'Using the word in its widest sense. I'm a Commonwealth man myself.'

Alleyn had to give himself a moment or two before he was able to respond to this declaration.

'What you are saying,' he ventured, 'in effect, is that the murderer must be one of the Italians on the premises. Is that right?'

'That,' said Mr Ruby, 'is dead right.'

'It narrows down the field of suspects,' said Alleyn drily.

'It certainly does,' Mr Ruby portentously agreed.

'Marco and Maria?'

'Right.'

During an uncomfortable pause Mr Ruby's rather bleary regard dwelt upon Signor Lattienzo in his windblown cape by the lakeside.

'And Signor Lattienzo, I suppose?' Alleyn suggested.

There was no reply.

'Have you,' Alleyn asked, 'any reason, apart from the grand opera theory, to suspect one of these three?'

Mr Ruby seemed to be much discomforted by this question. He edged with his toe at a grassy turf. He cleared his throat and looked aggrieved.

'I knew you'd ask that,' he said resentfully.

'It was natural, don't you think, that I should?'

'I suppose so. Oh yes. Too right it was. But listen. It's a terrible thing to accuse anyone of. I know that. I wouldn't want to say anything that'd unduly influence you. You know. Cause you to — to jump to conclusions or give you the wrong impression. I wouldn't like to do that.'

'I don't think it's very likely.'

'No? You'd *say* that, of course. But I reckon you've done it already. I reckon like everyone else you've taken the old retainer stuff for real.'

'Are you thinking of Maria?'

'Too bloody right I am, mate.'

'Come on,' Alleyn said. 'Get it off your chest. I won't make too much of it. Wasn't Maria as devoted as one was led to suppose?'

'Like hell she was! Well, that's not correct either. She was devoted all right but it was a flaming uncomfortable sort of devotion. Kind of dog-with-a-bone affair. Sometimes when they'd had a difference you'd have said it was more like hate. Jealous! She's eaten up with it. And when Bella was into some new "friendship" — know what I mean? — Maria as likely as not would turn plug-ugly. She was even jealous in a weird sort of way, of the artistic triumphs. Or that's the way it looked to me.'

'How did she take the friendship with Mr Reece?'

'Monty?' A marked change came over Mr Ruby. He glanced quickly at Alleyn as if he wondered whether he was unenlightened in some respect. He hesitated and then said quietly. 'That's different again, isn't it?'

'Is it? How, "different"?'

'Well—you know.'

'But I don't know.'

'It's platonic. Couldn't be anything else.'

'I see.'

'Poor old Monty. Result of an illness. Cruel thing, really.'

'Indeed? So Maria had no cause to resent him.'

'This is right. She admires him. They do, you know. Italians. Especially his class. They admire success and prestige more than anything else. It was a very different story when young Rupert came along. Maria didn't worry about letting everyone see what she felt about *that* lot. I'd take long odds she'll be telling you the kid done—did—it. That vindictive, she is. Fair go—I wouldn't put it past her. Now.'

Alleyn considered for a moment or two. Signor Lattienzo had now joined Rupert Bartholomew on the lakeside and was talking energetically and clapping him on the shoulder. Mr Reece and Miss Dancy still paced their imaginary promenade deck and the little Sylvia Parry, perched dejectedly on a rustic seat, watched Rupert.

Alleyn said: 'Was Madame Sommita tolerant of these outbursts from Maria?'

'I suppose she must have been in her own way. There were terrible scenes, of course. That was to be expected, wasn't it? Bella'd threaten Maria with the sack and Maria'd throw a fit of hysterics and then they'd both go weepy on it and we'd be back to square one with Maria standing behind Bella massaging her shoulders and swearing eternal devotion. Italians! My oath! But it was different, totally different—with the kid. I'd never seen her as far gone over anyone else as she was with him. Crazy about him. In at the deep end, boots and all. That's why she took it so badly when he saw the light about that little opera of his and wanted to opt out. He was dead right, of course, but Bella hadn't got any real musical judgement. Not really. You ask Beppo.'

'What about Mr Reece?'

'Tone deaf,' said Mr Ruby.

'Really?'

'Fact. Doesn't pretend to be anything else. He was annoyed with the boy for disappointing her, of course. As far as Monty was concerned the diva had said the opus was great, and what she said had got to be right. And then of course he didn't like the idea of throwing a disaster of a party. In a way,' said Mr Ruby, 'it was the Citizen Kane situation with the boot on the other foot. Sort of.' He waited for a moment and then said: 'I feel bloody sorry for that kid.'

'God knows, so do I,' said Alleyn.

'But he's young. He'll get over it. All the same, she'd a hell of a lot to answer for.'

'Tell me. You knew her as well as anybody, didn't you? Does the name "Rossi" ring a bell?'

'Rossi,' Mr Ruby mused. 'Rossi, eh? Hang on. Wait a sec.'

As if to prompt, or perhaps warn him, raucous hoots sounded from the jetty across the water, giving the intervals without the cadence of the familiar singing-off phrase 'Dah dahdy dah-dah. Dah *Dah*.'

Les appeared on deck and could be seen to wave his scarlet cap.

The response from the islanders was instant. They hurried into a group. Miss Dancy flourished her woollen scarf. Mr Reece raised his arm in a Roman salute. Signor Lattienzo lifted his Tyrolean hat high above his head. Sylvia ran to Rupert and took his arm. Hanley moved out of cover and Troy, Mrs Bacon and Dr Carmichael came out of the house and pointed Les out to each other from the steps. Mr Ruby bawled out, 'He's done it. Good on 'im, 'e's done it.'

Alleyn took a handkerchief from his breast pocket and a spare from his overcoat. He went down to the lake edge and semaphored: *Nice Work*. Les returned to the wheelhouse and sent a short toot of acknowledgement.

The islanders chattered excitedly, telling each other that the signal *must* mean the launch was mobile again, that the lake was undoubtedly calmer and that when the police did arrive they would be able to cross. The hope that they themselves would all be able to leave remained unspoken.

They trooped up to the house and were shepherded in by Mr Reece who said, with sombre playfulness, that 'elevenses' were now served in the library.

Troy and Dr Carmichael joined Alleyn. They seemed to be in good spirits. 'We've finished our chores,' Troy said, 'and we've got something to report. Let's have a quick swallow, and join up in the studio.'

'Don't make it too obvious,' said Alleyn, who was aware that he was now under close though furtive observation by most of the household. He fetched two blameless tomato juices for himself and Troy. They joined Rupert and Sylvia Parry who were standing a little apart from the others and were not looking at each other. Rupert was still white about the gills but, or so Alleyn thought, rather less distraught — indeed there was perhaps a hint of portentousness, of self-conscious gloom in his manner.

She has provided him with an audience, thought Alleyn. Let's hope she knows what she's letting herself in for.

Rupert said: 'I've told Sylvia about — last night.'

'So I supposed,' said Alleyn.

'She thinks I was right.'

'Good.'

Sylvia said: 'I think it took wonderful courage and artistic integrity and I do think it was right.'

'That's a very proper conclusion.'

'It won't be long now, will it?' Rupert asked. 'Before the police come?' He pitched his voice rather high and brittle with the sort of false airiness some actors employ when they hope to convey suppressed emotion.

'Probably not,' said Alleyn.

'Of course, I'll be the prime suspect,' Rupert announced.

'Rupert, *no*,' Sylvia whispered.

'My dear girl, it sticks out a mile. After my curtain performance. Motive. Opportunity. The lot. We might as well face it.'

'We might as well not make public announcements about it,' Troy observed.

'I'm sorry,' said Rupert grandly. 'No doubt I'm being silly.'

'Well,' Alleyn cheerfully remarked, 'you said it. We didn't. Troy, hadn't we better sort out those drawings of yours?'

'OK. Let's. I'd forgotten.'

'She leaves them unfixed and tiles the floor with them,' Alleyn explained. 'Our cat sat on a preliminary sketch of the Prime Minister and turned it into a jungle flower. Come on, darling.'

They found Dr Carmichael already in the studio. 'I didn't want Reece's "elevenses",' he said. And to Troy: 'Have you told him?'

'I waited for you,' said Troy.

They were, Alleyn thought, as pleased as Punch with themselves. 'You tell him,' they said simultaneously. 'Ladies first,' said the doctor.

'Come on,' said Alleyn.

Troy inserted her thin hand in a gingerly fashion into a large pocket of her dress. Using only her first finger and her thumb she drew out something wrapped in one of Alleyn's handkerchiefs. She was in the habit of using them as she preferred a large one and she had been known when intent on her work to confuse the handkerchief and her paint-rag, with regrettable results to the handkerchief and to her face.

She carried her trophy to the paint-table and placed it there. Then, with a sidelong look at her husband, she produced two clean hoghair brushes and, using them upside down in the manner of chopsticks, fiddled open the handkerchief and stood back.

Alleyn walked over, put his arm across her shoulders and

looked at what she had revealed.

A large heavy envelope, creased and burnt but not so extensively that an airmail stamp and part of the address was not still in evidence. The address was typewritten.

> The Edit
> *The Watchma*
> PO Bo
> NSW 14C
> SY
> Australia

'Of course,' Troy said after a considerable pause, 'it may be of no consequence at all, may it?'

'Suppose we have the full story?'

'Yes. All right. Here goes, then.'

Their story was that they had gone some way with their house-maiding expedition when Troy decided to equip herself with a box-broom and a duster. They went downstairs in search of them and ran into Mrs Bacon emerging from the study. She intimated that she was nearing the end of her tether. The staff, having gone through progressive stages of hysteria and suspicion, had settled for a sort of work-to-rule attitude and, with the exception of the chef who had agreed to provide a very basic luncheon and Marco who was, said Mrs Bacon, abnormally quiet but did his jobs, either sulked in their rooms or muttered together in the staff sitting-room. As far as Mrs Bacon could make out, the New Zealand ex-hotel group suspected in turn Signor Lattienzo, Marco and Maria on the score of their being Italians and Mr Reece whom they cast in the role of *de facto* cuckold. Rupert Bartholomew was fancied as an outside chance on the score of his having turned against the Sommita. Maria had gone to earth, supposedly in her room. Chaos, Mrs Bacon said, prevailed.

Mrs Bacon herself had rushed round the dining- and drawing-rooms while Marco set out the elevenses. She had then turned her attention to the study and found to her horror that the open fireplace had not been cleaned nor the fire relaid. To confirm this, she had drawn their attention to a steel ashpan she herself carried in her rubber-gloved hands.

'And that's when I saw it, Rory,' Troy explained. 'It was sticking up out of the ashes and I saw what's left of the address.'

'And she nudged me,' said Dr Carmichael proudly, 'and I saw it too.'

'And he behaved *perfectly*,' Troy intervened. 'He said: "Do let me take that thing and tell me where to empty it" And Mrs Bacon said, rather wildly: "In the bin. In the yard," and made feeble protestations and at that moment we all heard the launch hooting and she became distracted. So Dr Carmichael got hold of the ashpan. And I—well—I—got hold of the envelope and put it in my pocket among your handkerchief which happened to be there.'

'So it appears,' Dr Carmichael summed up, 'that somebody typed a communication of some sort to *The Watchman* and stamped the envelope which he or somebody else then chucked on the study fire and it dropped through the grate into the ashpan when it was only half-burnt. Or doesn't it?'

'Did you get a chance to have a good look at the ashes?' asked Alleyn.

'Pretty good. In the yard. They were faintly warm. I ran them carefully into a zinc rubbish bin already half-full. There were one or two very small fragments of heavily charred paper and some clinkers. Nothing else. I heard someone coming and cleared out. I put the ashpan back under the study grate.'

Alleyn bent over the trophy. 'It's a Sommita envelope,' said Troy. 'Isn't it?'

'Yes. Bigger than the Reece envelope but the same paper: like the letter she wrote to the Yard.'

'Why would she write to *The Watchman*?'

'We don't know that she did.'

'Don't we?'

'Or if she did, whether her letter was in this envelope.' He took one of Troy's brushes and used it to flip the envelope over. 'It may have been stuck up,' he said, 'and opened before the gum dried. There's not enough left to be certain. It's big enough to take the photograph.'

Dr Carmichael blew out his cheeks and then expelled the air rather noisily. 'That's a long shot, isn't it?' he said.

'Of course it is,' agreed Alleyn. 'Pure speculation.'

'If *she* wrote it,' Troy said carefully, 'she dictated it. I'm sure she couldn't type, aren't you?'

'I think it's *most* unlikely. The first part of her letter to the Yard was impeccably typed and the massive postscript flamboyantly handwritten. Which suggested that she dictated the beginning or told young Rupert to concoct something she could sign, found it too moderate and added the rest herself.'

'But why,' Dr Carmichael mused, 'was this thing in the study, on Reece's desk? I know! She asked that secretary of his to type it because she'd fallen out with young Bartholomew. How's that?'

'Not too bad,' said Alleyn. 'Possible. And where, do you suggest, is the letter? It wasn't in the envelope. And, by the way, the envelope was not visible on Reece's desk when you and I, Carmichael, visited him last night.'

'Really? How d'you know?'

'Oh, my dear chap, the cop's habit of using the beady eye, I suppose. It might have been there under some odds and ends in his "out" basket.'

Troy said: 'Rory, I think I know where you're heading.'

'Do you, my love? Where?'

'Could Marco have slid into the study to put the photograph in the postbag before Hanley had emptied the mailbox into it and could he have seen the typed and addressed envelope on the desk and thought there was a marvellous opportunity to send the photograph to *The Watchman*, because nobody would question it. And so he took out her letter or whatever it was and chucked it on the fire and put the photograph in the envelope and—'

Troy, who had been going great guns, brought up short. 'Blast!' she said.

'Why didn't he put it in the postbag?' asked Alleyn.

'Yes.'

'Because,' Dr Carmichael staunchly declared, 'he was interrupted and had to get rid of it quick. I think that's a damn good piece of reasoning, Mrs Alleyn.'

'Perhaps.' Troy said, 'her letter had been left out awaiting the writer's signature and — no, that's no good.'

'It's a lot of good,' Alleyn said warmly. 'You have turned up trumps, you two. Damn Marco. Why can't he make up his dirty little mind that his best move is to cut his losses and come clean. I'll have to try my luck with Hanley. Tricky.'

He went out on the landing. Bert had resumed his guard duty and lounged back in the armchair reading a week-old sports tabloid. A homemade cigarette hung from his lower lip. He gave Alleyn the predictable sideways tip of his head.

Alleyn said: 'I really oughtn't to impose on you any longer, Bert. After all, we've got the full complement of keys now and nobody's going to force the lock with the amount of traffic flowing through this house.'

'I'm not fussy,' said Bert which Alleyn took to mean that he had no objections to continuing his vigil.

'Well, if you're sure,' he said.

'She'll be right.'

'Thank you.'

The sound of voices indicated the emergence of the elevenses party. Miss Dancy, Sylvia Parry and Rupert Bartholomew came upstairs. Rupert, with an incredulous look at Bert and a scary one at Alleyn, made off in the direction of his room. The ladies crossed the landing quickly and ascended the next flight. Mr Reece, Ben Ruby and Signor Lattienzo made for the study. Alleyn ran quickly downstairs in time to catch Hanley emerging from the morning-room.

'Sorry to bother you,' he said, 'but I wonder if I might have a word. It won't take a minute.'

'But of *course*,' said Hanley. 'Where shall we go? Back into the library?'

'Right.'

When they were there Hanley winningly urged further refreshment. Upon Alleyn's declining, he said: 'Well, *I* will; just a teeny tiddler,' and helped himself to a gin-and-tonic. 'What can I do for you, Mr Alleyn?' he said. 'Is there any further development?'

Alleyn said: 'Did you type a letter to *The Watchman* some time before Madame Sommita's death?'

Hanley's jaw dropped and the hand holding his drink stopped half way to his mouth. For perhaps three seconds he maintained this position and then spoke.

'Oh Christmas!' he said. 'I'd forgotten. You wouldn't credit it, would you? I'd entirely forgotten.'

He made no bones about explaining himself and did so very fluently and quite without hesitation. He had indeed typed a letter from the Sommita to *The Watchman*. She had been stirred up 'like a hive of bees', he said, by the episode of the supposed intruder on the Island and had decided that it was Strix who had been sent by *The Watchman* and had arrived after dark the previous night, probably by canoe, and had left unobserved by the same means, she didn't explain when. The letter which she dictated was extremely abusive and threatened the editor with a libel action. She had made a great point of Mr Reece not being told of the letter.

'Because of course he'd have stopped all the nonsense,' said Hanley. 'I was to type it and take it to her to sign and then put it in the bag, all unbeknownst. She asked *me* to do it because of the row with the Wonder Boy. She gave me some of her notepaper.'

'And you did it?'

'My dear! As much as my life was worth to refuse. I typed it out, calming it down the least morsel, which she didn't notice. But when she'd signed it I bethought me that maybe when it had gone *she'd* tell the Boss-Man and he'd be cross with me for doing it. So I left the letter on his desk meaning to show it to him after the performance. I put it under some letters he had to sign.'

'And the envelope?'

'The envelope? Oh, on the desk. And then, I remember, Marco came in to say I was wanted on stage to refocus a light.'

'When was this?'

'When? I wouldn't know. Well—late afternoon. After tea sometime, but well before the performance.'

'Did Marco leave the study before you?'

'*Did* he? I don't know. Yes, I do. He said something about making up the fire and I left him to it.'

'Did Mr Reece see the letter, then?'

Hanley flapped his hands. 'I've no notion. He's said nothing to me, but then with the catastrophe — I mean, everything else goes out of one's head, doesn't it, except that nothing ever goes out of *his* head. You could ask him.'

'So I could,' said Alleyn. 'And will.'

Mr Reece was along in the study. He said at once in his flattest manner that he had found the letter on his desk under a couple of business communications which he was to sign in time for Hanley to send them off by the evening post. He did sign them and then read the letter.

'It was ill-advised,' he said, cutting the episode down to size. 'She had been over-excited ever since the matter of the intruder arose. I had told her Sir Simon Marks had dealt with *The Watchman* and there would be no more trouble in that quarter. This letter was abusive in tone and would have stirred everything up again. I threw it on the fire. I intended to speak to her about it but not until after the performance when she would be less nervous and tense.'

'Did you throw the envelope on the fire too?' Alleyn asked and thought: If he says yes, bang goes sixpence and we return to square one.

'The envelope?' said Mr Reece. 'No. It was not in an envelope. I don't remember noticing one. May I ask what is the significance of all this, Chief Superintendent?'

'It's really just a matter of tidying up. The half-burnt envelope stamped and addressed to *The Watchman* was in the ashpan under the grate this morning.'

'I have no recollection of seeing it,' Mr Reece said heavily. 'I believe I would remember if I had seen it.'

'After you burnt the letter, did you stay in the study?'

'I believe so,' he said and Alleyn thought he detected a weary note. 'Or no,' Mr Reece corrected himself. 'That is not right. Maria came in with a message that Bella wanted to see me. She was in the concert chamber. The flowers that I had ordered for her had not arrived and she was — distressed. I went to the concert chamber at once.'

'Did Maria go with you?'

'I really don't know what Maria did, Superintendent. I fancy — no, I am not sure but I don't think she did. She may have returned there a little later. Really, I do *not* remember,' said Mr Reece, and pressed his eyes with his thumb and forefinger.

'I'm sorry,' Alleyn said, 'I won't bother you any longer. I wouldn't have done so now but it just might be relevant.'

'It is no matter,' said Mr Reece. And then: 'I much appreciate what you are doing,' he said. 'You will excuse me, I'm sure, if I seem ungracious.'

'Good Lord, yes,' said Alleyn quickly. 'You should just hear some of the receptions we get.'

'I suppose so,' said Mr Reece heavily. 'Very likely.' And then with a lugubrious attempt at brightening up. 'The sun is shining continuously and the wind has almost gone down. Surely it can't be long, now, before the police arrive.'

'We hope not. Tell me, have you done anything about Marco? Spoken to him? Faced him with being Strix?'

And then Mr Reece made the most unexpected, the most remarkable statement of their conversation.

'I couldn't be bothered,' he said.

## III

On leaving the study, Alleyn heard sounds of activity in the dining-room. The door was open and he looked in to find Marco laying the table.

'I want a word with you,' Alleyn said, 'not here. In the library. Come on.'

Marco followed him there, saying nothing.

'Now, listen to me,' Alleyn said. 'I do not think, indeed I have never thought, that you killed Madame Sommita. You hadn't time to do it. I now think—I am almost sure—that you went into the study yesterday afternoon intending to put the photographs you took of her, in the mailbag. You saw on the desk a stamped envelope addressed in typescript to *The Watchman*. It was unsealed and empty. This gave you a wonderful opportunity, it made everything safer and simpler. You transferred the photograph from its envelope to this envelope, sealed it down and would have put it in the bag but I think you were interrupted and simply dropped it back on the desk and I dare say explained your presence there by tidying the desk. Now. If this is so, all I want from you is the name of the person who interrupted you.'

Marco had watched Alleyn carefully with a look, wary and hooded, that often appears on the faces of the accused when some telling piece of evidence is produced against them. Alleyn thought of it as the 'dock-face'.

'You *have* been busy,' Marco sneered. 'Congratulations.'

'I'm right, then?'

'Oh yes,' he said casually. 'I don't know how you got there but you're right.'

'And the name?'

'You know so much, I'd have thought you'd know that.'

'Well?'

'Maria,' said Marco.

From somewhere in the house there came a sound, normally unexceptionable but now arresting. A door banged and shut it off.

'Telephone,' Marco whispered. 'It's the telephone.'

'Did Maria see you? See you had the envelope in your hands? Did she?'

'I'm not sure. She might have. She could have. She's been — looking — at me. Or I thought so. Once or twice. She hasn't said anything. We haven't been friendly.'

'No?'

'I went back to the study. Later. Just before the opera and it had gone. So I supposed someone had put it in the mailbag.'

There was a flurry of voices in the hall. The door swung open and Hanley came in.

'The telephone!' he cried. 'Working. It's the—' He pulled up short, looking at Marco. 'Someone for you, Mr Alleyn,' he said.

'I'll take it upstairs. Keep the line alive.'

He went into the hall. Most of the guests were collected there. He passed through them and ran upstairs to the first landing and the studio where he found Troy and Dr Carmichael. He took the receiver off the telephone. Hanley's voice fluted in the earpiece: 'Yes. Don't hang up, will you? Mr Alleyn's on his way. Hold the line, please.' And a calm reply: 'Thank you, sir. I'll hold on.'

'All right, Hanley,' Alleyn said. 'You can hang up now,' and heard the receiver being cradled. 'Hullo,' he said. 'Alleyn speaking.'

'Chief Superintendent Alleyn? Inspector Hazelmere, Rivermouth Police, here. We've had a report of trouble on Waihoe Island and are informed of your being on the premises. I understand it's a homicide.'

Alleyn gave him the bare bones of the case. Mr Hazelmere repeated everything he said. He was evidently dictating. There were crackling disturbances on the line.

'So you see,' Alleyn ended, 'I'm a sort of minister without portfolio.'

'Pardon? Oh. Oh, I get you. Yes. Very fortunate coincidence, though. For us. We'd been instructed by head office that you were in the country, of course. It'll be an unexpected honour . . .' A crash of static obliterated the rest of this remark. '. . . temporary repair. Better be quick . . . should make it . . . chopper . . . hope . . . doctor . . .'

'There's a doctor here,' Alleyn shouted. 'I'd suggest a fully equipped homicide squad and a search warrant— can you hear?— and a brace and bit. Yes, that's what I said. Large. Yes, large. Observation purposes. Are you there? Hullo? Hullo?'

The line was dead.

'Well,' said Troy after a pause. 'This is the beginning of the end, I suppose.'

'In a way the beginning of the beginning,' Alleyn said wryly. 'If it's done nothing else it's brought home the virtues of routine. I'm not sure if they have homicide squads in New Zealand but whatever they do have they'll take the correct steps in the correct way and with authority. And you, my love, will fly away home with an untouched canvas.' He turned to Dr Carmichael. 'I really don't know what I'd have done without you,' he said.

Before Dr Carmichael could answer there was a loud rap at the door.

'Not a dull moment,' said Alleyn. 'Come in!'

It was Signor Lattienzo, pale and strangely unsprightly.

'I am *de trop*,' he said. 'Forgive me. I thought you would be here. I find the ambiance downstairs uncomfortable. Everbody asking questions and expressing relief and wanting above all to know when they can go away. And behind it all—fear. Fear and suspicion. Not a pretty combination. And to realize that one is in much the same state oneself, after all! That I find exceedingly disagreeable.'

Dr Carmichael said to Alleyn. 'They'll be wanting to know about the telephone call. Would you like me to go downstairs and tell them?'

'Do. Just say it *was* the police and they are on their way and the line's gone phut again.'

'Right.'

'That's a *very* nice man,' said Troy when he had gone. 'We never completed our bedmaking. I don't suppose it matters so much now but we ought at least to put our gear away, don't you think?'

She had managed to get behind Signor Lattienzo and pull a quick face at her husband.

'I expect you're right,' he said obediently and she made for the door. Signor Lattienzo seemed to make an effort. He produced a rather wan replica of his more familiar manner.

'Bedmaking! "Gear"?' he exclaimed. 'But I am baffled. Here is the most distinguished painter of our time whom I have, above all things, desired to meet and she talks of bedmaking as a sequence to murder.'

'She's being British,' said Alleyn. 'If there were any bullets about she'd bite on them. Pay no attention.'

'That's right,' Troy assured Signor Lattienzo. 'It's a substitute for hysterics.'

'If you say so,' said Signor Lattienzo and as an afterthought seized and extensively kissed Troy's hand. She cast a sheepish glance at Alleyn and withdrew.

Alleyn, who had begun to feel rather British himself, said he was glad that Signor Lattienzo had looked in. 'There's something I've been wanting to ask you,' he said, 'but with all the excursions and alarms, I haven't got round to it.'

'Me? But of course! Anything! Though I don't imagine that I can produce electrifying tidings,' said Signor Lattienzo. He sat down in the studio's most comfortable armchair and appeared to relax; 'Already,' he said, 'I feel better,' and took out his cigarette case.

'It's about Madame Sommita's background.'

'Indeed?'

'She was your pupil for some three years, wasn't she, before making her debut?'

'That is so.'

'You were aware, I expect, of her real name?'

'Naturally. Pepitone.'

'Perhaps you helped her decide on her professional name?

Sommita, which is as much as to say "The Tops", isn't it?'

'It was not my choice. I found it a little extravagant. She did not and she prevailed. You may say she has been fully justified.'

'Indeed you may. You may also say, perhaps, that the choice was a matter of accuracy rather than of taste.'

Signor Lattienzo softly clapped his hands. 'That is precisely the case,' he applauded.

'Maestro,' Alleyn said. 'I am very ignorant in these matters, but I imagine that the relationship between pedagogue and pupil is, or at least can be, very close, very intimate.'

'My dear Mr Alleyn if you are suggesting—'

'Which I am not. Not for a moment. There can be close relationships that have no romantic overtones.'

'Of course. And allow me to say that with a pupil it would be in the highest degree a mistake to allow oneself to become involved in such an attachment. And apart from all that,' he added with feeling, 'when the lady has the temperament of a wild cat and the appetite of a hyena, it would be sheer lunacy.'

'But all the same, I expect some kind of aseptic intimacy does exist, doesn't it?'

Signor Lattienzo broke into rather shrill laughter. ' "Aseptic intimacy",' he echoed. 'You are a master of the *mot juste*, my dear Mr Alleyn. It is a pleasure to be grilled by you.'

'Well, then: did you learn anything about a family feud—one of those vendetta-like affairs—between the Pepitones and another Sicilian clan: the Rossis.'

Signor Lattienzo took some time in helping himself to a cigarette and lighting it. He did not look at Alleyn. 'I do not concern myself with such matters,' he said.

'I'm sure you don't but did *she*?'

'May I first of all ask you a question? Do you suspect that this appalling crime might be traced to the Pepitone-Rossi affair? I think you must do so, otherwise you would not bring it up.'

'As to that,' said Alleyn, 'it's just a matter of avenues and stones, however unlikely. I've been told that Madame Sommita herself feared some sort of danger threatened her and that she suspected Strix of being an agent or even a member of the Rossi family. I don't have to tell you that Marco is Strix. Mr Reece will have done that.'

'Yes. But — do you think — '

'No. He has an unbreakable alibi.'

'Ah.'

'I wondered if she had confided her fears to you?'

'You will know, of course, of the habit of *omertà*. It has been remorselessly if erroneously, paraded in works of popular fiction with a mafioso background. I expected that she knew of her father's alleged involvement with mafioso elements although great care had been taken to remove her from the milieu. I am surprised to hear that she spoke of the Rossi affair. Not to the good Monty, I am sure?'

'Not specifically. But it appears that even to him she referred repeatedly, though in the vaguest of terms, to sinister intentions behind the Strix activities.'

'But otherwise — '

Signor Lattienzo stopped short and for the first time looked very hard at Alleyn. 'Did she tell that unhappy young man? Is that it? I see it is. Why?'

'It seems she used it as a weapon when she realized he was trying to escape her.'

'Ah! That is believable. An appeal to his pity. That I can believe. Emotional blackmail.'

Signor Lattienzo got up and moved restlessly about the room. He looked out at the now sunny prospect, thrust his plump hands into his trouser pockets, took them out and examined them as if they had changed and finally approached Alleyn and came to a halt.

'I have something to tell you,' he said.

'Good.'

'Evidently you are familiar with the Rossi affair.'

'Not to say familiar, no. But I do remember something of the case.'

Alleyn would have thought it impossible that Signor Lattienzo would ever display the smallest degree of embarrassment or loss of *savoir faire* but he appeared to do so now. He screwed in his eyeglass, stared at a distant spot somewhere to the right of Alleyn's left ear and spoke rapidly in a high voice.

'I have a brother,' he proclaimed. 'Alfredo Lattienzo. He is an Avvocato, a leading barrister, and he, in the course of his professional duties, has appeared in a number of cases where the mafioso element was—ah—involved. At the time of the Rossi trial, which as you will know became a *cause célèbre* in the USA, he held a watching brief on behalf of the Pepitone element. It was through him, by the way, that Isabella became my pupil. But that is of no moment. He was never called upon to take a more active part but he did—ah —he did learn— ah—from, as you would say, the horse's mouth, the origin and subsequent history of the enmity between the two houses.'

He paused. Alleyn thought that it would be appropriate if he said: You interest me, strangely. Pray continue your most absorbing narrative. However, he said nothing and Signor Lattienzo continued.

'*The origin*,' he repeated. 'The event that set the whole absurdly wicked feud going. I have always thought there must have been Corsican blood somewhere in that family. My dear Alleyn, I am about to break a confidence with my brother and one does not break confidences of this sort.'

'I think I may assure that whatever you may tell me I won't reveal the source.'

'It may, after all, not seem as striking to you as it does to me. It is this. The event that gave rise to the feud so many, many years ago, was the murder of a Pepitone girl by her Rossi bridegroom. He had discovered a passionate and explicit letter from a lover. He stabbed her to the heart on their wedding night.'

212

He stopped. He seemed to balk at some conversational hurdle.

'I see,' said Alleyn.

'That is not all,' said Signor Lattienzo. 'That is by no means all. Pinned to the body by the stiletto that killed her was the letter. That is what I came to tell you and now I shall go.'

## Chapter Eight

## THE POLICE

I

'From now on,' Alleyn said to Dr Carmichael, 'it would be nice to maintain a masterly inactivity. I shall complete my file and hand it over, with an anxious smirk, to Inspector Hazelmere in, please God, the course of a couple of hours or less.'

'Don't you feel you'd like to polish it off yourself? Having gone so far?'

'Yes, Rory,' said Troy. 'Don't you?'

'If Fox and Bailey and Thompson could walk in, yes, I suppose I do. That would be, as Noel Coward put it "*un autre pair de souliers*". But this hamstrung solo, poking about without authority, has been damned frustrating.'

'What do you suppose the chap that's coming will do first?'

'Inspect the body and the immediate environment. He can't look at my improvised dabs-and-photographs because they are still in what Lattienzo calls the womb of the camera. He'll take more of his own.'

'And then?'

'Possibly set up a search of some if not all of their rooms. I suggested he bring a warrant. And by that same token did your bedmaking exercise prove fruitful? Before or after the envelope-and-ashes episode?'

'A blank,' said Dr Carmichael. 'Hanley has a collection of bedside books with Wilde and Gide at the top and back-street Marseilles at the bottom but all with the same *leit-motif*.'

'And Ben Ruby,' said Troy 'has an enormous scrapbook of newspaper cuttings all beautifully arranged and dated and noted and with all the rave bits in the reviews underlined. For quotation in advance publicity, I suppose. It's got the Strix photographs and captions and newspaper correspondence, indignant and supportive. Do you know there are only seven European Strix photographs, one American, and four Australian, including the retouched one in *The Watchman*. Somehow one had imagined, or I had, a hoard of them. Signor Lattienzo's got a neat little pile of letters in Italian on his desk. Mr Reece has an enormous coloured photograph framed in silver of the diva in full operatic kit — I wouldn't know which opera except that it's not *Butterfly*. And there are framed photographs of those rather self-conscious, slightly smug walking youths in the Athens Museum. He's also got a marvellous equestrian drawing in sanguine of a nude man on a stallion which I could swear is a da Vinci original. Can he be as rich as all that? I really do swear it's not a reproduction.'

'I think he probably can,' said Alleyn.

'What a shut-up sort of man he is,' Troy mused. 'I mean, who would have expected it? Does he really appreciate it or has he just acquired it because it cost so much? Like the diva, one might say.'

'Perhaps not quite like that,' said Alleyn.

'Do you attach a lot of weight to Signor Lattienzo's observations. I don't know what they were, of course.'

'They were confidential. They cast a strongly Italian flavour over the scene. Beyond that,' said Alleyn, 'my lips are sealed.'

'Rory,' Troy asked, 'are you going to see Maria again? Before the police arrive?'

'I've not quite decided. I think perhaps I might. Very briefly.'

'We mustn't ask why, of course,' said Carmichael.

'Oh yes you may. By all means. If I do see her, it will be to tell her that I shall inform the police of her request to — attend to her mistress and shall ask them to accede to it.

When they've finished their examination of the room, of course.'

'You will?'

'That's the general idea.'

'Well, then . . . Are you going to explain why?'

'Certainly,' said Alleyn. And did.

When he had finished Troy covered her face with her hands. It was an uncharacteristic gesture. She turned away to the windows. Dr Carmichael looked from her to Alleyn and left the studio.

'I wouldn't have had this happen,' Alleyn said, 'for all the world.'

'Don't give it another thought,' she mumbled into his sweater and helped herself to his handkerchief. 'It's nothing. It's just the *fact* of that room along there. Off the landing. You know—behind the locked door. Like a Bluebeard's chamber. I can't stop thinking about it. It's kind of got me down a bit.'

'I know.'

'And now—Maria. Going in there. *Damn!*' said Troy and stamped. 'I'd got myself all arranged not to be a burden and now look at me.'

'Could it be that you've done a morsel too much self-arranging and I've done a morsel too much male chauvinism, although I must say,' Alleyn confessed, 'I'm never quite sure what the ladies mean by the phrase. Have a good blow,' he added as Troy was making gingerly use of his handkerchief. She obeyed noisily and said she was feeling better.

'What would Br'er Fox say to me?' she asked and answered herself. Alleyn joined in.

' "We'll have to get you in the Force, Mrs Alleyn",' they quoted in unison.

'And wouldn't I make a pretty hash of it if you did,' said Troy.

'You've done jolly well with the half-burnt envelope. Classic stuff that, and very useful. It forced Marco to come tolerably clean.'

'Well, come, that's something.'

'It's half an hour to lunch-time. How about putting a bit of slap on your pink nose and coming for a brisk walk.'

'Lunch!' said Troy, 'and Mr Reece's massive small-talk. And *food*! More *food*!'

'Perhaps the cook will have cut it down to clear soup and a slice of ham. Anyway, come on.'

'All right,' said Troy.

So they went out of doors where the sun shone, the dark wet trees glittered, the lake was spangled and the mountains were fresh, as if, it seemed, from creation's hand. The morning was alive with birdsong, sounds that might have been the voice of the bush itself, its hidden waters, its coolness, its primordial detachment.

They walked round the house to the empty hangar and thence, across the landing-ground, to the path through the bush and arrived at the lakeside.

'Wet earth and greenery again,' said Troy. 'The best smell there is.'

'The Maori people had a god-hero called Maui. He went fishing, and hauled up the South Island.'

'Quite recently, by the feel of it.'

'Geologically it was, in fact, thrust up from the ocean bed by volcanic action. I've no idea,' said Alleyn, 'whether it was a slow process or a sudden commotion. It's exciting to imagine it heaving up all of a sudden with the waters pouring down the flanks of its mountains, sweeping across its plains and foaming back into the sea. But I dare say it was a matter of aeons rather than minutes.'

'And you say there are now lots and lots of painters, busy as bees, having a go at —' Troy waved an arm at the prospect — 'all that.'

'That's right. From pretty peeps to competent posters and from factual statements to solemn abstractions. You name it.'

'How brave of them all.'

'Only some of them think so.' Alleyn took her arm. 'Some

217

have got pretty near the bones. If things had been different,' he said, 'would you have wanted to paint?'

'Not at once. Make charcoal scribbles, perhaps. And after a time make some more with paint. Bones,' said Troy vaguely. 'The anatomy of the land. Something might come of it.'

'Shall we see what happens if we follow round the shore?'

'If you like. We'll either fetch up in the front of the house or get ourselves bushed. After all we *are* on an island.'

'All right, smarty-pants. Come on.'

A rough track followed the margin of the lake, for the most part clear of the bush but occasionally cutting through it. In places storm-water poured across the path. They came to a little footbridge over a deep-voiced creek. Here the bush was dense but further on it thinned enough to allow glimpses, surprisingly close at hand, of the west wall of the house. They were walking parallel with the path that skirted the concert chamber. The ground here was soft under their feet.

They walked in single file. Alleyn stopped short and held up his hand. He turned and laid his finger on his lips.

Ahead of them, hidden by the bush, someone was speaking.

The voice was so low, so very quiet that it was almost toneless and quite without a personality. It was impossible to catch what was said or guess at who said it.

Alleyn signalled to Troy to stay where she was and himself moved soundlessly along the path. He was drawing closer to the voice. He remembered that at a point opposite the first window of the concert chamber there was a garden seat and he fancied the speaker might be sitting on it. He moved on and in another moment or two realized that he should be able to make out the sense of what was said and then that it was said in Italian.

Alleyn's Italian had been pretty fluent but it was several years since he had had occasion to use it and it had grown rusty. At first the phrases slid past incomprehensibly and then he began to tune in.

'—*I have acted in this way because of what is being*—

*hinted — suggested by you. All of you. And because when
these policemen come you may try —*'

Alleyn lost the next phrase or two. There were gaps as if
the speaker paused for a reply and none was forthcoming.
The voice was raised. '*— this is why — I have anticipated — I
warn you — can go further and if necessary I will. Now. How
do you answer? You understand, do you not? I mean what I
say? I will act as I have said? Very well. Your answer? Speak
up. I cannot hear you.*'

Nor could Alleyn. There had been some sort of reply —
breathy — short — incomprehensible.

'*I am waiting.*'

Into the silence that followed a bell-bird, close at hand,
dropped his clear remark ending with a derisive clatter.
Then followed, scarcely perceptible, a disturbance, an in-
trusion, nowhere — somewhere — coming closer and louder:
the commonplace beat of a helicopter.

Inside the house a man shouted. Windows were thrown
open.

'*Il alicottero!*' exclaimed the voice. There was a stifled
response from his companion and sounds of rapid retreat.

'Here are the cops, darling!' said Alleyn.

'Rapture! Rapture! I suppose,' said Troy. 'Will you go and
meet them?'

'It may be a case of joining in the rush, but yes, I think I'd
better.'

'Rory — what'll be the drill?'

'Unusual, to say the least. I suppose I introduce them to
Reece unless he's already introduced himself and when
that's effected I'll hand over my file and remain on tap for
questioning.'

'Will you use the studio?'

'I'd prefer the study but doubt if we'll get it. Look, my
love, after lunch will you take to the studio if it's available?
Or if you can't stand that any more, our room? I know you
must have *had* them both but perhaps you might suffer
them again, for a bit. Carmichael will look in and so will I,

219

of course, but I don't know—'

'I'll be as right as rain. I might even try a few tentative notes—'

'Might you? Truly? Marvellous,' he said. 'I'll see you round to the front of the house.'

Their path took a right turn through the bush and came out beyond the garden seat. On the gravel walk in front of the house stood Maria with her arms folded, a black shawl over her head, staring up at the helicopter, now close overhead and deafening.

'Good morning, Maria,' Alleyn shouted cheerfully. 'Here are the police.'

She glowered.

'I have been meaning to speak to you: when they have completed their examination I think you'll be permitted to perform your office. I shall recommend that you are.'

She stared balefully at him for under her heavy brows. Her lips formed a soundless acknowledgement. '*Grazie tante.*'

Hanley came running out of the house, pulling on a jacket over his sweater.

'Oh, hul-*lo*, Mr Alleyn,' he cried. 'Thank goodness. I'm the Official Welcome. The Boss-Man told me to collect you and here you are. *Ben' troveto*, if that's what they say. You *will* come, won't you? I thought *he* ought to be there in person, but no, he's receiving them in the library. You haven't seen the library, have you, Mrs Alleyn? My dear, *smothered* in synthetic leather. Look! That contraption's alighting! Do let us hurry.'

Troy went up the front steps to the house. Signor Lattienzo was there, having apparently stepped out of the entrance. Alleyn saw him greet her with his usual exuberance. She waved.

'Mr Alleyn, *please*!' cried the distracted Hanley and led the way at a canter.

They arrived at the clearing as the helicopter landed and were raked with the unnatural gale from its propeller.

Hanley let out an exasperated screech and clutched his blond hair. The engine stopped.

In the silence that followed Alleyn felt as if he was involved in some Stoppard-like time-slip and was back suddenly in the middle of a routine job. The three men who climbed out of the helicopter wore so unmistakably the marks of their calling, townish suits on large heavily muscled bodies, felt hats, sober shirts and ties. Sharp eyes and an indescribable air of taking over. Their equipment was handed down: cases and a camera. The fourth man who followed was slight, tweedy and preoccupied. He carried a profesional bag. Police surgeon, thought Alleyn.

The largest of the men advanced to Alleyn.

'Chief Superintendent Alleyn?' the large man said. 'Hazelmere. Very glad indeed to see you, sir. Meet Dr Winslow. Detective-Sergeant Franks, Detective-Sergeant Barker.'

Alleyn shook hands. The police all had enormous hands and excruciating grips and prolonged the ceremony with great warmth.

'I understand you've had a spot of bother,' said Inspector Hazelmere.

'If I *may* butt in,' Hanley said anxiously. 'Inspector, Mr Reece hopes—' and he delivered his invitation to the library.

'Very kind, I'm sure,' acknowledged Hazelmere. 'You'll be his secretary, sir? Mr Hanley? Is that correct? Well now, if it's all the same to Mr Reece I think it might be best if we took a look at the scene of the fatality. And if the Chief Superintendent would be kind enough to accompany us he can put us in the picture, which will save a lot of time and trouble when we see Mr Reece.'

'Oh,' said Hanley. 'Oh yes. I see. Well—' he threw a troubled glance at Alleyn— 'if Mr Alleyn will—'

'Yes, of course,' said Alleyn.

'Yes. Well, I'll just convey your message to Mr Reece. I'm sure he'll understand,' said Hanley uneasily.

'I suggest,' said Alleyn, 'that you might ask Dr Carmichael

to join us. I'm sure Dr Winslow would be glad to see him.

'Are you? Yes. Of course.'

'Thank you very much, Mr Hanley,' said Hazelmere
blandly dismissive.

Hanley hesitated for a second or two, said, 'Yes, well —
again and set off for the house.

Alleyn said: 'I can't tell you how glad I am to see you
You'll understand what a tricky position I've been in. N
official authority but expected to behave like everybody'
idea of an infallible sleuth.'

'Is that a fact, sir?' said Mr Hazelmere. He then paid
Alleyn some rather toneless compliments, fetching up with
the remark that he knew nothing beyond the information
conveyed by Les, the launchman, over a storm-battered
telephone line that a lady had been, as he put it, made awa
with and could they now view the remains and would Alleyn
be kind enough to put them in the picture.

So Alleyn led them into the house and up to the first land
ing. He was careful, with suitable encomiums, to introduc
Bert who was laconic and removed his two armchairs from
their barrierlike position before the door. Dr Carmichael
arrived and was presented, Alleyn unlocked the door and
they all went into the room.

Back to square one. Blades of cool air slicing in throug
the narrowly opened windows, the sense of damp curtains
dust, stale scent and a pervasive warning of mortality
shockingly emphasized when Alleyn and Dr Carmichae
drew away the black satin sheet.

Hazelmere made an involuntary exclamation which h
converted into a clearance of the throat. Nobody spoke o
moved and then Detective-Sergeant Franks whispered
'Christ!' It sounded more like a prayer than an oath.

'What was the name?' Hazelmere asked.

'Of course,' Alleyn said, 'you don't know, do you?'

'The line was bad. I missed a lot of what the chap was say
ing.'

'He didn't know either. We communicated by variou

forms of semaphore.'

'Is that a fact? Fancy!'

'She was a celebrated singer. In the world class. The tops, in fact.'

'*Not*,' exclaimed Dr Winslow, 'Isabella Sommita? It can't be!'

'It is, you know,' said Dr Carmichael.

'You better have a look, doc,' Hazelmere suggested.

'Yes. Of course.'

'If you're thinking of moving her we'll just let Sergeant Barker and Sergeant Franks in first, doc,' said Hazelmere. 'For photos and dabs.'

Alleyn explained that he had used his own professional camera and had improvised fingerprinting tactics. 'I thought it might be as well to do this in case of postmortem changes. Dr Carmichael and I disturbed nothing and didn't touch her. I dare say the results won't be too hot and I think you'd better not depend on them. While they're doing their stuff,' he said to Hazelmere, 'would you like to get the picture?'

'Too right I would,' said the Inspector and out came his notebook.

And so to the familiar accompaniment of clicks and flashes, Alleyn embarked on an orderly and exhaustive report, event after event as they fell out over the past three days including the Strix-Marco element, the puzzle of the keys and the outcome of the opera. He gave a list of the inmates and guests in the Lodge. He spoke with great clarity and care, without hesitation or repetition. Hazelmere paused, once, and looked up at him.

'Am I going too fast?' Alleyn asked.

'It's not that, sir,' Hazelmere said. 'It's the way you give it out. Beautiful!'

Succinct though it was, the account had taken some time. Franks and Barker had finished. They and the two doctors, who had covered the body and retired to the far end of the room to consult, now collected round Alleyn, listening.

When he had finished he said: 'I've made a file covering all this stuff and a certain amount of background— past history and so on. You might like to see it. I'll fetch it, shall I?'

When he had gone Dr Winslow said: 'Remarkable.'

'Isn't it?' said Dr Carmichael with a slightly proprietary air.

'You'll never hear better,' Inspector Hazelmere pronounced. He addressed himself to the doctors. 'What's the story, then, gentlemen?'

Dr Winslow said he agreed with the tentative opinion formed by Alleyn and Dr Carmichael: that on a superficial examination the appearances suggested that the deceased had been anaesthetized and then asphyxiated and that the stiletto had been driven through the heart after death.

'How long after?' Hazelmere asked.

'Hard to say. After death the blood follows the law of gravity and sinks. The very scant effusion here suggested that this process was well advanced. The post-mortem would be informative.'

Alleyn returned with the file and suggested that Inspector Hazelmere, the two doctors and he go to the study leaving Sergeants Barker and Franks to extend their activities to the room and bathroom. They had taken prints from the rigid hands of the Sommita and were to look for any that disagreed with them. Particularly, Alleyn suggested, on the bottom left-hand drawer of the dressing-table, the gold handbag therein and the key in the bag. The key and the bag were to be replaced. He explained why.

'The room had evidently been thoroughly swept and dusted that morning so anything you find will have been left later in the day. You can expect to find Maria's and possibly Mr Reece's but we know of nobody else who may have entered the room. The housekeeper Mrs Bacon may have done so. You'll find her very co-operative.'

'So it may mean getting dabs from the lot of them,' said Hazelmere.

'It may, at that.'

'By the way, sir. That was a very bad line we spoke on. Temporary repairs after the storm. Excuse me, but did you ask me to bring a brace and bit?'

'I did, yes.'

'Yes. I thought it sounded like that.'

'*Did* you bring a brace and bit, Inspector?'

'Yes. I chanced it.'

'Large-sized bit?'

'Several bits. Different sizes.'

'Splendid.'

'Might I ask—'

'Of course. Come along to the studio and I'll explain. But first—take a look at the fancy woodwork on the wardrobe doors.'


## II


The conference in the studio lasted for an hour and at its conclusion Dr Winslow discussed plans for the removal of the body. The lake was almost back to normal and Les had come over in the launch with the mail. 'She'll be sweet as a millpond by nightfall,' he reported. The police helicopter was making a second trip bringing two uniform constables and would take Dr Winslow back to Rivermouth. He would arrange for a mortuary van to be sent out and the body would be taken across by launch to meet it. The autopsy would be performed as soon as the official pathologist was available: probably that night.

'And now,' said Hazelmere, 'I reckon we lay on this—er—experiment, don't we?'

'Only if you're quite sure you'll risk it. Always remembering that if it flops you may be in for some very nasty moments.'

'I appreciate that. Look, Mr Alleyn, if you'd been me would you have risked it?'

'Yes,' said Alleyn. 'I would. I'd have told myself I was a bloody fool but I'd have risked it.'

'That's good enough for me,' said Hazelmere. 'Let's go.'

'Don't you think that perhaps Mr Reece has been languishing rather a long time in the library?'

'You're dead right. Dear me, yes. I'd better go down.'

But there was no need for Hazelmere to go down. The studio door opened and Mr Reece walked in.

Alleyn thought he was probably very angry indeed.

Not that his behaviour was in any way exceptionable. He did not scold and he did not shout. He stood stock still in his own premises and waited for somebody else to perform. His mouth was tightly closed and the corners severely compressed.

With his head metaphysically lowered to meet an icy breeze, Alleyn explained that they had thought it best first to make an official survey and for Inspector Hazelmere, whom he introduced and who was given a stony acknowledgement, to be informed of all the circumstances before troubling Mr Reece. Mr Reece slightly inclined his head. Alleyn then hurriedly introduced Dr Winslow who was awarded a perceptibly less glacial reception.

'As you are now at liberty,' Mr Reece pronounced, 'perhaps you will be good enough to come down to the library where we will not be disturbed. I shall be glad to learn what steps you propose to take.'

Hazelmere, to Alleyn's satisfaction, produced his own line of imperturbability and said blandly that the library would no doubt be very convenient. Mr Reece then pointedly addressing himself to Alleyn, said that luncheon had been postponed until two o'clock and would be in the nature of a cold buffet to which the guests would help themselves when so inclined. It was now one-twenty.

'In the meantime,' Mr Reece magnificently continued, 'I will take it as a favour if you will extend my already deep obligation to you by joining us in the library.'

Alleyn thought there would be nothing Hazelmere would enjoy less than having him, Alleyn, on the sideline, a silent

226

observer of his investigatory techniques.

He said that he had promised to look in on Troy. He added (truthfully) that she suffered from occasional attacks of migraine and (less truthfully) that one had threatened this morning. Mr Reece expressed wooden regrets and hoped to see him as soon as it was convenient. Alleyn felt as if they were both repeating memorized bits of dialogue from some dreary play.

Mr Reece said: 'Shall we?' to Hazelmere and led the way out of the studio. Hazelmere turned in the doorway and Alleyn rapidly indicated that he was returning to the bedroom. The Inspector stuck up his vast thumb and followed Mr Reece to the stairs.

Alleyn shut the door and Dr Carmichael, who had continued his now familiar role of self-elimination, rose and asked if Hazelmere really meant to carry out The Plan.

'Yes, he does and I hope to God he'll do himself no harm by it.'

'Not for the want of warning.'

'No. But it was I who concocted it.'

'What's the first step?'

'We've got to fix Maria asking for or being given unasked permission to lay out the body. Hazelmere had better set it up that she'll be told when she may do it.'

'Suppose she's gone off the idea?'

'That's a sickening prospect, isn't it? But we're hoping the opportunity it offers will do the trick. I'm going along now to get those two chaps on to it.'

Dr Carmichael said, 'Alleyn, if you can spare a moment would you be very kind and go over the business about the keys. I know it, but I'd like to be reminded.'

'All right. There are three keys to the bedroom. Maria had one which I took possession of when I first was in the bedroom, the Sommita another, and young Bartholomew the third. Mrs Bacon held the fourth. When Reece and the Sommita went upstairs after the concert they found Maria waiting. If the door had been locked she had let herself in with her own key. The Sommita threw a violent temperament, gave them what for, kicked them out and locked the door after them. They have both said individually that they distinctly heard the key turn in the lock. Twenty minutes later Maria returned with a hot drink, let herself in with her own key and found her mistress murdered. There was no sight anywhere on any surface or on the floor or on the body of the Sommita's key. I found it subsequently in her evening bag neatly disposed and wrapped at the bottom of a drawer. Reece is sure she didn't have the bag when they took her upstairs. The people who fussed round her in her dressing-room say she hadn't got it with her and indeed in that rig it would have been an incongruous object for her to carry—even offstage. Equally it's impossible to imagine her at the height of one of her towering rages getting the key from wherever it was, putting it in the lock in the fraction of time between Reece or Maria closing the door behind them and them both hearing the turn of the lock, and then meticulously getting out her evening bag, putting her key in it and placing it in the drawer. It even was enclosed in one of those soft cloth bags women use to prevent gold mesh from catching in the fabric of things like stockings. That's the story of the keys.'

'Yes. That's right. That's what I thought,' said Dr Carmichael uneasily.

'What's the matter?'

'It's just—rather an unpleasant thought.'

'About the third key?'

'Yes!'

'Rupert Bartholomew had it. Maria came to his room very late in the night and said I'd sent her for it.'

'Did she, by God!'

'He gave it to her. Bert, asleep in the chairs across the doorway, woke up to find Maria trying to stretch across him and put the key in the lock.'

'She must have been dotty. What did she think she'd do? Open the door and swarm over his sleeping body?'

'Open the door, yes. It opens inwards. And chuck the key into the room? She was hell-bent on our finding it there. Close the door, which would remain unlocked: she couldn't do anything about that. And when, as is probable, Bert wakes, throw a hysterical scene with all the pious drama about praying for the soul of the Sommita and laying her out.'

'Actually what did happen?'

'Bert woke up to find her generous personal equipment dangling over him. She panicked, dropped the key on him and bolted. He collected it and gave it to me. So she is still keyless.'

'Could you ever prove all these theories?'

'If the plan works.'

'Maria, eh?' said Dr Carmichael. 'Well, of course, she does look — I mean to say —'

'We've got to remember,' Alleyn said, 'that from the time Maria and Reece left the room and went downstairs and he joined his guests for dinner, Maria was in the staff sitting-room preparing the hot drink. Mrs Bacon and Marco and others of the staff can be called to prove it.'

Carmichael stared at him. 'An alibi?' he said. 'For Maria? That's awkward.'

'In this game,' Alleyn said, 'one learns to be wary of assumptions.'

'I suppose I'm making one now. Very reluctantly.'

'The boy?'

'Yes.'

'Well, of course, he's the prime suspect. One can turn on all the clichés: "lust turned to hatred", "humiliation", "breaking-point" — the lot. He was supposedly in his room at the crucial time but could have slipped out and he had his key to her room. He had motive and opportunity and he was in an extremely unstable condition.'

'Do the rest of them think — ?'

'Some of them do. Hanley does, or behaves and drops hints as if he does. Maria, and Marco I fancy, have been telling everyone he's the prime suspect. As I dare say the rest of the domestic staff believe, being aware, no doubt, of the changed relationship between the boy and the diva. And of course most of them witnessed the curtain speech and the fainting fit.'

'What about Lattienzo?'

'Troy and I overheard the jocund maestro in the shrubbery or near it, and in far from merry pin, threatening an unseen person with an evidently damaging exposure if he or she continued to spread malicious gossip. He spoke in Italian and the chopper was approaching so I missed whole chunks of his discourse.'

'Who was he talking to?'

'Somebody perfectly inaudible.'

'Maria?'

'I think so. When we emerged she was handy. On the front steps watching the chopper. Lattienzo was not far off.'

'I thought Lattienzo was not in his usual ebullient form when he came up here just now.'

'You were right,' said Alleyn and gave an account of the interview.'

'The Italian element with a vengeance,' said the doctor thoughtfully.

'I must go along and fix things up in that room and then hie me to the library and Mr Reece's displeasure. Look in on Troy, like a good chap, would you, and tell her this studio's free? Do you mind? She's in our bedroom.'

'I'm delighted,' said the gallant doctor.

And so Alleyn returned to the Sommita's death chamber and found Sergeants Franks and Barker in dubious consultation. A brace and a selection of bits was laid out on a sheet of newspaper on the floor.

'The boss said you'd put us wise, sir,' said Franks.

'Right,' said Alleyn. He stood with his back to one of the exuberantly carved and painted wardrobe doors, felt behind him and bent his knees until his head was on a level with the stylized sunflower which framed it like a formalized halo. He made a funnel of his hand and looked through it at the covered body on the bed. Then he moved to the twin door and went through the same procedure.

'Yes,' he said, 'it'll work. It'll work all right.'

He opened the doors.

The walk-in wardrobe was occupied but not crowded with dresses. He divided them and slid them on their hangers to opposite ends of the interior. He examined the inside of the doors, came out and locked them.

He inspected the bits.

'This one will do,' he said and gave it, with the brace, to Sergeant Franks. 'Plumb in the middle,' he said, putting his finger on the black centre of the sunflower. 'And slide that newspaper under to catch the litter. Very careful, now. No splintering whatever you do. Which of you's the joiner?'

'Aw heck!' said Franks to Barker, 'what about you having a go, Merv.'

'I'm not fussy, thanks,' said Barker, backing off.

They looked uncomfortably at Alleyn.

'Well,' he said, 'I asked for it and it looks as if I've bought it. If I make a fool of myself I can't blame anyone else, can I? Give it here, Franks. Oh God, it's one of those push-me-pull-you brutes that shoot out at you when you least expect it.' He thumbed a catch and the business end duly shot out. 'What did I tell you? You guide it, Franks, and hold it steady. Dead centre. Anyone'd think we were defusing a bomb. Come on.'

'She's new, sir. Sharp as a needle and greased.'

'Good.'

He raised the brace and advanced it. Franks guided the point of the bit. 'Dead centre, sir,' he said.

'Here goes, then,' said Alleyn.

He made a cautious preliminary pressure. 'How's that?'

'Biting, sir.'

'Straight as we go, then.' Alleyn pumped the brace.

A little cascade of wood dust trickled through the elaborate carving and fell on the newspaper.

'Nearly there,' he grunted presently and a few seconds later the resistance was gone and he disengaged the tool.

At the black centre of the sunflower was a black hole as wide as the iris of an eye and very inconspicuous. Alleyn blew away the remnants of wood dust that were trapped in curlicues, twisted a finger in the hole and stood back. 'Not too bad,' he said.

He opened the door. The hole was clean cut.

'Now for the twin,' he said and gave the companion door the same treatment.

Then he went into the wardrobe and shut the doors. The interior smelt insufferably of La Sommita's scent. He looked through one of the holes. He saw the body. Neatly framed. Underneath the black satin cover its arm, still raised in cadaveric spasm, seemed to point at him. He came out, shut and locked the wardrobe doors and put the key in his pocket.

'It'll do,' he said. 'Will you two clean up? Very thoroughly? Before you do that I think you should know why you've been called on to set this up and what we hope to achieve by it. Don't you?'

They intimated by sundry noises that they did think so and he then told them of the next steps that would be taken, the procedure to be followed and the hoped-for outcome. 'And now I think perhaps one of you might relieve poor old Bert on the landing and I'd suggest the other reports for duty to Mr Hazelmere who will probably be in the library. It opens off the entrance hall. Third on the right from the front. I'm going down there now. Here's the key to this room. OK?'

'She'll be right, sir,' said Franks and Barker together.

So Alleyn went down to the library.

It came as no surprise to find the atmosphere in that utterly neutral apartment tepid, verging on glacial. Inspector Hazelmere had his notebook at the ready. Mr Reece sat at one of the neatly laden tables with the glaze of boredom veiling his pale regard. When Alleyn apologized for keeping him waiting he raised his hand and let it fall as if words now failed him.

The Inspector, Alleyn thought, was not at the moment happy in his work though he put up a reasonable show of professional *savoir-faire* and said easily that he thought he had finished 'bothering' Mr Reece and believed he was now fully in the picture. Mr Reece said woodenly that he was glad to hear it. An awkward silence followed which he broke by addressing himself pointedly to Alleyn.

'Would you,' he said, 'be good enough to show me where you found that book? I've been wondering about it.'

Alleyn led the way to the remote corner of the library and the obscure end of a top shelf. 'It was here,' he said, pointing to the gap. 'I could only just reach it.'

'I would require the steps,' said Mr Reece. He put on his massive spectacles and peered. 'It's very badly lit,' he said. 'The architect should have noticed that.'

Alleyn switched on the lights.

'Thank you. I would like to see the book when you have finished with it. I suppose it has something to do with this family feud or vendetta or whatever that she was so concerned about?'

'I would think so, yes.'

'It is strange that she never showed it to me. Perhaps that is because it is written in Italian. I would have expected her to show it to me,' he said heavily. 'I would have expected her to feel it would give validity to her theory. I wonder how she came by it? It is very shabby. Perhaps it was second-hand.'

'Did you notice the name on the fly-leaf? "M. V. Rossi"?'

'Rossi? *Rossi*!' he repeated, and stared at Alleyn. 'But that was the name she *did* mention. On the rare occasions when she used a name. I recollect that she once said she wished my name did not resemble it. I thought this very far-fetched but she seemed to be quite serious about it. She generally referred simply to the *nemico* — meaning the enemy.'

'Perhaps, after all, it was not her book.'

'It was certainly not *mine*,' he said flatly.

233

'At some time – originally, I suppose – it has been the property of the "enemy". On wouldn't have expected her to have acquired it.'

'You certainly would not,' Mr Reece said emphatically. 'Up there, was it? What sort of company was it keeping?'

Alleyn took down four of the neighbouring books. One, a biography called *Il Voce*, was written in Italian and seemed from cover to cover to be an unmodified rave about the Sommita. It was photographically illustrated beginning with a portrait of a fat-legged infant, much be-frilled, be-ringleted and be-ribboned, glowering on the lap according to the caption, of '*La Zia Guilia*' and ending with La Sommita receiving a standing ovation at a royal performance of *Faust*.

'Ah yes,' said Mr Reece. 'The biography. I always intended to read it. It went into three editions. What are the others?'

One in English, one in Italian – both novels with a strong romantic interest. They were gifts to the Sommita, lavishly inscribed by admirers.

'Is the autobiography there?' asked Mr Reece. 'That meant a helluva lot to me. Yes, sir. A helluva lot.'

This piece of information was dealt out by Mr Reece in his customary manner: baldly as if he were citing a quotation from Wall Street. For the first time he sounded definitely American.

'I'm sure it did,' Alleyn said.

'I never got round to reading it right through,' Mr Reece confessed and then seemed to brighten up a little. 'After all,' he pointed out, 'she didn't write it herself. But it was the thought that counted.'

'Quite. This seems, doesn't it, to be a corner reserved for her own books?'

'I believe I remember, now I come to think of it, her saying something about wanting some place for her own books. She didn't appreciate the way they looked in her bedroom. Out of place.'

'Do you think she would have put them up there herself?'

Mr Reece took off his spectacles and looked at Alleyn as if

e had taken leave of his senses. 'Bella?' he said. 'Up there? On the steps?'

'Well, no. Silly of me. I'm sorry.'

'She would probably have told Maria to do it.'

'Ah, apropos! I don't know,' Alleyn said, 'whether Mr Hazelmere has told you?' He looked at the Inspector who lightly shook his head. 'Perhaps we should —?'

'That's so, sir,' said Hazelmere. 'We certainly should.' He addressed himself to Mr Reece. 'I understand, sir, that Miss Maria Bennini has expressed the wish to perform the last duties and Mr Alleyn pointed out that until the premises had been thoroughly investigated the *stattus*, (so Mr Hazelmere pronounced it) '*quow* must be maintained. That is now the case. So, if it's acceptable to yourself, we will inform Miss Bennini and in due course —'

'Yes, yes. Tell her,' Mr Reece said. His voice was actually unsteady. He looked at Alleyn almost as if he appealed to him. 'And what then?' he asked.

Alleyn explained about the arrangements for the removal of the body. 'It will probably be at dusk or even after dark when they arrive at the lakeside,' he said. 'The launch will be waiting.'

'I wish to be informed.'

Alleyn and Hazelmere said together: 'Certainly, sir.'

'I will —' he hunted for the phrase — 'I will see her off. It is the least I can do. If I had not brought her to this house —' He turned aside, and looked at the books without seeing them. Alleyn put them back on their shelf. 'I'm not conversant with police procedure in New Zealand,' Mr Reece said. 'I understand it follows the British rather than the American practice. It may be quite out of order, at this juncture, to ask whether you expect to make an arrest in the foreseeable future.'

Hazelmere again glanced at Alleyn who remained silent. 'Well, sir,' Hazelmere said, 'it's not our practice to open up wide, like, until we are very, very sure of ourselves. I think I'm in order if I say that we hope quite soon to be in a position to take positive action.'

'Is that your view, too, Chief Superintendent?'

'Yes,' Alleyn said. 'That's my view.'

'I am very glad to hear it. You wish to see Maria, do you not? Shall I send for her?'

'If it's not putting you out, sir, we'd be much obliged,' said Inspector Hazelmere who seemed to suffer from a compulsion to keep the interview at an impossibly high-toned level.

Mr Reece used the telephone. 'Find Maria,' he said, 'and ask her to come to the library. Yes, at once. Very well, then, find her. Ask Mrs Bacon to deal with it.'

He replaced the receiver. 'Staff coordination has gone to pieces,' he said. 'I asked for service and am told the person in question is sulking in her room.'

A long silence followed. Mr Reece made no effort to break it. He went to the window and looked out at the lake. Hazelmere inspected his notes, made two alterations and under a pretence of consulting Alleyn about them said in a slurred undertone: 'Awkward if she won't.'

'Hellishly,' Alleyn agreed.

Voices were raised in the hall, Hanley's sounding agitated, Mrs Bacon's masterful. A door banged. Another voice shouted something that might have been an insult and followed it up with a raucous laugh. Marco, Alleyn thought. Hanley, all eyes and teeth, made an abrupt entrance.

'I'm terribly sorry, sir,' he said. 'There's been a little difficulty. *Just* coming.'

Mr Reece glanced at him with contempt. He gave a nervous titter and withdrew only to reappear and stand, door in hand, to admit Maria in the grip of Mrs Bacon.

'I'm extremely sorry, Mr Reece,' said Mrs Bacon in a high voice. 'Maria has been difficult.'

She released her hold as if she expected her catch would bolt and when she did not, left the arena. Hanley followed her, shutting the door but not before an indignant contralto was heard in the hall: 'No,' it said, 'this is too much. I can take no more of this,' said Miss Dancy.

236

'You handle this one, eh?' Hazelmere murmured to Alleyn.

But Mr Reece was already in charge.

He said: 'Come here.' Maria walked up to him at once and waited with her arms folded, looking at the floor.

'You are making scenes, Maria,' said Mr Reece, 'and that is foolish of you: you must behave yourself. Your request is to be granted, see to it that you carry out your duty decently and with respect.'

Maria intimated rapidly and in Italian that she would be a model of decorum, or words to that effect, and that she was now satisfied and grateful and might the good God bless Signor Reece.

'Very well,' said Mr Reece. 'Listen to the Chief Superintendent and do as he tells you.'

He nodded to Alleyn and walked out of the room.

Alleyn told Maria that she was to provide herself with whatever she needed and wait in the staff sitting-room. She would not be disturbed.

'You found her. You have seen what it is like,' he said. 'You are sure you want to do this?'

Maria crossed herself and said vehemently that she was sure.

'Very well. Do as I have said.'

There was a tap on the door and Sergeant Franks came in.

Hazelmere said: 'You'll look after Miss Bennini, Franks, won't you? Anything she may require.'

'Sir,' said Sergeant Franks.

Maria looked as if she thought she could do without Sergeant Franks and intimated that she wished to be alone with her mistress.

'If that's what you want,' said Hazelmere.

'To pray. There should be a priest.'

'All that will be attended to,' Hazelmere assured her. 'Later on.'

'When?'

'At the interment,' he said flatly.

She glared at him and marched out of the room.

'All right,' Hazelmere said to Franks. 'Later on. Keep with it. You know what you've got to do.'

'Sir,' said Sergeant Franks and followed her.

'Up we go,' said Alleyn.

He and Hazelmere moved into the hall and finding it empty, ran upstairs to the Sommita's bedroom.


### III

It was stuffy in the wardrobe now they had locked themselves in. The smell was compounded of metallic cloth, sequins, fur, powder, scent and of the body when it was still alive and wore the clothes and left itself on them. It was as if the Sommita had locked herself in with her apparel.

'Cripes, it's close in here,' said Inspector Hazelmere.

'Put your mouth to the hole,' Alleyn suggested.

'That's an idea, too,' Hazelmere said and began noisily to suck air through his peephole. Alleyn followed his own advice. Thus they obliterated the two pencils of light that had given some shape to the darkness as their eyes became adjusted to it.

'Makes you think of those funny things jokers on the telly get up to,' Hazelmere said. 'You know. Crime serials.' And after a pause. 'They're taking their time, aren't they?'

Alleyn grunted. He applied his eye to his peephole. Again, suddenly confronting him, was the black satin shape on the bed: so very explicit, so eloquent of the body inside. The shrouded limb, still rigid as a yardarm, pointing under its funeral sheet—at him.

He thought: But shouldn't the rigidity be going off now? And tried to remember the rules about cadaveric spasm as opposed to rigor mortis.

'I told Franks to give us the office,' said Hazelmere. 'You know. Unlock the door and open it a crack and say something loud.'

'Good.'

'What say we open these doors, then? Just for a second or two? Sort of fan them to change the air? I suffer from hay fever,' Hazelmere confessed.

'All right. But we'd better be quick about it, hadn't we? Ready?'

Their keys clicked.

'Right.'

They opened the doors wide and flung them to and fro, exchanging the wardrobe air for the colder and more ominously suspect air of the room. Something fell on Alleyn's left foot.

'Bloody hell!' said Hazelmere, 'I've dropped the bloody key.'

'Don't move. They're coming. Here! Let me.' Alleyn collected it from the floor, pushed it in the keyhole and shut and locked both doors. He could feel Hazelmere's bulk heaving slightly against his own arm.

They looked through their spyholes. Alleyn's was below the level of his eyes and he had to bend his knees. The bedroom door was beyond their range of sight but evidently it was open. There was the sound of something being set down, possibly on the carpet. Detective-Sergeant Franks said: 'There you are, then, lady. I'll leave you to it. If you want anything, knock on the door. Same thing when you've finished. Knock.'

And Maria: 'Give me the key. I let myself out.'

'Sorry, lady. That's not my orders. Don't worry. I won't run away. Just knock when you're ready. See you.'

The bedroom door shut firmly. They could hear the key turn in the lock.

Alleyn could still see, framed by his spyhole, the body and beyond it a section of the dressing-table.

As if by the action of a shutter in a camera they were blotted out. Maria was not two feet away and Alleyn looked into her eyes. He thought for a sickening moment that she had seen the hole in the sunflower but she was gone only to reappear by the dressing-table: — stooping — wrenching open a drawer — a bottom drawer.

Hazelmere gave him a nudge. Alleyn remembered that he commanded a slightly different and better view than his own of the bottom left-hand end of the dressing-table.

But now Maria stood up and her hands were locked round a gold mesh bag. They opened it and inverted it and shook it out on the dressing-table and her right hand fastened on the key that fell from it.

Hazelmere shifted but Alleyn, without moving his eye from the spyhole, reached out and touched him.

Maria now stood over the shrouded body and looked at it, one would have said, speculatively.

With an abrupt movement, more feline than human, she knelt and groped under the shroud — she scuffled deep under the body, which jolted horridly.

The black shroud slithered down the raised arm and by force of its own displaced weight slid to the floor.

And the arm dropped.

It fell across her neck. She screamed like a trapped ferret and with a grotesque and frantic movement rolled away and scrambled to her feet.

'Now,' Alleyn said.

He and Hazelmere unlocked their doors and walked out into the room.

Hazelmere said: 'Maria Bennini, I arrest you on a charge —'

*Chapter Nine*

## DEPARTURE

I

The scene might have been devised by a film director who had placed his camera on the landing and pointed it downwards to take in the stairs and the hall beneath where he had placed his actors, all with upturned faces. For sound he had used only the out-of-shot Maria's screams, fading them as she was taken upstairs by the two detective-sergeants to an unoccupied bedroom. This would be followed by total silence and immobility and then, Alleyn thought, the camera would probably pan from face to upturned face: from Mr Reece half way up the stairs, pallid and looking, if anything, scandalized, breathing hard, and to Ben Ruby immensely perturbed and two steps lower down, to Signor Lattienzo with his eyeglass stuck in a white mask. Ned Hanley, on the lowest step, held on to the banister as if in an earthquake. Below him Miss Dancy at ground level, appropriately distraught and wringing every ounce of star-quality out of it. Further away Sylvia Parry clung to Rupert Bartholomew. And finally, in isolation, Marco stood with his arms folded and wearing a faint, unpleasant smile.

Removed from all these stood Mrs Bacon in command of her staff who were clustered behind her. Near the door into the porch, Les and Bert kept themselves to themselves in close proximity to the pregnant nude whose smirk would no doubt he held in shot for a second or two providing an enigmatic note. Finally, perhaps, the camera would dwell upon the remaining stiletto and the empty bracket where its opposite number had hung.

Alleyn supposed this company had been made aware of what was going on by Hanley and perhaps Mrs Bacon and that the guests had been at their buffet luncheon and the staff assembled for theirs in their own region and that Maria's screams had brought them out like a fire-alarm.

Mr Reece, as ever, was authoritative. He advanced up the stairs and Inspector Hazelmere met him at the top. He, too, in his professional manner was impressive and Alleyn thought: He's going to handle this.

'Are we to know,' Mr Reece asked at large, 'what has happened?'

'I was coming to see you, sir,' said Inspector Hazelmere. 'If you'll excuse me for a moment—' he addressed the company— 'I'll ask everybody at the back, there, if you please, to return to whatever you were doing before you were disturbed. For your information, we have been obliged to take Miss Maria Bennini into custody—' he hesitated for a moment— 'you may say protective custody,' he added. 'The situation is well in hand and we'll be glad to make that clear to you as soon as possible. Thank you. Mrs—er—'

'Bacon,' Alleyn murmured.

'Mrs Bacon—if you would be kind enough—'

Mrs Bacon was kind enough and the set was, as it were, cleared of supernumeraries.

For what, Alleyn thought, might well be the last time, Mr Reece issued a colourless invitation to the study and was at some pains to include Alleyn. He also said that he was sure there would be no objection to Madame's singing maestro for whom she had a great affection, Signor Lattienzo, and their old friend and associate, Mr Ben Ruby, being present.

'They have both been with me throughout this dreadful ordeal,' Mr Reece said drearily, and added that he also wished his secretary to be present and take notes.

The Inspector controlled any surprise he may have felt at this request. His glance which was of the sharp and bright variety rested for a moment on Hanley before he said there was no objection. In fact, he said, it had been his intention to ask for a general discussion. Alleyn thought that if there had been a slight juggling for the position of authority, the Inspector had politely come out on top. They all proceeded solemnly to the study and the soft leather chairs in front of the unlit fireplace. It was here, Alleyn reflected, that this case had taken on one of its more eccentric characteristics.

Inspector Hazelmere did not sit down. He took up his stance upon that widely accepted throne of authority, the hearthrug. He said:

'With your permission, sir, I am going to request Chief Superintendent Alleyn to set out the events leading up to this crime. By a very strange but fortunate coincidence he was here and I was not. Mr Alleyn.'

He stepped aside and made a very slight gesture handing over the hearthrug, as it were, to Alleyn, who accordingly took his place on it. Mr Reece seated himself at his desk which was an ultra-modern affair, streamlined and enormous. It accommodated two people facing each other across it. Mr Reece signalled to Hanley who hurried into the second and less opulent seat and produced his notebook. Alleyn got the impression that Mr Reece highly approved of these formalities. As usual he seemed to compose himself to hear the minutes of the last meeting. He took a leather container of keys from his pocket, looked as if he was surprised to see it, and swivelled round in his chair with it dangling from his fingers.

Alleyn said: 'This is a very unusual way to follow up an arrest on such a serious charge but I think that, taking all the circumstances which are themselves extraordinary, into consideration, it is a sensible decision. Inspector Hazelmere and I hope that in hearing this account of the case and the difficulties it presents you will help us by correcting anything I may say if you know it to be in the smallest degree, mistaken. Also we do beg you, if you can add any information that will clear up a point, disprove or confirm it, you will stop me and let us all hear what it is. That is really the whole purpose of the exercise. We ask for your help.'

He paused.

For a moment or two nobody spoke and then Mr Reece cleared his throat and said he was sure they all 'appreciated the situation'. Signor Lattienzo, still unlike his usual ebullient self, muttered '*Naturamente*' and waved a submissive hand.

'OK, OK,' Ben Ruby said impatiently. 'Anything to wrap it up and get shot of it all. Far as I'm concerned, I've always thought Maria was a bit touched. Right from the start I've had this intuition and now you tell me that's the story. She did it.'

Alleyn said: 'If you mean she killed her mistress singlehanded, we don't think she did any such thing.'

Mr Reece drew back his feet as if he was about to rise but thought better of it. He continued to swing his keys.

Signor Lattienzo let out a strong Italian expletive and Ben Ruby's jaw dropped and remained in that position without his uttering a word. Hanley said '*What!*' on a shrill note and immediately apologized.

'In that case,' Mr Reece asked flatly, 'why have you arrested her?'

The others made sounds of resentful agreement.

'For impaling the dead body with the stiletto thrust through the photograph,' said Alleyn.

'This is diabolical,' said Signor Lattienzo. 'It is disgusting.'

'What possible proof can you have of it?' Mr Reece asked. 'Do you know now, positively, that Marco is Strix and took the photograph?'

'Yes. He has admitted it.'

'In that case how did she obtain it?'

'She came into this room when he was putting it into an envelope addressed to *The Watchman* in typescript, on Madame Sommita's instructions, by Mr Hanley.'

'That's right —' Hanley said. 'The envelope was meant for her letter to *The Watchman* when she'd signed it. I've told you —' And then, on a calmer note. 'I see what you mean. Marco would have thought it would be posted without —

244

anybody— *me*— thinking anything of it. Yes, I see.'

'Instead of which we believe Maria caught sight of Marco pushing the photograph into the envelope. Her curiosity was aroused. She waited until Marco had gone, and took it out. She kept it, and made the mistake of throwing the envelope into the fire. It fell, half-burnt, through the bars of the grate into the ashpan from where we recovered it.'

'If this is provable and not merely conjecture,' said Mr Reece, swinging his keys, 'do you argue that at this stage she anticipated the crime?'

'If the murder was the last in a long series of retributive crimes it would appear so. In the original case an incriminating letter was transfixed to the body.'

There followed a long silence. 'So she was right,' said Mr Reece heavily. 'She was right to be afraid. I shall never forgive myself.'

Ben Ruby said Mr Reece didn't want to start thinking that way. 'We none of us thought there was anything in it,' he pleaded. 'She used to dream up such funny ideas. You couldn't credit them.'

Signor Lattienzo threw up his hands. 'Wolf. Wolf,' he said.

'I've yet to be convinced,' Mr Reece said. 'I cannot believe it of Maria. I know they used to fall out occasionally but there was nothing in that. Maria was devoted. Proof!' he said still contemplating his keys. 'You have advanced no proof.'

'I see I must now give some account of the puzzle of the keys.'

'The keys? Whose keys?' asked Mr Reece, swinging his own.

Alleyn suppressed a crazy impulse to reply 'The Queen's keys' in the age-old challenge of the Tower of London. He merely gave as clear an account as possible of the enigma of the Sommita's key and the impossibility of her having had time to remove it from a bag in the bottom drawer of the dressing-table and lock the bedroom door in the seconds

245

that elapsed between her kicking out Mr Reece and Maria and them hearing it click in the lock.

Mr Reece chewed this over and then said: 'One can only suppose that at this stage her bag was not in the drawer but close at hand.'

'Even so: ask yourself. She orders you out, you shut the door and immediately afterwards hear it locked: a matter of perhaps two seconds.'

'It may have already been in her hand.'

'Do you remember her hands during the interview.'

'They were clenched. She was angry.'

'Well—it could be argued, I suppose. Just. But there is a sequel,' Alleyn said. And he told them of Maria's final performance and arrest.

'I'm afraid,' he ended, 'that all the pious protestations, all her passionate demands to perform the last duties were an act. She realized that she had blundered, that we would, on her own statement, expect to find her mistress's key in the room, and that she must at all costs get into the room and push it under the body where we would find it in due course.'

'What did she say when you arrested her?' Lattienzo asked.

'Nothing. She hasn't spoken except—'

'Well? Except?'

'She accused Rupert Bartholomew of murder.'

Hanley let out an exclamation. Lattienzo stared at him 'You spoke, Mr Hanley?' he said.

'No, no. Nothing. Sorry.'

Ben Ruby said: 'All the same, you know—well, I mean, you *can't* ignore—I mean to say, there *was* that scene, wasn't there? I mean, she had put him through it, no kidding. And the curtain speech and the way he acted. I mean to say, he's the only one of us who you could say had motive and opportunity—I mean—'

'My good Ben,' Lattienzo said wearily, 'we all know in general terms what you mean. But when you say "opportunity" what *precisely* do you mean? Opportunity to murder? But Mr Alleyn tells us he does not as yet accuse the perpetrator of the dagger-and-photograph operation of the murder. And Mr Alleyn convinces me, for what it's worth that he knows what he's talking about. I would like to ask Mr Alleyn if he links Maria, who has been arrested for the photograph abomination, with the murder and if so what that link is. Or are we to suppose that Maria, on re-entering the room, hot drink in hand, discovered the dead body and was inspired to go downstairs, unobserved by the milling crowd, remove the dagger from the wall, collect the photograph from wherever she'd put it, return to the bedroom, perform her atrocity and then raise the alarm? Is that, as dear Ben would put it, the story?'

'Not quite,' said Alleyn.

'Ah!' said Lattienzo. 'So I supposed.'

'I didn't say we don't suspect her for murder: on the contrary. I merely said she was arrested on the charge of mutilating the body, not on a charge of murder.'

'But that may follow?'

Alleyn was silent.

'Which is as much as to say,' Ben Ruby said, 'that you reckon it's a case of conspiracy and that Maria is half of the conspiracy and that one of us — I mean of the people in this house — was the principal. Yeah?'

'Yes.'

'Charming!' said Mr Ruby.

'Are we to hear any more?' Mr Reece asked. 'After all, apart from the *modus operandi* in Maria's case, we have learnt nothing new, have we? As, for instance, whether you have been able to clear any of us of suspicion. Particularly the young man — Bartholomew.'

'Monty, my dear,' said Lattienzo who had turned quite pale, 'how right you are. And here I would like to say with the greatest emphasis that I resist vehemently any suggestion, open or covert, that this unfortunate boy is capable of such a crime. Mr Alleyn, I beg you to consider! What does such a theory ask us to accept? Consider his behaviour.'

'Yes,' Alleyn said, 'consider it. He makes what amounts to a public announcement of his break with her. He puts himself into the worst possible light as a potential murderer. He even writes a threatening message on a greetings card. He is at particular pains to avoid laying on an alibi. He faints, is taken upstairs, recovers and hurries along to the bedroom where he chloroforms and asphyxiates his victim and returns to his own quarters.'

Lattienzo stared at Alleyn for a second or two. The colour returned to his face, he made his little crowing sound and seized Alleyn's hands. 'Ah!' he cried. 'You agree! You see! You see! It is impossible! It is ridiculous!'

'If I may just pipe up,' Hanley said, appealing to Mr Reece. 'I mean, all this virtuous indignation on behalf of the Boy-Beautiful! Very touching and all that.' He shot a glance at his employer and another at Lattienzo. 'One might be forgiven for drawing one's own conclusions.'

'That will do,' said Mr Reece.

'Well, all right, then, sir. Enough said. But I mean— after all, one would like to be officially in the clear. I mean: take me. From the time you escorted Madame upstairs and she turned you and Maria out until Maria returned and found her—dead—I was in the dining-room and hall calming down guests and talking to Les and telling you about the lake and making a list for Les to check the guests by. I really could not,' said Hanley on a rising note of hysteria, 'have popped upstairs and murdered Madame and come back, as bright as a button, to speed the parting guests and tramp about with umbrellas. And anyway,' he added, 'I hadn't got a key.'

'As far as that goes,' said Ben Ruby, '*she* could have let you in and I don't mean anything nasty. Just to set the record straight.'

'Thank you very much,' said Hanley bitterly.

'To return to the keys,' Mr Reece said slowly, still swinging his own as if to illustrate his point. 'About the third key, *her* key.' He appealed to Hazelmere and Alleyn. 'There must be some explanation. Some quite simple explanation. Surely.'

Alleyn looked at Hazelmere who nodded very slightly.

'There is,' said Alleyn, 'a *very* simple explanation. The third key was in the bag in the bottom drawer where it had lain unmolested throughout the proceedings.'

Into the silence that followed there intruded a distant pulsation: the chopper returning, thought Alleyn.

Mr Reece said: 'But when Maria and I left — we — heard the key turn in the lock. What key? You've accounted for the other two. She locked us out with her own key.'

'We think not.'

'But Maria heard it too. She has said so. I don't understand this,' said Mr Reece. 'Unless . . . But no. No, I don't understand. Why did Maria do as you say she did? Come back and try to hide the key under — ? It's horrible. *Why* did she do that?'

'Because, as I've suggested, she realized we would expect to find it.'

'Ah. Yes. I take the point but all the same — '

'Monty,' Signor Lattienzo cried out. 'For pity's sake *do* something with those accursed keys. You are lacerating my nerves.'

Mr Reece looked at him blankly. 'Oh?' he said. 'Am I? I'm sorry.' He hesitated, examined the key by which he had suspended the others and, turning to his desk, fitted it into one of the drawers. 'Is that better?' he asked and unlocked the drawer.

Ben Ruby said in a voice that was pitched above its normal register: 'I don't get any of this. All I know is we better look after ourselves. And as far as our lot goes — you, Monty, and Beppo and me — we were all sitting at the dinner table from the time you left Bella alive and throwing a temperament, until Maria raised the alarm.' He turned on Alleyn. 'That's right, isn't it?' That's correct? Come on — isn't it?'

'Not quite,' said Alleyn. 'When Mr Reece and Maria left

249

Madame Sommita she was not throwing a temperament. She was dead.'

## II

In the bad old days of capital punishment it used to be said that you could tell when a verdict of guilty was about to be returned. The jury always avoided looking at the accused. Alleyn was reminded now, obliquely, of this dictum. Nobody moved. Nobody spoke. Everyone looked at him and only at him.

Inspector Hazelmere cleared his throat.

The helicopter landed. So loud, it might have been on the roof or outside on the gravel. The engine shut off and the inflowing silence was intolerable.

Mr Reece said: 'More police, I assume.'

Hazelmere said: 'That is correct sir.'

Somebody crossed the hall and seconds later Sergeant Franks walked past the windows.

'I think, Chief Superintendent Alleyn,' said Mr Reece, 'you must be out of your mind.'

Alleyn took out his notebook. Hazelmere placed himself in front of Mr Reece. 'Montague Reece,' he said, 'I arrest you for the murder of Isabella Sommita and I have to warn you that anything you say will be taken down in writing and may be used in evidence.'

'Hanley,' Mr Reece said, 'get through to my solicitors in Sydney.'

Hanley said in a shaking voice: 'Certainly, sir.' He took up the receiver, fumbled and dropped it on the desk. He said to Alleyn: 'I suppose — is it all right? I mean —'

Hazelmere said: 'It's in order.'

'Do it,' Mr Reece said. And then, loudly to Hazelmere. 'The accusation is grotesque. You will do yourself a great deal of harm.'

Alleyn wrote this down.

Mr Reece looked round the room as if he was seeing it for the first time. He swivelled his chair and faced his desk. Hanley, drawn back in his chair with the receiver at his ear, watched him. Alleyn took a step forward.

'Here *are* the police,' Mr Reece observed loudly.

Hazelmere, Lattienzo and Ruby turned to look.

Beyond the windows Sergeant Franks tramped past, followed by a uniform sergeant and a constable.

'*No*!' Hanley screamed. '*Stop him*! *No*!'

There was nothing but noise in the room.

Alleyn had not prevented Mr Reece from opening the unlocked drawer and snatching out the automatic but he had knocked up his arm. The bullet had gone through the top of a window-pane and two succeeding shots had lodged in the ceiling. Dust fell from the overhead lampshades.

Two helmets and three deeply concerned faces appeared at the foot of the windows, slightly distorted by pressure against the glass. The owners rose and could be heard thundering round the house.

Alleyn with Mr Reece's arms secured behind his back said, a trifle breathlessly: 'That was a very silly thing to do, Signor Rossi.'


III

. . . almost the only silly thing he did,' Alleyn said. 'He showed extraordinary coolness and judgement throughout. His one serious slip was to say he heard the key turn in the lock. Maria set that one up and he felt he had to fall in with it. He was good at avoiding conflicts and that's the only time he told a direct lie.'

'What I *can't* understand,' Troy said, 'is his inviting you of all people to his party.'

'Only, I think, after the Sommita or perhaps Hanley told him about her letter to the Yard. It was dated a week before his invitations to us. Rather than un-pick her letter he decided to confirm it. And I'm sure he really did *want* the portrait. Afterwards it could have been, for him, the equivalent of a scalp. And as for my presence in the house, I fancy it lent what the mafiosi call "elegance" to the killing.'

'My God,' said Signor Lattienzo, 'I believe you are right.'

'There was one remark he made that brought me up with a round turn,' Alleyn said. 'He was speaking of her death to Ben Ruby and he said, "And now she no longer casts a shadow." '

'But that's — isn't it — a phrase used by —'

'The mafiosi? Yes. So I had discovered when I read the book in the library. It was not in Mr Reece's usual style, was it?'

Signor Lattienzo waited for a little and then said, 'I assure you, my dear Alleyn, that I have sworn to myself that I will not pester you but I immediately break my resolution to say that I die to know how you discovered his true identity. His name. "Rossi".'

'Have you ever noticed that when people adopt pseudonyms they are so often impelled to retain some kind of link with their old name? Often it is the initials, often there is some kind of assonance — Reece — Rossi. M.V. Rossi — Montague V. Reece. He actually had the nerve to tell me his Bella had confided that she wished his surname didn't remind her of the "enemy". The M.V. Rossi signature in the book bears quite a strong resemblance to the Reece signature, spiky letters and all. He seems to have decided very early in life to opt out of the "family" business. It may even have been at his father's suggestion. Papa Rossi leaves a hefty swag of ill-gotten gains which Monty Reece manipulates brilliantly and with the utmost propriety and cleanest of noses. I think it must have amused him to plant the book up there with the diva's bi-and auto-biographies. The book has been instructive. The victim in the case it deals with was a Rossi girl — his sister. A paper was stabbed to her heart. She had a brother, Michele-Vittorio Rossi, who disappeared.'

'Our Mr Reece?'

'It's a good guess.'

'And Maria?'

'The widow Bennini? Who wouldn't tell me her maiden name. I wouldn't be surprised if it turns out to have been Rossi. He is said to have picked her up at the Italian Embassy. He may even have planted her there. Obviously they were in heavy cahoots. I imagine them enjoying a good gloat over the Strix on-goings.'

Signor Lattienzo said: 'Was Strix in Monty's pay?'

'So far there's no proof of it. It would fit in very tidily, wouldn't it? But all this is grossly speculative stuff. At best, merely Gilbertian "corroborative detail". The case rests on the bedrock fact that once you accept that the crime was committed at the earlier time, which the medical opinion confirms, everything falls into place and there are no difficulties. Nobody else could have done it, not even young Bartholomew who was being tended in his room by you and Dr Carmichael. The rest of us were at dinner. The doctors will testify that the stab was administered an appreciable time after death.'

'And—he—Monty, took Bella up to her room and—he—?'

'With Maria's help, chloroformed and stifled her. I've been told that the diva, after cutting up rough, always without fail required Maria to massage her shoulders. Maria actually told me she offered this service and was refused, but perhaps it was Maria, ready and waiting, who seized the opportunity to grind away at Madame's shoulders and then use the chloroform while Mr Reece who—all inarticulate sympathy—had been holding the victim's hands, now tightened his grip and when she was insensible went in for the kill. He then joined us in the dining-room as you will remember and told us she was not very well. Maria meanwhile prepared the hot drink and collected the dagger and photograph.'

'So that extra touch was all her own?'

'If it was I feel sure he approved it. It was in the mafioso manner. It had, they would consider, style and elegance.'

'That,' observed Signor Lattienzo, 'as Monty himself would say, "figures".'

Bert came into the hall. He said they were ready and opened the front doors. There, outside, was the dawn. Bell-birds chimed through the bush like rain distilled into sound. The trees, blurred in mist, were wet and smelt of honey-dew. The lake was immaculate and perfectly still.

Troy said: 'This landscape belongs to birds: not to men, not to animals: huge birds that have gone now, stalked about in it. Except for birds it's empty.'

Bert shut the doors of the Lodge behind them.

He and Alleyn and Troy and Signor Lattienzo walked across the gravelled front and down to the jetty where Les waited in the launch.

# Ngaio Marsh

'The finest writer in the English language of the pure, classical, puzzle whodunit. Among the Crime Queens, Ngaio Marsh stands out as an empress.' *Sun*. 'Her work is as near flawless as makes no odds: character, plot, wit, good writing and sound technique.' *Sunday Times*. 'The brilliant Ngaio Marsh ranks with Agatha Christie and Dorothy Sayers.' *Times Literary Supplement*.

DIED IN THE WOOL  £1.35
GRAVE MISTAKE  £1.25
LAST DITCH  £1.25
COLOUR SCHEME  £1.25
TIED UP IN TINSEL  £1.00
VINTAGE MURDER  £1.25
FINAL CURTAIN  £1.25
THE NURSING HOME MURDER  £1.25
BLACK AS HE'S PAINTED  £1.35
SWING BROTHER SWING  £1.25

Fontana Paperbacks

# Fontana Paperbacks

Fontana is a leading paperback publisher of fiction and non-fiction, with authors ranging from Alistair MacLean, Agatha Christie and Desmond Bagley to Solzhenitsyn and Pasternak, from Gerald Durrell and Joy Adamson to the famous Modern Masters series.

In addition to a wide-ranging collection of internationally popular writers of fiction, Fontana also has an outstanding reputation for history, natural history, military history, psychology, psychiatry, politics, economics, religion and the social sciences.

All Fontana books are available at your bookshop or newsagent; or can be ordered direct. Just fil! in the form and list the titles you want.

---

FONTANA BOOKS, Cash Sales Department, G.P.O. Box 29, Douglas, Isle of Man, British Isles. Please send purchase price, plus 8p per book. Customers outside the U.K. send purchase price, plus 10p per book. Cheque, postal or money order. No currency.

NAME (Block letters)

ADDRESS